AN
AMERICAN
TYPE

OTHER WORKS BY HENRY ROTH

Call It Sleep

Shifting Landscape

Mercy of a Rude Stream: Volume I
A Star Shines over Mt. Morris Park

Mercy of a Rude Stream: Volume II
A Diving Rock on the Hudson

Mercy of a Rude Stream: Volume III
From Bondage

Mercy of a Rude Stream: Volume IV
Requiem for Harlem

HENRY ROTH

AN
AMERICAN
TYPE

A NOVEL

Edited by Willing Davidson

W. W. NORTON & COMPANY

NEW YORK LONDON

Frontispiece: courtesy of Hugh Roth

For information about permission to reproduce selections from this book,
write to Permissions, W. W. Norton & Company, Inc.,
500 Fifth Avenue, New York, NY 10110

For information about special discounts for bulk purchases, please contact
W. W. Norton Special Sales at specialsales@wwnorton.com or 800-233-4830

Manufacturing by Courier Westford
Book design by Ellen Cipriano
Production manager: Anna Oler

Library of Congress Cataloging-in-Publication Data

Roth, Henry.
An American type : a novel / Henry Roth ; edited by Willing Davidson. — 1st ed.
p. cm.
ISBN 978-0-393-07775-9 (hardcover)
1. Authors—Fiction. 2. Yaddo (Artist's colony)—Fiction.
3. Reminiscing in old age—Fiction. 4. New York (State)—Saratoga Springs—
History—20th century—Fiction. 5. Jewish fiction. 6. Domestic fiction.
I. Davidson, Willing. II. Title.
PS3535.O787A8 2010
813'.52—dc22

2010011906

W. W. Norton & Company, Inc.
500 Fifth Avenue, New York, N.Y. 10110
www.wwnorton.com

W. W. Norton & Company Ltd.
Castle House, 75/76 Wells Street, London W1T 3QT

1 2 3 4 5 6 7 8 9 0

To the memory of Leah, my mother:

*"Just see, my child, how some fruit ripens
at a glance of the sun, and some fruit
takes all summer."*

CONTENTS

PROLOGUE
At Times in Flight   1

PART ONE
Albuquerque, New York   9

PART TWO
Cincinnati, Los Angeles   59

PART THREE
New York   171

PART FOUR
Albuquerque   263

EDITOR'S AFTERWORD   275

PROLOGUE

....

At Times in Flight

I was courting a young woman, if the kind of brusque, uncertain, equivocal attentions I paid her might be called courting: it was for me at any rate, never having done it before.

I had met her at Yaddo, the artists' colony, a place you've probably heard of, where writers, painters, and musicians were invited for the summer, or part of it, in the hope that, relieved of their usual pressures and preoccupations, and provided with abundant leisure, they would create. Unfortunately it didn't work that way, as you've probably also heard. Most of us needed pressure and preoccupation, since, once there, we loafed or spent a great deal of time in frivolity and idle chatter. It was during the time of the Spanish Civil War, in 1938 to be exact, and of course that formed a part of our conversation, the fact that the Loyalists seemed on the verge of victory and yet incapable of gaining it. There was also at that time a kind of projec-

1

tion of the Marxist mood among young intellectuals. I mention these things to recall the mood of the time as it seemed to me.

I was then engaged in writing a second novel, which I had agreed to complete for my publisher. I had already written quite a section, and this opening section had been accepted and extolled. It was only necessary for me to finish it. But it went badly from then on; in fact, it had gone badly before I reached Yaddo—I can't blame Yaddo for that: they provided me with the necessary environment to write in. It had gone badly—aims had become lost, purpose, momentum lost. A profound change seemed to be taking place within me in the way I viewed my craft, in my objectivity. It is difficult to say. I am, unfortunately, not analytical enough to be capable of isolating the trouble, though I don't know what good that would have done either.

That was the time, the general mood, the predicament out of which this story comes. The young woman I was courting—we shall call her M—was a very personable, tall, fair-haired young woman, a pianist and composer, a young woman with a world of patience, practicality, and self-discipline, bred and raised in the best traditions of New England and the Middle West, the most wholesome traditions. I was, at that time, sufficiently advanced and superior to be somewhat disdainful of those traditions. I wondered whether there was any reality to my courtship, any future, whether, in short, anything would come of it. I was so committed to being an artist—in spite of anything.

The colony was close to Saratoga Springs, and I owned a Model A Ford, and in the early morning hours before breakfast I would drive down from Yaddo to the spa. There was a kind of public place there in those days, a place where paper cups could be bought for a penny, and a sort of fountain where the water bubbled through a slender pipe into a basin—and I say bubbled because that was one of its attractions, the fact that it did bubble.

Ever since childhood I have regarded carbonated water as some-

thing of a treat, something not easily obtainable, in fact, only by pur-
chase, remembering the seltzer-water man on the East Side laboring
up the many flights of stairs with his dozen siphons in a box. And
here it was free, and not only free but salutary. The water had a
slightly musty or sulfurous flavor to go with its effervescence, but its
properties were surpassingly benign.

I happened to mention the effectiveness and bracing qualities
of the waters of the spring to a small group standing in front of the
main building of Yaddo, and invited at large anyone who wished to
accompany me in the morning. The response was almost universally
negative. "Drink that water? That stuff?" was the tenor of their
comments. "I'd sooner drink mud water," said one of the poets. But
one person did reply in the affirmative. That was M. She liked the
water; it shortly became apparent that she liked it as much as I did.

So we were soon driving together in the morning, from Yaddo
to the spa, traversing the mile or so of highway that led past the
racetrack under the morning trees. The racing season was about to
begin, and as a kind of added incentive to the ride, we could see the
preliminary training of the horses—whether this was on the track
itself or a subsidiary one beside it, I no longer remember. But as we
drove past in the early morning, we would see what I suppose was
one of the usual sights at racetracks, but to us a novelty: the grooms
or trainers bent low over their mounts and urging them on for a longer or shorter gallop. A horse is a beautiful thing—a fleet, running
horse—and we would stop sometimes on our way and watch one
course along the white railing. Enormously supple and swift, they
seemed at times in flight. The dirt beneath them seemed less spurned
by their hooves than drawn away in their magnificent stride.

The racing season opened. Neither of us had ever been to a horse
race, and we decided it might be a worthwhile experience to attend
one, especially since the track itself was so accessible, and as an additional inducement again, in view of the traditional impecuniousness

of artists, free. The racetrack adjoined Yaddo at one side, and it was just a short walk through the woods of the estate before one came to a turn of the track—or so we had been told. What could be more pleasant to lovers, or quasi-lovers, than a walk through the forest on a summer day. We set out in the afternoon.

We more or less sensed the way, though I think as we approached we could hear a murmur through the woods, and so oriented ourselves. We arrived at a fairly steep embankment, which we climbed, and came to a halt before the iron palings of a fence. The track lay before us—at a peculiar angle, one might say, to the normal. We were not in the grandstand or near it; we were far away from it. In fact, the grandstand with its throng was mostly a blur of color, and the horses being paraded in front of it were tiny and remote figures. Perhaps memory diminishes the scene. We seemed to be, as we virtually were, in some coign or niche where we could watch the excitement in a remote and almost secret way. I can't recall what we said there; I know we were both enchanted by the spectacle, miniature though it was, as if it were a racetrack in an Easter egg. There was an undercurrent of sound that reached us from the grandstand—the band playing, the mingled voices—a certain far-off animation and stir that even at this distance communicated itself.

The horses cavorted, shied, sidled restively as they were brought to the post. The crowd hushed immediately, and the bugle sounded insistent and clear, and suddenly the race began.

The pack headed in a direction away from us, toward the opposite curve of the track, and, if anything, they were tinier than before, toy horses, toy riders, far off, and almost leisurely with distance. Then they rounded the far curve and came toward us, and now they appeared to gain in impetus and in size. They were no longer toy horses and toy riders. They were very real, and growing in reality every second. One could see the utter seriousness of the thing, the supreme effort, the rivalry as horse and man strained every muscle to

4

forge to the front. Oh, it was no toy spectacle; they were in fierce and bitter competition, vying, horse and man, vying for the lead, and the glowing eyeballs and the shrunken jockeys, the quiet, the enormous suppleness, and the cry. They struck the left-hand turn of the track and rounded it; each horse and the whole band centered as one in their striving to stay close to the inner railing. And then my attention was drawn to something strange—I don't know why. Perhaps what was about to happen was already happening—a jockey close to the lead, or in the forward half of the pack, a jockey in pale green silks, seemed to be toppling.

I couldn't believe my eyes, and in fact my mind seemed to cancel the sight and give it another interpretation. But he was toppling—and in another moment, he and his mount disappeared. And then in a furious rush the whole pack pounded by, a haze of hues. I glanced at M. She was following the leaders as they rounded the turn on our right and entered the straightaway, and I was almost tempted to look that way, too, such was the suction of their swerve, but instead I looked back. The jockey in green was on the ground, still rolling. The horse had fallen a short way from him and was pawing air and ground trying to regain his footing. The jockey arose, ducked under the inner railing, and limped across the greensward rubbing his dusty white riding breeches; officials were hurrying toward him. And now the horse arose and began running after the pack. But he no longer ran like a racehorse. There was something terribly ungainly and grotesque about his motion, and suddenly I realized why—his further hind leg had been broken. It flopped along beneath him as ludicrous as a stuffed stocking, and as incapable of bearing weight.

"Look," I said. "Look, M." She withdrew her rapt eyes from the finish line, questioningly. "He's broken his leg."

Her expression changed to one of horror, and that was the word she uttered: "Horrors!"

"Yes," I said. "Just now."

"Oh, that beautiful animal!"

The horse lurched past us, ran a few more steps, and careened against the inner railing. His legs milled beneath him, but he could no longer rise.

"Isn't that simply ghastly!" said M.

"Yes."

"How did it happen?"

"I'm not sure. Jolted, I imagine. I could see something break the rhythm of the race, and then—"

"That poor, beautiful animal."

"I guess he's done for."

"Why?"

I pointed.

Across the infield, a small truck had been set in motion, a mortuary truck, I supposed. Booted men clung to the sides of the cab. M still regarded me questioningly.

"They're going to shoot him."

"Oh, no!" she exclaimed. "No!"

"Well, what on earth are they going to do with him? He's done for."

She uttered a cry and suddenly began running down the embankment.

"Wait a minute!" I stretched out a restraining hand.

"No! Please!"

"What's the matter?"

"I don't want to be shot!"

"You?"

"Bullets ricochet. I'm afraid."

"Just a minute then. I want to see what happens."

I had gone a few steps down the embankment, and now I climbed up again. The truck was rolling to a stop beside the animal. Men had already jumped off. Some kneeled, others squatted about the horse, examining him. There was a brief conference. And then the cluster opened up into a kind of expectant semicircle, out of which one man strode forward with a pistol and held it close to the horse's head. The report that followed seemed oddly insignificant for so grave and dread an event. I watched them load the carcass aboard the truck, and for some reason a similar scene on the East Side from long ago returned—an image from long-vanished childhood of a cop shooting a horse fallen in the snow, and the slow winch of the big green van that hauled the animal aboard later.

She was smiling now, a little placatingly. "I'm sorry I'm such a sissy."

I shrugged. "What's the difference? I hope I wasn't rude."

"No. You were just yourself."

I laughed. "We come here once in a lifetime, and once in a thousand or a million this happens. And so close by."

"Disappointed?"

"No, I didn't bet on him. But when I saw him going down, I felt a sense of loss."

She regarded me sympathetically. "We can see another race if you want to."

"No, not unless you do."

She shook her head.

"Well, lead the way back," I said. "You've got a better sense of direction than I have." I followed her into the narrow and rather somber band of trees that bordered the racetrack. Beyond lay a glade with a measure of sunlight, and behind us was a scene that I should muse on a great deal, of a horse destroyed when the race became real.

PART ONE

....

Albuquerque,
New York

CHAPTER 1

He had awakened early, at four-thirty, and then lain in bed another hour hoping to fall asleep again. Formerly, he would have been fairly certain of doing that. He reserved his Valium tablet (self-doled out at one a day), for just that hour, four or five in the morning. But taking the tranquilizer at bedtime instead of early morning seemed to ensure a longer night's sleep. The change in program appeared to keep his unpredictable gut at rest for the night, obviating his having to haul himself out of bed and to the toilet at one or two in the morning, a groaning zombie wracked with arthritic hurt. Today, he had gotten up at a few minutes after five, plodded through his aching routine of washing down a half tablet of the strong analgesic Percocet together with a whole tablet of generic Tylenol with a glass of warm water, then raised the thermostats in the study and living room. When the glass kettle on the stove began its wavering whistle, he concocted a half cup of mixed instant coffee combined with powdered chocolate—mocha coffee, he supposed it would be called—ensconced himself on a high stool, because it was less painful to stand up from it than from an ordinary chair, and commenced sipping the hot drink. Ingestion of the brew seemed to abate somewhat the dismal ache of his existence.

Passing through the living room on his way to the shower, he had stopped and turned on Channel 9 on the color TV. Scenes of war's preparations, war's grief-stricken separations, were depicted on the tube: the weeping wife and children of U.S. servicemen, the tearful parents at dockside; in the foreground the hugging and embracing, in the background the military transport, the sleek cruiser. In other scenes, a few dedicated antiwar protesters displayed their placards. It was the eve of the Gulf War, he was alone in Albuquerque, New Mexico, and his wife was dead.

He had lost incentive to write, lost inspiration, to do as he had done in the past. Whether his élan would return, he couldn't say. He rather doubted it. With his eighty-fifth year less than three months away, it was to be expected that his vitality would increasingly ebb. A negative increase with time, like a battery, the derivative of V, where V was Vitality, with respect to Time, T, equaled minus T, which resulted in an exponential equation. He felt that way, infirm, unsteady, flagging mentally. Foolish to expect vibrant, inspired surges of prose. Better to devote himself to putting every last detail of his affairs in order, before the end, instead of cudgeling the dull, decrepit ass of fancy— to borrow an Elizabethan's metaphor.

He had already accomplished a great deal since the death of his wife, accomplished a great deal toward putting his house in order. His last will and testament was finally drawn up. Yesterday, he had received a letter from his lawyer saying that M's will had successfully passed through probate. There remained the customary two-week-long notice in the local newspapers advising all legitimate claimants to M's estate to come forward, make known their claims, or forever after hold their peace. A formality. He couldn't think of anyone who had a legitimate claim to M's estate. So, in a few weeks, all that had been hers, or that they had shared, would be legally his—her gold and silver ornaments in the safe-deposit box in the bank, and the clothes still hanging in "Her" closet in his study, as well as those in the two chests of drawers in the bedroom.

Enough time had passed now, nine months, that he had become accustomed to M's absence. He no longer expected to hear her stirring at the other end of the house, nor sounding a group of notes on the piano—the piano had been sold—nor hear her coming through the long hall of the mobile home toward him, to stand tall and distinguished in the study doorway, and inclining her devoted, lined face, perhaps set off by a new hairdo, the gray mushroom she fancied in her last years, announce that supper was ready.

All the feeling that he had wanted to pour out about M, his lost wife, his beloved, was still locked up within him. He could never give literary form to his grief, only suffer in scarcely articulate sorrow: *Ahz vey iz mir. Ahz vey iz mir.* He could feel the tears beginning to brim, his sinuses swollen. *Ahz vey iz mir. Ahz vey iz mir.* He had written about her in early spring, when leaves on trees outside his study window were translucent and tender. And now, in late autumn, the arboreal cycle was at an end: boughs had grown shaggy, foliage drear and lusterless. Spring would return, but not she, not she; return only in his mind. *Ahz vey iz mir.* How salty the taste of his upper lip. He blew his nose, swallowed; ears clicked, retrieving his hearing. You are not required to finish. He had comforted himself with that Talmudic dictum on other occasions.

He switched on his computer again.

CHAPTER 2

With its characteristic hop, skip, and jump, the little Ford, Ira at the wheel, entered the town of Saratoga Springs. The day was bright, the weather warm, the time early afternoon. He had made the trip without incident, starting out at sunup. And now turned into the main street of town, too preoccupied as usual with what lay ahead, with what he would say by way of felicitous introduction to the (how often stressed) strict, proper, critical Mrs. Ames, stewardess of the colony—too preoccupied with suave preenactments of a self he wasn't, and still hoped people wouldn't know it, to get much of an impression of the town. He had been here once before, when Edith had been a guest, and he had barged in off the highway, thumbing his way—and laid her in the woods back of the formal gardens and nymphs. Now Edith was at home, in New York, waiting for his return. It was the year 1929 then. It was 1938 now: nine years later, and he an acknowledged writer of promise. Ira snubbed the thought. Some promise: hung up on the meat hook of a second novel, but don't tell anybody. Writer of promise. Author of a book, a novel that had won wide critical acclaim, except from the Communist Party, his comrades. That was in 1934. 1934 to 1938. Four years wasted, up the flue.

Saratoga Springs was a placid, unhurried resort: little stores, little shops, leisurely pedestrians, fat mamas quaffing mineral water at the springs. And the fine trees along the avenue, as if the place had been preserved under a bell jar. Had the horse races begun? The racetrack lay along this very main street. And beyond the racetrack, Yaddo. But he'd better ask where Yaddo was to make sure.

Ira eased toward the scattering of parked cars, saw ahead an unoccupied stretch, an easy parking space, and pulled in. He had counted on sprucing up before he drove to the mansion for the interview.

The ignition shut off, keys pocketed, he got out, and walked back in search of a barbershop. A short distance ahead he spied the endless, tireless spiral turning alternate red and white stripes within the glass cylinder. Ha, boyoboy, progress. Remember the stationary ones with the gold knob on top? On Park Avenue, under the railroad trestle in slummy old Harlem? Two bits for a trim. Teutonic Jewish barber, stiff and haughty; you'd think the guy was a Prussian, the imperious way he said "Next!" and snapped the striped haircloth. And here was the same, slouchy Ira, product of East Side ghetto and slum Harlem, an invited guest at Yaddo. Ai, Americhka, as Mom would have said, where else but in Americhka? Still, he'd rather be in some goddamn hole in the wall, and busy at his writing, than in this luxurious state of a loser at loose ends.

He entered the shop: standard arrangement of three barber chairs, a row of regular chairs against the wall, coat hooks, mirrors, and the narrow marble shelf below the mirrors, with its armory of hair tonics, pomades, witch hazels, and what the hell. Ira looked for directions from the lone barber, who put down his newspaper and said friendly-voiced as he stood up, "Any chair." Fairly husky man, probably Italian.

Duly seated, pumped up to the proper height, and haircloth tucked in about his neck: "Just a trim," Ira directed. "Leave most of it on, okay?"

"Shave?" asked the voice above the clippers' snip, voice of the amiable face in the mirror.

"No, I shaved this morning."

"Shampoo?"

"Uh-uh. No, thanks." The old ploys. He'd rather the guy didn't talk, got it over with.

"Here for the races?"

"No."

"The springs? They're good for you." That deepening in the throat not reassuring, and definitely Italian.

"I hope so." Not to show prejudice.

"You can buy a paper cup for a penny, and drink all you want. Real healt'y."

"Yeah." Should he wait prudently until the end of the operations of the minuscule ordeal, before he asked? Or ask now? The guy was bound to palaver. "Say, where's this place called Yaddo?"

"Is that where you're goin'?"

"No, I know somebody staying there."

"You come by car?"

"Yeah."

"Where you parked?"

"Across the street."

"You're headin' right straight for the place. You know where the racetrack is?"

"I seem to remember."

"You drive right past the place. Short distance. There's a sign, I think." He made transition to shears. "A little one that says the name. Your friend stayin' there or workin' there?"

"No, she's a guest." Why she, not he? Plausibility.

"Real nice place. I drove around there once. Millionaire's place, once. Next door to the racetrack, too, but now it's got them long-haired people in it."

"Yes, I've been there once myself."

Thankful for a lull in the talk, Ira watched comb and scissors move up and down sideburns in the mirror, as the real ones grazed and twittered next to his ear. Edith had said, "Your hair looks a little wild," when he'd kissed her good-bye that morning. Otherwise he wouldn't have bothered getting a haircut. And what was the difference? He'd been invited. But still, first impressions counted. Your hair looks a little wild. It wouldn't after the tonsorial taming: wavy, no longer curly as once. With his eyeglasses on the shelf at the bottom of the mirror, he had to squint: tentatively smiling, ambiguous face, his, above the blue pinstriped haircloth. Ambiguous or ambivalent? Tentative, that was sure, undecided, indecisive—he moved his head obediently before the barber's rectifying finger. Become absent. Wished the guy'd come to the terminal short-shave sideburns and back of neck lather . . .

Lather at last, edged imminence of razor, the soft whisk of brush sweeping freshly clipped hair from sideburn and nape. Ira waited for the barber to raise the small mirror that would reflect the job well done in the larger mirror—and lead at last to unfrocking of neck, and liberation. Instead, something rounded, like a spoon, was being pressed against the nape of his neck, and Ira heard the barber's commiserating "Tch, tch."

"What's the matter?"

In his large, pink palm, a quarter-inch, gray wormlike form lay motionless. "Pore worms," he said. "You got 'em pretty bad."

"Poor—pore worms! You mean that came outta the pores in the back of my neck?"

"Yeah." The barber considerately pressed the spoonlike instrument against the nape of Ira's neck, and brought within view a mate to the first.

"I don't see how—how could that get in the back of my neck?"

"You mighta been layin' in the grass or somethin'."

"Doesn't seem possible." Ira squinted at the thing. "I haven't been near the grass."

"Well, you never know where you pick 'em up. Some women has them under their hair—heavy."

There was something about the barber's mien, his gentle concern, the way one hand, the hand holding the instrument in a fist rested on his hip, and the improbability of the little wormlike shapes in the man's hand that just didn't seem right, aroused faintest doubt.

"They get rotten under your skin after a while. They're real bad for you." The barber's gentle concern increased. "Tell you what: I can get 'em all out for you for three dollars."

Ira hesitated. Jesus, there was no telling: a whole headful of those things? Was it possible? He felt the nape of his neck, felt newly shaved smoothness. A worm and no wriggle? It wasn't possible. "I'll get somebody to look at it," he said curtly. "A doctor, somebody like that."

"Suit yourself." The barber threw the two small specimens into the wastebasket and proceeded to undo the haircloth. "Want your eyeglasses?"

"I'll say. I should have had them on first."

"You'da seen how bad they was."

"Yeah."

That sonofabitch. Ira crossed the street to the Ford.

I'll bet a dollar to a doughnut those were some kind of goddamn worms. He felt the back of his neck again as he got into the car. Maggots, I'll bet, weevils. That bastard. He shoved the ignition key into the lock. I must look like a sucker. He stepped on the self-starter. Thank God for a little zoology, anyway.

And he drove through the wide tree-lined avenue, past spa and racetrack, recalling the youth, alternately brash and callow, who had hitchhiked there to visit Edith, already an established poet and NYU professor. He drove up to the mansion, stopped before the richly carved oak door, got out, and rang the bell. The young domestic who answered said that Mrs. Ames was out, would be back in an hour, and would he please wait. She escorted him past dark furniture in a sumptuous living room to a warm, sunny, carpeted receiving chamber, and invited him to be seated there. The long drive, the heat of the day, and now the strain of waiting for Mrs. Ames in a sitting room that seemed to grow more stifling with every passing minute, made him feel nauseated. Could it be the egg salad sandwich he had ordered for lunch? He and his unpredictable gut. He asked one of the uniformed maids where the bathroom was, was shown, and went in and retched. Jesus, what a way to begin his stay in a famous artists' colony: puke up your toes.

Feeling wan and bedraggled, he returned to the sitting room, hoping for a few minutes to regain his composure before the arrival of his formidable hostess. No such luck. Panting, he had scarcely sat down again to catch his breath when Mrs. Ames, in a white dress, a thin, erect, severely self-controlled woman in her late forties, entered and introduced herself, at the same time extending her hand to Ira. He apologized for what he described as his rumpled appearance, and tried to explain why. She was sympathetic. She said she hoped he would recover and hoped he would like his stay here. He was sure he would. They talked briefly. In his letter of application his handwriting had appealed to her, she said. When two applicants seemed equally deserving, she often chose the one whose handwriting was the more interesting. He was glad she did, lucky she did, he told her, because in elementary school, try as his teachers might to inculcate in him the Palmer method of writing, they failed. She seemed politely amused and went on to give him the particulars pertaining to lodgings, studio, and meals.

They parted. He was absolutely certain that as usual he had made the world's worst impression. Lucky if he didn't get his ass booted out of here in a week, if not before, from what he had heard about Mrs. Ames. Hell, what could he do? He had congratulated himself on being a slum-bred Yiddle who had made it to Yaddo— he was still a slum-bred Yiddle. God, to be able to put on a front, a veneer, act like a literary peer, at least show some of the influence Edith had exerted on him these ten years. *Lemakh*, as Pop would say. *Shlimazl*. Bullshit. And he had to puke, too. Christ sake. He made a U-turn, as she had suggested, toward the white farmhouse where his sleeping quarters would be. That sonofabitch barber with those maggots or angle worms, or what the hell they were, purportedly pressed out of the nape of a guy's neck. And having heaved up that goddamn egg salad sandwich he got in Albany—or was it Troy?—talking to her, his breath must have been as fragrant as soured milk. Yech.

Two women, both young, were reclining against the sunny railings above the steps that led up to the door of the white farmhouse. One, bright of countenance, with curly auburn hair and eyeglasses, was short of stature, girlish in a crinkly dress, like an undergraduate. The other was tall, not only tall for a woman, but taller, Ira suspected, unconsciously bridling, than he was, with long legs in split blue bloomers, or whatever the hybrids were called. You could forget the first woman after an hour; she fitted into the average American type, whatever you felt it was. The other you'd never forget. Her height alone made her conspicuous, but more than that, and Ira started more at the recognition, unmistakably lesbian: that cool remote patina over her features. Brown-eyed, blond-hair bobbed, secondary features, as it were, compared to that cool, male-unperturbed distance. He got out of the car. "Good afternoon," he said, trying to palliate the testy gruffness of his tone. "I'm scheduled for a room here."

They both laughed suddenly, but there was a difference about the way they laughed, the shorter woman girlishly, the taller woman as if withdrawing.

"I'm sorry, I forgot. I'm Ira Stigman, and Mrs. Ames said I had a room on the second floor of the white framed building."

"Oh, you're the new guest coming in," the shorter woman said with eager friendliness. "I'm Nettie Dellburn. My husband and I share the same floor with you. And the bath, too," she smiled.

"Oh, then this is it."

"Yes. Would you like me to show you the vacant room? I'm sure that's the one. It's—"

"There's only one vacancy?"

"It's right above us. That's the window."

"I can find it, I guess. Let's see, I turn around in the hall, then I'm looking this way."

"That's right."

"Okay. I'll find it. Thanks."

He realized when he turned away how brusque he was; he hadn't even given her—what was her name? Nettie—a chance to introduce her friend. Oh, snub before you're snubbed, even if it means behaving like a boor—so? As he unlocked the rumble seat, he could see them out of the corner of his eye walking along the blacktop toward the main house. Lesbians always have that glassy, supercilious look, he thought as he dragged out the big brown canvas duffel bag. He had stuffed it full, the new solid cowhide and brass-fitted satchel Edith had consented to his buying—on sale—at Rogers Peet. What a satchel.

Didn't she have fine regular features, though? Aristocratic. He heaved the duffel bag over his shoulder. Tall. What funny blue bloomers—oh, he knew the name: sansculottes, they called them.

He mounted the steps and looked into the open door of the large sunny room that was to be his for the duration of his stay. Comfortable. A walk-in closet, empty bookshelves waiting for his possessions, a writing table, lamps and scatter rugs and easy chairs, a wide bed. And this was only his lodgings. Tomorrow he would walk out to his studio in the woods. What more could he ask to make a fresh start on that prologue to his new novel? In the first person this time.

He unloaded the duffel bag on the bed. "I, the author, torn by allegiances, yes, wrenched by the moral considerations arising from the Civil War and yet susceptible to the courtly and sybaritic, to the point of immobility." That was an elegant turn of phrase. He went downstairs to fetch his beautiful new satchel.

Such was his first day, or afternoon. Introductions to the other guests came at dinner, in a kind of random fashion, introducing one-self to whoever was nearby or with whom one sat at table. And later again at the general gathering presided over by Mrs. Ames in the palatial drawing room—large as a ballroom. Some names he was already familiar with, left-wing writers and poets, Muriel R, Kenneth F, Daniel F, Leonard E. Some who had read his novel already knew him. There was conversation, tinged with the requisite under-tone of cynicism about the place, the lavish food, the impeccable service, the governess of the colony. Ira learned that his neighbor at the table also shared the same floor in the white farmouse. He was a historian, cordial and portly, a university professor of history, who together with his young wife, a graduate student, was engaged in writing a biography of the late President Warren G. Harding. The tall woman with the serenely aloof features was a composer, an instructor of music theory at a midwestern college. Luigi Russo, a young Italian painter, who spoke with a decided accent, was staying downstairs in the farmhouse.

And almost at once it became apparent that the youthful Jewish novelist, perhaps a year or two younger than Ira, Leonard E, whose novel about the fierce abolitionist John Brown had won widespread praise, particularly from the left-wing press, was the object of special concern from Mrs. Ames. The stately, straitlaced lady all but hovered over him with a solicitude too pronounced to be concealed. He didn't appear in the dining room with the rest of the guests, was in some way privileged not to; nor did it take Ira long to guess why, and with whom Leonard probably was having his dinner. Well, for Christ sake. In Leonard's bearing toward Mrs. Ames—and hers toward him, her forbearance, her troubled tenderness—and in Leonard's withdrawn, self-gnawing, reserved, and deeply distracted look, Ira recognized both his own frustration as writer and his own relation to Edith. Jesus, right here in Yaddo. Another CCNY boy gone wrong. But no joking, Ira rebuked himself, no joking. He could see the frustration tearing the guy apart. The guy was talented, sensitive, a hell of a lot more refined than he was, Ira reflected, and yet his only haven, his only security, or hope of it, was won not by his art but by the total surrender, the permissiveness that was the other face of this severe woman, almost as it was with him and Edith. With all kinds of social connections, power, one could well say, having at her beck and call this opulence to confer or withhold, for all her doting, she still couldn't vouchsafe what the guy wanted, any more than Edith could for Ira.

"That Leonard E," Ira feinted with a question, like a boxer with his right. "He wasn't—I didn't see him in the dining hall."

"No." Kenneth F, foremost cynic among the guests, removed his cigarette. "He was too busy tearing up last week's chapter of his novel," Kenneth snickered. "He and Mrs. Ames have dinner together."

How familiar, how fatally familiar. Ira covertly studied Leonard's delicately featured, ascetic, and harried face: Penelope, undoing all she had done the day before. Ira sat down in one of the finely carved chairs to participate in the game of charades being organized by the handsome, assured, nervously energetic Chester C—whom Ira had previously observed with envy, exercising virtuoso dexterity when it came to helping himself to salad at dinner, manipulating the large wooden salad fork and spoon with one hand. "God, the guy's to the manner born," Ira had remarked to Kenneth, who shared the same table.

"All-American homo," Kenneth quipped.

"Aw, come on."

"He's in advertising, writes movie scripts in his spare time."

Now Chester was busily arranging opposing teams for charades. In the other team across the baronial hall sat cool what-was-her-name in a brown dress, beside the young wife of the historian. Boy, you have to think about this: look at that situation. If you'd just write about that, you'd objectify your own predicament, present an objective correlative, as Eliot says, and in this setting right here: an American *Zauberberg*. He knew all about the embraces of an older woman, their total surrender—and their armor plate against the typical masculine male. Boy, it's all laid out for you. Forget it. Bear down on that prologue tomorrow; that's what you're here for. That tall gal's countenance is so smooth, composed, frictionless: everything glances off her. Not mannish—nunlike; well, that tells you the whole story.

He had never played charades previously, but before the evening was over, he was lauded on all sides for his exceptional aptitude at divining the mimed syllables of concealed words sooner than anyone else, and after only the most meager of hints, what the word in concealment was. Chester threw up his hands in elite despair: "There he goes again!"

"You must have a marvelous intuition," Mrs. Ames complimented.

"Nah, just beginner's luck."

The next morning, after a hearty breakfast, which he consumed with such gusto that the serving maid smiled at his appreciation, all was prepared for him to tackle his writing. The studio in the clearing in the woods offered celestial solitude: the knotty-pine interior; a couch for restful meditation; even the pencils on the old-fashioned desk, with its new green blotter, were newly sharpened. He threw himself into his work: a fresh beginning. What the hell is the matter with you? You don't have to sanction history. Get away from that fixation. Announce it. What did Joyce say? History was a nightmare from which he was trying to awake. I'll bet a buck he didn't want to awake. Boy, nice chair this, swivels, tilts. Argus-eyed pine walls' unblinking surveillance of you. Howdy, howdy. No, but there's really nothing to it. Confess the effect of the two vectors on you: force equals ass times acceleration. Oof. And having done so, gracefully, go on to the yarn: party of surveyors in the Dakotas—doesn't have to be for a railroad; could be topographic—accompanied by a detachment of soldiers. And lo and behold, Ira looked about at the knotty pine and chuckled. On every crest and ridge, at every point of the compass, outlined against the burnished blue sky, mounted Sioux warriors—*des peaux-rouges criards*, said Rimbaud—mounted Sioux warriors astride their pinto ponies, mustangs, cayuse, interdicted all movement—forward or backward. Oh, legend, legend. They're immobilized. So are you. Get goin'. Ira was trying to write true to life, true to material conditions, as the comrades in the Communist Party would say. He would trace back the ancestry of his hero, his friend, dockworker, and Party member, Bill Loem, a true American type.

His first day's output was cause for celebration. Exulting, he left the studio in midafternoon. Jesus, he practically had it licked. A few emendations here, a little qualification there, better cadence, and he'd be out in the clear, out of the Dakotas, out of the Badlands, once again free to exercise the one gift he could rely on, could move in confidently—the very one the goddamn quicksand of history had imprisoned him. "Pissmire!" he uttered aloud, pulling the cottage door shut. "Pissmire of history," he repeated contemptuously. Hell, just say so. He hadn't said it quite emphatically enough. Well, tomorrow he would. And better get in touch with Bill before he left for the West Coast. Right. Get those details about his escape from the reformatory, about freight train travel. Right. All right. After the whore that broke the kid in when he slept in the newspaper distributing depot. Hey, you know the stuff's beginning to fade? I'll tell

25

you something. You know? Why should you have to go any further into that family-life business. Ira halted among the trees. Take it that far, that's enough, into postadolescence. About as far as he himself had gotten. Ira resumed walking again. He could handle that. He'd tell Max Perkins that's as far as he could go.

There were obvious pairings off: Ira went along once or twice on a drinking spree in the evening, with Kenneth F and others, to the dim-lit café table and the inebriate hilarity that seemed desperate—he could think of no other way to describe it—like Kenneth's cynicism, impregnable negativism, desperately sterile, a bizarre, homeopathic defense against sterility itself. Ira recognized the state, but he wasn't ready for it, not yet. Maybe he wasn't clever enough, too stolidly protective of a remnant of hope, of affirmation. They soon stopped inviting him.

The sprightly, dark young sculptress who taught art at an Iowa High School, and wore glasses that magnified her brown eyes, asked him to drop in on her at her studio the week before she was due to leave. Strange how the small white body, tense in the opposition of play, discouraged him, and then suddenly surrendered limp, flaccid, larval, arousing him to work his will. Three, four days of driving about with her in the cool evenings after dinner followed, and strolling off afterward into the dark, anywhere, as he had once done with Edith. Perhaps that was why he was successful: she looked so much like Edith, except milk-white, where Edith was dusky in shadow. Three, four days when the sharp, magnified eyes behind her glasses contemplated him, speculatively—and then she was gone. He had offered to take her to the train, but she declined—she would take a taxi. She declined, taking leave of him that last evening they were together, teasing him as if she had determined to make sport of reminiscence.

In how many ways the time passed—other than when engaged at writing: softball games when one became carefree, for an hour they were paroled from artistic sentence, even Leonard. Or comparing notes received from Mrs. Ames. Enlarging one's acquaintance with the other guests—the strange, Egyptian-born Jewish composer, the wiseacre, also Jewish musicologist with whom Ira got into a furious dispute over whether, as the other maintained, jazz was a form of folk music. Listening for the first time to records of Gregorian chants in the chapel-like room adjoining the commons hall. How moving they were within their limited modulations, like the davening he had heard on the East Side as a kid, awakening the long-dormant yearning to pray. David F, one of the few married guests at Yaddo, who lived in a cottage with wife and child, and was author of a trilogy, lectured Ira on the futility of writing novels, of receiving so little remuneration for all one's striving. He was giving that up for good; he was going to Hollywood, where his services would at least be handsomely paid for. He urged Ira to do likewise. "You can't live on favorable reviews," David said, "especially if you've got a family to support, a child to feed and clothe."

"Yeah, but how can you give it up—voluntarily I mean?"

"Of course you can. It isn't that hard. It's a rational decision."

Ira went away unconvinced, returned to his study, and pondered. No. It was not a rational decision; it was a rationalization on David's part. You don't desert that kind of—what?—intensity, whereby you fulfilled yourself, unless it deserts you; and then you make the best of it, put the best face on it, as they say. Same thing, same thing: Leonard, petted, cherished, up there in his study next to Mrs. Ames's apartment, tearing up the previous week's writing, as Kenneth had gibed; and Kenneth himself, irrigating his barren fancy with liquor; David embellishing the void with a rationalization. And Ira, back in the old rut again, the prologue before the Badlands, with a sentence now and then to simulate progress.

27

Jesus, what was happening? Was the place really as unconducive to work as Kenneth had said it was, too luxurious, too sheltered? Or was it them? He hadn't been any better before Yaddo. Were the others? And there were so many others who seemed entangled in the same web of futility, so many brilliant guys gone to Hollywood, friends such as George, Lynn R. Either echoing themselves or seeking asylum in academia—or dead. And Hal W, poet, now talking about painting. Shallow, Edith had said. Well, hell, then he was, too. Some were thwarted to madness, some prudently gave up. What had got into them? The Party said, the Marxists said, that it was the times: history had raised a wall against the old ways. What did that mean? Old interpretations, tried and true, reliable perceptions, second-nature responses, the sensory surface play they once were satisfied to find words for, words to match. They no longer were. It was no longer sufficient. They sensed an abstraction troubling the surface from below, and they didn't know how to deal with it. That was the rub. But change, holy cow, how could they change? How could he change? Change to meet the changed way you engage with externals, with the same spontaneity? Boyoboy, were they licked. That was it, wasn't it? He wasn't merely whipping up a froth of words. Or was he? Finding alibis for indolence, for self-indulgence.

He sat in his studio a long while. Should he quit trying, or go on? A lousy little incident in the Dakotas, and he was stymied, stuck. But that was what they were all saying, each in his own quandary: a lousy little incident in the Dakotas. Jesus, if you were a poet, you could treat that as trope, entity, discreet, within definite confines. T. S. Eliot and his aridities, you in the Badlands; it caught up with you. Who could help you? All right, Argus in the woodwork, stop the leering.

He felt an urge to reread the slender sheaf of typescript he had accumulated in the bottom drawer of his desk, but fought it off.

In the mood he was in, the pages would go the way of Leonard's, Leonard upstairs in his tower above the stained-glass windows at the landings, ripping up his first two chapters.

The notice on the bulletin board stated that Miss M was giving a recital this afternoon in the chapel adjoining the drawing room, a piano recital: some music of her own composition, some of it the work of others—what did it say? *The White Donkey* by Cabriolet, no, Chabriolet. Better than sitting there slumped over on his ass incubating another boil, whoever Miss M was. He swiveled about on his chair and stood up. Besides, it was good form: Show Mrs. Ames a little respect. Helped you survive here.

Many, perhaps most of the audience, had already gathered—it was hard to tell in such a large room filled with chairs whether the recital was relatively well attended or not.

Still, he would have ventured to say that nearly every guest in Yaddo was there, and some in attendance Ira didn't recognize, friends of guests perhaps, or visitors: It was Sunday afternoon. He slipped into a chair. A religious sentiment, a spiritual vagary, had imbued Mrs. Peabody, wife of a railroad tycoon—was that what Edith said?—who had bequeathed the place as an artist's colony in memory of her deceased child, the small boy who purportedly gave the colony its name, on trying to say the word, shadow, which he spied on the ground. Adjacent to the drawing room, and illuminated by stained-glass windows, was a chapel, raised from the drawing room by a few steps, and furnished with an organ. At the moment, a grand piano occupied the center of the raised floor, as on a stage. Miss M appeared to a scattering of applause, which she acknowledged with modest smile, and seated herself at the piano. It was the tall lesbian, Ira realized.

Little enough could Ira follow in her toccata and fugue, little enough could he grasp, or appreciate, with his scanty exposure to modern music. But that was the trouble with modern music: either you were a trained professional, or you had to hear it a dozen times before musical figures took shape.

Attention wandered off. But wasn't she beautiful, though, ethereal, otherworldly. God, that bishop who said those angles were angels sure had it right: the regularity of her features, the sublimity in classic repose. What a pity she was a lesbian. Couldn't even talk to her. When she wasn't with that married couple, she consorted with that poet even taller than she was, spindly spinster with eyeglasses. What're you gonna do about that? Boy, the purity, austerity, pale aloofness: probably slap you down if you said boo to her, slap you down like a matzoh.

It happened very fast, without preliminaries or approaches, though Ira was tentative at first. The more he was with her, the more he wanted to be with her, the more girlish and tentative he perceived her to be, one (like himself) whose maturity was pent up, whose maturity strove to be released. However different they might be otherwise—in breeding, tradition, temperament, artistic direction and aspiration, in outward appearance—in this most fundamental respect, they complemented each other. They both stood at the portentous crossroads of maturity. They talked about it a great deal—Ira talked about it obsessively—when they drove out evenings in the Model A, or found a table in the big, green-painted noisy spa, or simply strolled about the grounds in the earlier-arriving dusk, holding hands. She listened, replied hesitantly, looked at him often with soft, brown, tender eyes. She surrendered to him the few times he embraced her, saying to him once, "You're stronger than I am." But he couldn't take her, scarcely tried to—it was enough to be with her; she implied no demand. So different this: desire subordinate to the need to find out each other in each other, to find out whether for each there was a viable path in the other—to oneself, whatever that self would be. Such need, need! It was like those dreams he had two or three times lately, dreaming that he couldn't find his way to his lodgings, or the Model A; and at the same time, as if one lobe of the brain were speaking to its counterpart, saying, I know why you're lost; you're still asleep. He couldn't begin to describe his need, only vouch for the immensity of it, how crucially it meshed with hers, though far less than her need for him.

She was so much more intelligent than he was—smarter, he would have said; compared with his own abysmal academic performance, hers had earned her a Phi Beta Kappa. But not only that: quick of mind, grasping an idea, grasping a direction, retaining instruction, oriented without anxiety. And attractive personally: you could see in other people's countenance their pleasure at the sight of her, the trust they immediately reposed in her—as against that questioning and askance reaction to him. Her calm, Anglo-Saxon radiance, her blond, bobbed hair, which the summer sun had bleached. Hers was an inherent nobility, hers all the virtues and amenities of breeding and tradition. What the hell would she want him for, or want with him?

She was the daughter of an erstwhile Baptist minister, a graduate of Brown University and all-American tackle at the turn of the century. Son of the American Revolution, his ancestor of the same name stood in bronze in Boston Common, a captain of the Revolutionary Army who had lost his life in battle. Her mother was the daughter of a very wealthy wholesale meat dealer; he disapproved of her marriage to the idealistic—and impecunious—young minister who was determined to heed the call to preach to the wild and riotous lumberjacks of Oregon. M's mother had moved in the best social circles in New York, and traced her ancestry back to the *Mayflower*. Chicago was the place of upbringing of M herself, of M and

31

her three siblings: two brothers, the first—and firstborn—a hard-driving sales manager for a giant food-processing corporation, the second, associate actuary of a prominent company of fire insurance underwriters; the sister was younger, a social worker in New York. Though all of M's siblings had shown at one time or another signs of rebellion against their parents, the two brothers marrying either clandestinely or without parental approval, Betty had rebelled most strenuously of all. Pretty, she had danced in the pony line of burlesque shows during college vacation in the summer. And against the stormy objection of her parents, she married John Miller, graduate of the University of Chicago, a freelance photographer. Only M had conformed—outwardly. And Father, after a year or two of preaching the gospel in lumber camps, his evangelical fervor diminished, had accepted a post as administrative head of the central YMCA in Chicago. He served there a number of years, then was offered the position of executive secretary of Kiwanis International, a civic organization dedicated to good fellowship and the fostering of civic virtue. He had served in that capacity for many years, and in another two would be retired.

M, seemingly conforming, M with her façade of cool impersonality, had also grown up and been educated in Chicago—first in the Oak Park schools (in due time, Ira was to learn about the rigid, unspoken, middle-class Protestant exclusiveness of Oak Park, home of Ernest Hemingway, of all people), and then at the University of Chicago. M had begun the study of piano at a very early age: Mother was ingenious at contriving piano lessons for her daughter without payment of cash—the family was ostensibly strapped in those early years. In exchange for use of piano and parlor for instruction of other pupils in the neighborhood, on the day M had her lesson, her lesson was free. "Mother always cooked a tuna fish casserole for supper that evening, and invited the piano teacher," said M. She majored in music at the University of Chicago, attended the American Conservatory in Chicago, took advanced work there, and was awarded a master's degree. She had three degrees in all.

In 1930 (the same year, Ira reflected, that he had begun his one and only novel in the Peterboro Inn, close at hand to the MacDowell Colony, where Edith was a guest), M had studied composition with Madame Boulanger in Paris—thanks to the generosity of a fairly well-to-do hotelier uncle, named Bub. Until this summer she had taught music and musical theory at Western College near Cincinnati, Ohio. Her six-month sabbatical would begin after Yaddo, which she planned to spend in New York, composing music.

So much Ira had learned in their growing friendship. How different they were, how different! And yet that didn't seem to matter (how different he and Edith were—even more). Under their differences, he was certain, a stronger bond than all their disparity existed, a bond that continually confirmed their kinship, nourished their need for each other, made feasible, made durable, the seemingly precarious, and tenuous, affinity. It was her estrangement, so like his own—so like Edith's, and yet not like—unrebellious, sad, and surpassingly gentle and without attitude, crust of posture, one might say, as he himself had. Somewhere, sometime early in childhood, the little girl recognized the first tokens of the irreparable gap between genteel pieties, Christian sufferance, and aphorism—and the actualities of behavior, of act, of dealing. So she herself told Ira: She recognized the hypocrisy that riddled the fabric of outward show of goodness—as with her parents, so with those about them— in respectable Oak Park. And she grieved, never to be the same, continually diverging without rebellion against the hearty falsity of grown-ups, without asserting her views, as her sister, Betty, did. Instead, she harbored protest till it settled within her, like a stratum of disenchantment. It was that, probably, the inveteracy of compliance, that gave her features their distant, unruffled look. And at the same time, how practical and competent she was—obedience had trained her—patient, domestic, thrifty, methodical, and forbearing, all the virtues and attributes she would need. How selfish and crass of him to put it that way, but selfish and crass was the way he was. Unlike Edith, smoldering with rebellion, swift to take offense, M laughed like a girl at the novelty of his brusqueness, neutralized his forebodings with her equanimity, her natural steadfastness, ancestral, pioneer steadfastness before the untried, staunch before difficulties that daunted him, and girlishly timid before small violence. She allayed him with her welcome normalcy. She awoke in him a nascent protectiveness for another—something he had never felt before, to face the world, so often intimidating and askance, on behalf of another. How the hell had nobody snapped her up long before this, that he was so lucky? He knew from what she told him she was attached to a certain married man, also in the music department at Western College—and with a certain single woman in the English Department, with whom she shared a multitude of recreations and excursions, from driving to Cincinnati for a hamburger to break the fearsome monotony of institutional meals, to driving together to New York. And that before she began teaching at Western College, a position entailing all sorts of extracurricular duties, from chaperone to organist at chapel, for all of which she received $1,800 per year, she had been deeply involved with a kind of preceptor in musical composition, Thomford H, handsome and winning in appearance and personality, as M described him. Probably she was in love with the man; probably that was the key affair, and the key heartbreak in her life. Ira never asked. It was none of his business: that was the realm of her privacy, with regard to anything in her past she kept reserved. He just felt he was lucky. That guy, whoever he was, and for whatever reason, had missed out on acquiring the very grace of their common tradition. Tough luck.

And because she disdained allure, was taller than average, not pretty but beautiful, not clever but underneath sobriety and auster-

ity, uniquely, scathelessly witty and aware, she was everything he
wanted. If only he didn't have to earn her. She said she wanted to
be loved singly and passionately, and who could argue with that?
She wanted to feel sheltered in another's emotion, and who could
argue with that either? But it meant, it implied a demand on him
that he was unprepared for, one that had never been made upon
him. His very acquiescence filled him with misgiving.

Their attachment, virtual inseparability, once work was done,
was evident to all at Yaddo, and it excited the imagination of the
young, soft-spoken Italian painter, fellow occupant of the white
farmhouse. With only a few days remaining before the sojourn of
Yaddo's guests came to an end (except that of Leonard's, quipped
the waggish Kenneth, with a chuck of the head toward the mansion, "He's got tenure"), Luigi Russo asked Ira for a favor: Would he,
with M beside him, sit for an afternoon or two—a couple of hours—
while Luigi painted them. Ira consented; he was sure M would, too.
Where? That field on the way to his studio, said Luigi.

"Open. A little wild . . . how you call?" asked Luigi.

"Oh, yeah. Meadow."

"Yeah, yeah, meadow," said Luigi eagerly. "I like how it grow:
natural."

The way painters thought, or didn't think, and yet arrived at
relevance, at fitting juxtaposition: the untended meadow of late summer, and the ripening of his own love for M. Neither of them was
in the first flush of youth: she had turned thirty in April, he thirty-
two in February. She thought it would be fun, when he told her.
And on the following afternoon, in sunny, dry August, while she
sat on the ground in white blouse and blue sansculottes, and he lay
outstretched beside her, chatting, randomly plucking weeds, Luigi
painted. They asked whether they could look at his work, when the
session was over; smiling absently, as if still in the reverie of vision,
he nodded. And what they saw was charming, unfinished, fleeting,

languid, spontaneous: the vegetation, the tree, and the two figures, identifiable if one knew them, though not by feature, simply by conformation, held together in the attitude of lovers as much by nearness as by atmosphere.

They congratulated Luigi. But that was the last sitting they would have time for. It rained the following day, and the day after was filled with preparations for departure—and for Ira, the onset of anxieties. He had decided that M contained in her some kind of complementary freedom that he needed. Within hours now the crisis, the wholly unpredictable outcome of telling Edith of his new attachment, of his firm attachment, of his resolve, of the thousand and one things he had meditated on, persuaded himself about, fortified himself with, all would be put to the test soon against the foreseeable, the unnerving opposition of Edith. Oh, people spoke glibly of crucibles. Cords would be more like it, cords of apprehension that tightened about crown and bosom. Jesus, the petite little woman, dark, olive-skinned, sober and tender, intense, relentless, that his worry summoned before his eyes. Nobody knew the trait, Edith's trait, that had barely stirred his recognition early on, when some assistant professorship was at stake at the university: her competitiveness, her stormy competitiveness. Edith's fury at being rejected. Hers was an endless bounty matched by an equal possessiveness. He'd have to face that—and hold his own against it.

Boy. Ira winced. Cold fingertips chafed cold fingertips. That last moment of tranquillity. Yes, he wanted that memento. He stood up from the bed beside his yawning, prestigious satchel, bought with her dough, walked down the flight of stairs and knocked at Luigi's door. And after greetings, questioned him.

"Mind if I borrow that painting for a few days?" Ira asked.

Luigi demurred gently. "It's not finished."

"I know. But it's got the tone. Listen," Ira explained. "I'll tell you why I want to borrow it. M's brother-in-law is a freelance photographer, you understand. I'd like him to take a picture of it. You live in Manhattan. You give me your address, I'll return it."

"I like it, you know. Maybe never finish. Doesn't need to finish." His bright eyes sharpened to a glint.

"I'll return it," Ira stressed.

They entered his room, like Ira's in a disarray of packing—with the addition of painter's gear, easel, brushes protruding from canvas parcel, paintings. "My brother drive me back to New York tomorrow."

"Oh, yeah? I'm driving M back."

"I tell you. I lend you this, you know why?" he produced the painting.

"Ah," Ira admired it. "No, why?"

"I owe you apawlgy. Something I say."

"Something you said?"

"You forget?"

"Oh! Oh!" Ira broke into a nervous laugh. "Is that all? That's a compliment."

"I didn't know she was gonna be—" Luigi finished with a gesture.

"Nah!" Ira scoffed. "Okay? I'll return it in a few days. I promise."

He climbed the stairs again. Jesus, that should be his worst worry. The guy was sensitive though. "She have flat breast," Luigi had remarked when he first saw Ira squiring M. "But she have nice ass." The thorough Italian craftsman's unfailing objectivity.

CHAPTER 3

Chaos. Fear. Palpitations of doubt as he drove the car, Manhattan-bound, with M at his side . . . trepidation and remorse, and grim anticipation of what awaited him. It was like the fear and anguish he had felt that doomsday afternoon almost twenty years ago, when he had been expelled from Stuyvesant High School for stealing a classmate's silver-filigreed pen and contemplated throwing himself into the Hudson River before confessing to Pop and Mom. Now he glanced over at M. Her serene, relaxed enjoyment of the passing countryside vexed him, in the throes of his mood: nervous, disoriented, fearful of getting a job, earning his own living.

He chided M for her sour breath—and she laughed. Yes, she agreed, she shouldn't have drunk that glass of milk this morning at their last breakfast in Yaddo. It didn't agree with her. Buttermilk did. She was sorry. He assured her that it was all right, didn't matter; they would stop for a bit of lunch in an hour. He apologized, tried to explain. "I'm scared of what I have to go through, I guess."

He could feel her gentle, compassionate gaze resting on him. "I wish I could help, Ira, but I can't. It's something you'll have to do yourself."

"I know. Just don't, don't be affronted if I'm impolite."

"I'm not. And you're not impolite."

"Thanks."

He drove on. And after a silence, he said, "I love the way you read a map. I'd have taken the wrong turn at least twice."

"It always helps to have a navigator along," she agreed.

"Yeah, but the way you seem to get right inside a map, that's what I envy."

"The top is always north," she smiled at him.

"Glad tidings," he laughed at last, painfully.

"Weren't you ever a Boy Scout?" she asked.

"Lot of good it did me. I have to turn a map upside down when I'm going south. Every direction for me is north." She smiled at him fondly.

"Fact," he continued. "For me there's only uptown, downtown, and crosstown. Maybe it's because you lived in Chicago. The streets go the same as New York? East and west?"

"Oh, yes."

"Then my theory is no good."

"We say, walk east until your hat floats."

"The lake?"

"Yes. Lake Michigan."

"By the shores of Gitchee Goomey. So when'd you learn to drive?"

"Thirteen, fourteen. Whenever my father bought our first Buick. He didn't know how to drive. Somebody had to drive."

Ira laughed. "So who taught you?"

"Taught?" It was her turn to laugh. "Nobody. My brothers said, this is the clutch, and this the brake, and this the gas."

"Didn't you need a license?"

"Not in those days."

"Boy, no license." He felt better. He removed his hand from the wheel, patted the long, slender, pianist's hand on the seat beside him, slack, the way it joined the loose wrist. Let the miles grow fewer, the confrontation with Edith nearer; he had to do it. He needed M too desperately not to do it. But he was too much of a coward to make the break immediately, without lulling Edith. Over M's protestations, he went home to Edith. "Just for a little bit," he said weakly.

It came up a few days later. Stonily, Edith listened to him; and he as obdurately to her. She accepted not one word of his plea that he had to get out, stand on his own feet; that his dependence on her was ruinous; that he could feel himself degenerating. Rubbish, that was all so much rubbish, as far as she was concerned. She, too, had hoped—a long time—that he would reach this decision with respect to her, to stand on his own two feet, assume the responsibilities he owed her, accept this necessity he was talking about, and confirm their relation of ten years in a way that would end its indefiniteness, confirm it in the usual way: by marriage. But no—flinty and taut, she continued to berate. Now that he gave evidence of grown-up attitudes, he had turned—and it wasn't merely to another woman—to a conventional, middle-class midwesterner. Oh, she knew the type: that common American housewife who expected to be supported, the kind who expected him to provide a conventional middle-class existence. Edith maintained her tirade, despite his denials that M was an artist, a composer, self-sufficient, self-supporting, independent, and thoroughly unconventional.

Sessions of pleading alternated with sessions of acrimony, followed by tender solicitude and reasonableness. What of his writing? Did he realize the kind of relationship he was so foolishly insisting on committing himself to would mean the end of his art?

"Maybe. I don't know. If it can't sustain itself, I mean provide enough financial support, I have no choice but to let it end."

"Fiddlesticks! If you'd get down to the business of writing a novel, as you set out to do, instead of that second-rate lyricism you wrote at Yaddo—"

"How would you know it was second-rate lyricism?" His voice coiled, even as he sensed within himself a sinking of spirit, the validity of her detraction.

"Oh, I didn't stand on ceremony," she went on. "I wanted to see what you had done."

"You mean you pried into my papers?"

"If you choose to call it that. It seems to me I have some sort of right to know about your progress, if any. And I would say it was nil."

"Thanks." Ira let the flat irony hang in the air.

"You expect me to be polite? What about yourself? Why, you have an affair with a piano teacher, and say nothing about it."

"But I did."

"You wrote not a single word."

"I don't see it would have made any difference."

"Oh, no, you weren't going to allow me to disturb your idyll. That would be too much. I can just tell the dreamworld you were living in by that pretty painting you brought home."

"Don't tell me you dug that out of the closet, too?"

"Of course I did. You needn't shake your head."

She was so uncompromising, her prominent, relentless, brown eyes in a small, unyielding face—her petiteness itself, middle-aged petiteness, concentrated reproach—as she sat in her wonted place, with back to the wall, on the black velvet-covered couch under the van Gogh reproduction.

"If you had written, I might have kept this from becoming the absurd commitment you've made of it—something that deserved to be nothing more than a summer fling. Now, of course, you've given her all sorts of promises: you're bound by your vows. And you're going to do something you'll regret the rest of your life—when you

find out what marrying a conventional midwesterner means, marrying into a conventional middle-class family."

"My disclaimers don't seem to do much good."

"No, because you don't know what you're doing; you don't know
what you're getting into."

"Okay, fine."

Her tone shifted into tenderness. "Don't you realize, darling,
that kind of involvement will ruin you as an artist? You'll become
the kind of person I've seen so many others become—who moan
afterwards that they let the best years of their lives go into doing all
kinds of practical things, business, profession, family, all the demands
made on them—until it was too late. Too late to realize their gifts
or their real ambitions in life. I don't want to sermonize, darling, I'm
sure I could have been a better poet if I had refused the obligations of
my family and friends, and dedicated myself to writing only. I don't
blame anybody but myself. You're the only worthwhile obligation I
have. Don't you see your whole life will go down the drain if you go
through with this insane sentimentality?" Her words slowed, each
spaced for emphasis. "I'm just trying to keep that from happening."

"I don't think you can." He knew by her angry glare she misunderstood him. "It's down the drain already—I think. The art is.
I may be wrong."

"Rubbish!"

"Rubbish? Look at the work that I brought back home from
Yaddo."

It was hopeless. They could go on like that for hours. That's how
these breakups, divorces, severances took place, Ira reflected afterward. That was their—call it what you will—piling up on a barrier
reef: wreckage. Experienced by others, by millions, now by him. It
was like life or death: not a goddamn new observation could you
contribute toward any of it. You went from irrelevance to rancor and
back to irrelevance again. You couldn't patch it up, that's all.

42

Ira looked out from the height of his former study window. Edith had moved to Waverly Place to be nearer the university. (She didn't like the new apartment: it was one of those narrow, railroad remodeled domiciles—"without graciousness," she said.) And she had gone to the extra expense of having the young and pretty Negro domestic come in three afternoons a week, and serve dinner, so that Ira could feel he was living connubially, a settled home life. *S'hut nisht geholfen*, he told himself in Yiddish, ironically: it didn't help. Oh, the trouble was obvious, or he thought it was: Edith had seen him through his writing of a novel of childhood, fostered the novel as she maternally nurtured him. That phase was over four years ago. And where the hell could he go now?

And where the hell was Dalton in all of this? Rich, calm, devoted to Edith—everything Ira wasn't. Her eternal suitor, a rich lawyer who had made it clear for years that he would take care of her if Ira were to fail her. Hell, he had even offered to take care of Ira, too, to support him while he wrote his novel. There were no limits to his generosity, though it seemed to Ira to come with soft shackles. Why didn't she say, all right, I have Dalton, devoted, older, man of affairs, go chase yourself? But she held on fiercely to this tandem, span, her dual chargers. One thing was clear though: he had to get out of here. Pull his freight, or most of it, go live some- where else, break this disastrous round of acrimony and entreaty. He had been to bed with her twice since returning from Yaddo, once at her request, fondling each other stark naked before the tall mirror she had bought to go in the hallway: she could be imagined ready to walk into the mirror, so avidly did she consume her image, one hand on his stalk, one hand on his hand, on her small dusky breast. Eye photo. How endearing, whispering on his yearning. It wasn't fair to M; it was betrayal. No. He had to get out, leave the premises.

He could never get away from Edith, break the enormous bond

of the past ten years, the writing, her inculcations in taste, behavior, his physical and financial dependency. Never, if he lived anywhere within range of turning to her for aid: The habit was too deep, his will too weak. Broke, where would he get a meal, where would he sleep?

He left to take a walk and think. And Bill Loem—with a new baby added to the family, little Foster, and news from Billy Jr., in Loyalist Spain, news that he had been badly wounded in the left foot—all you could get from Bill was savage harangue. Oh, but there was a possible solution! Bill had announced his determination to leave as soon as possible, for the West Coast, for LA, while his wife, Bea, took the bus there. They had heard that the welfare system in California was more generous, and with the warm weather one could live on much less. Bea was long-suffering, and had stuck with Bill through all sorts of travails. A sturdy—nay large—woman of even temperament, she was eager to leave for California, where she had spent some time in the twenties. There was the opportunity: go out there with Bill in the Model A, and get as far out of range of Edith's benefactions as he could. He wouldn't be able to resist otherwise.

Hell, he couldn't even go home, he stormed at himself. He had barred himself more effectively than if he had deliberately, cunningly planned it all: he had quarreled with Pop, before Yaddo, a near-altercation at Max and Laura Farb's home, second cousins, with whom he was staying. They actually squared off against each other—Ira leading with a left, and the old coot, glasses removed, head lowered to charge in, Ira thought. He'd have belted the old bastard, except for Max and Laura. What the hell. Ira could only sneak home to Brooklyn to see Mom in daylight hours now, while the old guy was tending his little luncheonette concession in a bakery on Pitkin Avenue.

He was just going over the same ground. Reality was like something dull, immovable, obdurate, rooted in the ground like a pyramid. He was stuck, too, and there was only one way.

It wasn't so bad, he tried to mitigate his apprehensive brooding. He envisaged himself reaching the West Coast, LA. There might be an opening for him in filmmaking. He was a writer. He might achieve independence, and then come back for M. It was all very vague, sure, but it was a prospect, it was a chance. Lynn R, Edith's friend who so obviously liked him, and whose company Ira enjoyed so greatly, a person with inventive repartee, endlessly entertaining—a fairy, yeah, had made advances at Ira when tipsy—was out there in Hollywood writing scripts. What dough to be made. Turn to him for introductions. And if not, again Ira felt that rearing of hope, he might find a new approach in his writing, writing that would hold him, as his first novel had, despite indolence, misgiving, and self-indulgence. There was a chance. But chiefly, once in LA, those first days, weeks, he would have Bill to guide him, help orient him—garrulous Bill was, yes, sure, wearing, but somebody to turn to, before going on his own. And as important as anything, Bill's iron will would prevent backsliding, permit no retreat, once the journey began. It was Bill's own needs that would guarantee that, impervious to Ira's wavering and regression. Already he envisaged their driving out west in the Model A; envisaged arriving, staying there, far from Edith's blandishments, breaking at last the ties, the umbilicus that held him to her.

He voiced his plans to M. She listened, as always, attentively, meditatively, comprehending the necessity that drove him to the steps he proposed taking, yet hesitant, demurring at the extremes he was going to, demurring, agreeing. If there was no other way to break his relationship with Edith, then drastic as this way was, what else could he do? He reminded her of the ingredient of practicality in his plans: Hollywood, film writing. He reminded her of Daniel F in Yaddo, his "rational decision" to abandon novel writing for Hollywood.

"Do you think you're the kind?"

And he looked at her, poised on the piano bench, her bobbed, fair hair luminous against the piano in the shadow of her neat basement studio. Oh, she knew so much more than she let on, or surmised so much more, but still deferred to him. He was almost tempted to plead: all right, you guide me, you suggest. But he didn't. "I don't know," he admitted. "I don't know whether I am the kind. Then I'll write fiction while I'm there. But one thing is sure. Once out there in LA, I can't go running to Edith."

It was only after he left that he realized he could have construed M's clement, level gaze as meaning he would be far away from her, too, leaving everything suspended in air, everything in flux, when instead, they could be building a life together. She would await the outcome, biding, abiding. By contrast, his own decisions were head-long and precipitous. He could glimpse their nature, but could do nothing about them.

And Mom, too, regarded him with grave, steady brown eyes when he explained. "You leave her brokenhearted; you leave an adoring woman desolate. You're willing to do that?"

"I can't help it. There's the lawyer. You know about him. She lives with him, too. I've got to save myself, that's all."

"And the other, the *fräulein*? What do you wish with her?"

"I want to marry her."

"And she you?"

"I think so."

"Then why don't you both marry? What stays you?" Mom put her workaday, thick hand to her lips; above them, the heavy face, the gray bobbed hair, with the sunken eyes between, narrowing to scrutinize. "Once married, *noo*, the other love affair is finished. She knows you have put an end to it. That you break her heart I don't condone, but you're my son."

"Well, I can't help—" Ira chafed, then gesticulated rebelliously.

"We don't know each other—I mean M and I—with minds made up. You understand?"

"Yours isn't. I understand quite well. What? You need to tell me? Ten years with a woman. She made a mensch out of you. She gave you a worthy presence, a bearing. She made a writer out of—"

"I know all that! But it's over. It'll be worse for me if I stay with her. Maybe worse for both of us. I've got to get rid of her." He scowled sullenly. "I've got to get rid of all that holds me to Edith. What do you want? The same kind of—what's the Yiddish word?—*Hass*? *Traurigkeit*? In English they'd say unhappiness, the same kind of feeling you and Pop have for each other?"

"Ah," Mom shook her head. "The same kind it couldn't be. Two cultivated people. And," Mom stressed with a disparaging grimace at Ira's analogy, "she loves you, no?"

"But I'll go crazy," he warned. "I feel I'm going to pieces, Mom. I have no other way. I've said it."

"Things fare well with me," her mournful tone excluded irony. "*Noo*. Money you'll need. I have two hundred and fifty dollars you may have. My heart's blood. I don't need to tell you with what strife each penny is pried from his niggardliness."

"I know, Mom."

"May the event prosper. Before we meet again, I'll go to the bank."

"Thanks, Mom."

"You won't squander?"

"Aw, Mom."

"*Noo*, we'll see with what credit you defray. Promise me now, you'll write?"

"Of course I'll write, Mom."

"God watch over you. You'll return next week. We'll part."

Ira left the ground floor of the two-story, nondescript frame house in a row of the same in Brooklyn. His parents had left the

Bronx because Pop had a *gesheft* there, a little "concession" in a bakery. Musing as he walked through the dingy street, musing as always with that peculiar overtone of anxiety that had become inescapable ever since he had made up his mind to leave Edith, he turned toward Pitkin Avenue. A veritable trace of grandeur, a vein of sublimity, his homey mother, shapeless, fleshy, Jewish. What if he could have drawn indefinitely on that rich Jewish world that Mom represented, only that and nothing else, known nothing else, from youth to the end of life? Ah, known nothing else. Too late now, much too late. Oh, hell, he never knew. He headed for the subway station.

CHAPTER 4

In the first week of October, Bea and the two children took the bus for LA. Ira would have helped get them to the bus station, except that the Ford, stripped down, was out of service. He had contracted with Victor, the younger brother of the service station owner at the foot of Morton Street, a kid still in his teens—and still illiterate—to overhaul the Ford for forty dollars, provided Ira lent a hand. The kid was entertained by Ira's eagerness—and ineptitude. And yet it was a learning process he relished greatly: it was a relief—more than that, a joy—to roll around under the small automobile, now raised on blocks, and undo the crankcase and camshaft, and watch the specialist called in to rebore the cylinders. He rejoiced in all that was entailed in overhauling the car, secure in the kid's knowledge of what went with what, and only his own muscles to exert. Sunny days. The car to one side of the filling station, and the overly tight crankshaft to be taken apart again, and new shims added, and crankshaft reassembled. Forgetful respite. Assume the carefree mood of the mechanic, find release in the camaraderie of work, nepenthe in evenly tightening the lugs of the oil pan.

When the job was done, the Ford smartly responding to the new battery, Ira the apprentice was invited by Victor to stay at his aunt's house in Atlantic City. They would drive out together, give the Ford a short workout, have pizzas and beer for supper—good pizzas, Victor assured. "Like homemade. Real Eyetollian pizza pie." Go for an evening walk on the boardwalk. In the morning have breakfast with his aunt and cousins, and go for another walk on the boardwalk, enjoy the ocean and the ocean breeze in daylight—until they felt like coming back.

It was to be the last ease of mind: jollity experienced in the Italian beer parlor, where he coped warily with the bubbling-hot wedges of pizza, pristine, savory, and so hot they held at bay the ravenousness they tantalized. Guzzling beer. And afterward, sated, surrendering totally to the earthy contentment of a full stomach, relishing each minute of precious interlude from apprehension, he joined Victor, simple, unschooled young Victor, in an evening stroll on the boardwalk. Talk wore out; healthy, welcome weariness set in. They headed for Victor's aunt's house a few blocks inland. Would that the night wind and the hypnotic clash of breakers meant for him what they meant for Victor: an untroubled night's sleep on the cot in the vacant bedroom upstairs, a good night's sleep with only the prospect of a morrow spent in enjoyment of idleness with friends and family. Which was how they spent the next day: Ira the bystander, entertained and comfortable, in the midst of Latin cheeriness until the sun canted westward, and time came for the two to return to Greenwich Village and the beginning of an absolutely unfathomable future.

The apartment was empty when he came back to Waverly Place. Edith had probably gone off with Dalton. Just as well. See what he could pack into the rumble seat of the Model A while she was gone. He could finish the rest of the job Monday, when she was at class. Easiest way. And when she came home from the university, tell her he was moving to the Twenty-third Street YMCA. Without fuss, he hoped, minus outbursts. Be packed anyway, ready to go. He loaded up his luxurious Rogers Peet satchel with books, lugged them down the three flights of carpeted stairs, and stowed them nervously and over-carefully into the rumble seat as compactly as he could. Then he did the same a second and third time, made the trip upstairs and down, hardening himself against meeting residents and the glances of passersby. The books for the most part were those Bill had sold him for eighty dollars. Marxist classics, and those Ira had acquired after graduation from CCNY at the end of the twenties during that period of intensive humanist discipline—delving into Dante and Goethe, Virgil and Homer before he wrote his first novel. That done, he partly packed his satchel and duffel bag with his other possessions, stowed them out of sight in the clothes closet, and awaited the arrival of Edith.

Tension gave him a hard-on. Should he jack off, or wait for Edith? She'd do anything, suck his prick, coax him to backscuttle her before the mirror. And she would be returning home from a weekend with Dalton. No, he'd masturbate. More honorable, faithful to M. And there was M in her one-room apartment a few minutes' ride uptown. Why didn't he ride uptown and fuck his love? That was it, that was the trouble: he couldn't merge the one with the other, fucking with love. He went into the bathroom . . .

Followed another bright day in October. He tried reading a few articles in the *New York Times*, but felt too edgy to complete more than the lead dispatches, the ones that concerned him most: the increasing number of Jews fleeing the persecution of the Nazis in the Third Reich; the Republican Loyalists definitely losing ground before Franco's insurrectionaries in the Spanish Civil War. He interspersed his reading with short periods of concentration in an attempt to recall anything else he ought to pack in to the Ford at the curb. He lolled worriedly in an armchair. Edith would soon return from class. He wanted to say good-bye and to assure her that he would write. He wanted to thank her for everything she had done for him; to part friends, yes, in spite of everything. The rumble seat was almost full. He had more things, apparel mostly, to load aboard, but because he knew Bill would need some room for belongings that he wanted to transfer to LA, Ira was leaving the balance of his own possessions behind. Someday he might call for them. He stood up, walked to the window, front window of a once-upon-a-time "front room."

He could see the Model A three flights down, ready at the curb. He looked east toward NYU: out of sight, unless he opened the window and leaned out. Standing at the angle he was, only the near corner of Washington Square Park came into view, and with the realization he might never stand there again, he sought to fix in mind the pipe railings that fenced in the park, the grass behind the pipe railings and the scattering of fallen leaves in the grass. Trees still in leaf, the leaves dry and lusterless but thick, the grass beneath bright green. Students by the score coming out of the park, entering Waverly Place on their way to the Sixth Avenue El, the Seventh Avenue subway line. No sign of Edith.

Memories rolled about, impinging. What had Mom said, when he came home that last time to collect the $250 he now had in his pocket? "You'll break her heart. You'll destroy her." Nah, he had scoffed in arrogant disclaimer. "She has Dalton; she has a rich lawyer to comfort her, an adult." Still, her colitis had worsened lately. Her doctor had recommended that she lie on a bed or couch after dinner, with hips propped up by several pillows; and she did, to everyone's amusement, including her own, with buttocks perfectly proportioned to her size, sleek and shapely, tilted up in the air. Nah, she'd be all right. He wouldn't break her heart.

In a lightweight coat, its tufts of wool in varied pattern of brown and black, and dark felt cloche on her head, she entered the room, still carrying her leather briefcase. Just when he hadn't been watching, and too involved within himself to hear her enter the apartment.

He stood up, greeted her. "I was watching for you awhile."

"Were you?" In good spirits, the color of her olive skin heightened by her brisk walk, affection wreathing her features, she kissed him. "The one good thing about this apartment is its closeness to the university. I can get home to a pair of sweet brown eyes sooner."

"Yes? Before you get knocked flat by a stiff wind?"

"But that's all it's good for. You've been busy?"

"Moderately." He helped her off with her coat.

"Thank you, precious. Have you been home all this time?"

"Oh, yeah."

"Doing what, if I may ask?"

"I'll wait till you put your coat away."

"Oh. Something important." She went into the hall, into the bedroom, came out sans hat, coat, briefcase, and turned toward the bathroom. "I'll be right back."

"No hurry."

"Any phone calls?"

"No."

She went into the bathroom, leaving the door open. "I was hoping Gleason of the *Times Book Review* would call. Horace has been pulling every string he could to get his book of poems in my hands, and I think he's succeeded. I hope he has—with Marya's help. She's the literary politician. Fortunately. You need to be to get anywhere. It happens that I like his poems."

"I do, too. That one about Valerius Catullus. And the one that goes, 'What you want for your money? Only more sleep.' I think quite a few of his poems can stand on their own feet, without pulling strings. I'm mixing figures—"

"I know what you mean. But not in today's literary world. The publicity goes to the best string-pullers. And rewards often do, too. You ought to hear Marya on the subject."

Leaving the sudden rush of water behind her, Edith stepped into the hall again. She sat down in the padded captain's chair, which used to be in her sunporch study, but now stood beside the oak end table with cigarette package and ashtray on it. "I'm ready."

"Well, I—" he lowered his eyes to the parquet floor, took a deep breath. "It's come, that's all. You're in such a good mood, I hate to . . . disturb it. Maybe I won't. But I don't know what else to do."

Even as he spoke, her face hardened, hardened and darkened at each word. "I thought when Dalton and I came home last night you were cheerful, and you were relaxed. 'He's beginning to come to his senses,' I thought. Evidently not. Or have you changed? What is it you're planning to do?"

"Well . . . I've packed up most of my stuff. I'm leaving."

She shook her head incredulously. "I don't believe it."

"It's true."

"How can I believe it? Despite everything everyone has done to help you see what a terrible mistake you're making. All that Dalton has done. I've done. I know he's asked you how much money you thought you'd need to live elsewhere on your own. With no restrictions. No restraints. I don't even ask that you see me. Only that you act reasonably for your own good. Find a place, your own place, in New York. Keep writing."

"I can't do it. I can't stay in New York. I've told you over and over again, I've got to establish my own independence."

"In what way would Dalton's helping you interfere with your independence? I'm not helping you. I'm not going to—"

"No." Ira warped skepticism into his grimace.

"I'm not!" Voice and sharp tip of her head combined in emphasis. "I'll not contribute a thing if that's what you object to. Dalton has offered to do it entirely on his own. He feels—as I do—that anyone with your gifts as a writer, as an artist, should not have to sacrifice them just to keep alive. I'm willing to refrain, if it takes that to preserve your gifts. I'll let Dalton and you make arrangements entirely between yourselves, deal with you entirely alone. He loves you very much, you know."

"Yeah. I don't know whether it's a question of having to sacrifice my gifts or not."

"What do you mean?"

"Whether I have any gifts left. So-called gifts—"

"Oh, poppycock!"

"You can poppycock all you like. I've had all the breaks I could possibly have. Your generosity—"

"I don't care about my generosity. I care about you!" Inflexible, adamant in her affirmation, something elemental imbued her declarations, like a gathering storm. "Darling, don't you see it's in your interest? Dalton is trying to help—leave me out of the picture."

"I'd be just where I've been."

"That's so much nonsense!"

"And I'm telling you that I can feel if I continue—I don't know. I'll go to pieces. I'll degenerate."

"Then let's get help."

"Help?"

"Let's get therapy. Psychoanalysis. That may be just what you need at this point."

"I don't want it. I'm not going to have anybody burrow into the mess I am."

"But that's the whole idea. To relieve you of the burden of it. You are in crisis, child."

"I don't care. I don't want it."

"And you think that going all the way to Los Angeles with an illiterate, fanatic Communist, who is actually manipulating you for his own ends, is going to be of any help to you in getting out of the terrible mental state you're in. What kind of help?"

"I don't ask him to help. I'm just asking to accompany him so far that I can't turn to you—I can't turn to you, or Dalton."

She seemed stunned into silence, her features coated as if in bronze, and body rigid in the wine-colored frock she wore, her gaze, even her protrusive brown eyes seemed sightless though fixed on him, unswervingly. He had nullified all of her. What blows one had to strike to sunder love. How the words swirled about in his mind, bereft of meaning. She wouldn't let go, couldn't let go, wouldn't comprehend, couldn't comprehend that he was convinced her immense affection for him incapacitated him. Worse: his whole interior structure—how to explain? Graphically, incontestably— had already parted from itself out of sheer frustration into a new irreversible phase, one that utterly loathed what he was, and even more, except for M, might become even more loathsome, and without M, without a minuscule of a chance to become the person he could accept, yearned to be.

"Do you realize what a mistake you're making?" Edith's importunity intensified. "Do you have any, any, the least notion of the ghastly mistake you're making?"

"Maybe not. But I've got to make it. Staying is a greater mistake." She was extracting from him every declaration he didn't wish to utter. And yet it was almost as if they weren't speaking the same language.

"I didn't say staying. Staying here. We've ruled that out. I mean going to Los Angeles with Bill."

"There's one practical consideration: Hollywood."

"You're the most unfitted person for Hollywood I have ever known."

"Thanks."

"If I thought you had the least ability in that direction, I'd encourage you, despite the crazy way you're going about it—without introductions, without anything—even at the expense of your literary career, even if you never wrote anything worthwhile again. You did—once—and that's more than most."

"Hollywood is only secondary; that's all I'm trying to say."

"The primary thing is that other woman. A very conventional middle-class one at that. About whom you have fantastic, romantic notions. That's the primary thing. You're in some sort of trance."

"Maybe. I'm fighting for my survival. That's the primary thing."

"And Dalton and I are trying to help you, help you get through."

"And you can't. You won't."

"Oh!" She lifted her eyes in scorn.

"I'd go even further," he insisted with raised voice. "It's nothing less than regeneration of some sort that I'm after. And neither you nor Dalton can help me. M can."

His last words overlapped hers: "Did anyone ever hear of such utter romantic rot! Yes, rot!"

"Okay."

She brought her two small hands together, ladylike and quiet; and so with her voice, as if resigned: "And when do you plan to leave?"

"New York? In a few days. Very few."

"Then why have you packed?"

He was at a loss for an answer, a suitable, tactful, mitigating one, knowing nothing would mollify. "I don't think it's fair to stay here."

"That's very considerate of you. And very late, I might add."

"I'm sorry."

And then what happened seemed to express the whole sense of their opposition, a discharge that was fraught with relief and finality. The little black ashtray that she had brought back from Silver City, jet-black ashtray fashioned by an unusually gifted Navajo crafts-woman, he had been told, sailed toward him across the intervening space, but only toward him—it would miss him, he could see, by so wide a margin, he needn't trouble to move his head; he could watch it go by. It passed wide of his right shoulder, struck the wall behind him, and broke in two before it fell to the floor, each black piece pure white within.

"You damn fool!" She burst into tears, into heartbroken sobs.

....

PART TWO

Cincinnati,
Los Angeles

CHAPTER 5

The ship was cheered, the harbour cleared,
Merrily did we drop
Below the kirk, below the hill,
Below the lighthouse top.

With Coleridge's lines in Ira's ears, and the shining Capitol dome in view—built by capitalist America, Bill didn't fail to remind Ira—the two stopped to eat their lunch, hard-boiled eggs Bill had cooked in the morning and packaged bread. Doris, Bill's daughter by his first wife, was expected to sell whatever bulky furniture Bill hadn't been able to sell, and send him the proceeds. The rest—all that pertained to little Dian, and would soon be needed by the infant Foster, Bill's child with Bea—was stowed somehow in the rumble seat and on top of it, crib and mattress and playpen, lashed down securely by Bill's powerful hand after other household items, utensils that would be needed by Bea, were packed in with Ira's books and belongings. The Model A no longer bounded onward in saucy fashion, but clung staidly to the road.

Cincinnati was the first goal. Too late, Ira realized that the route he had chosen to get there, the one that looked shortest on the map, was anything but that, a mountain road, full of windings and climbings and abrupt hairpin curves: a mistake. So was his proposal that they bivouac beside the road that night to save expenses: baloney sandwiches and milk for supper. Dusk turning cobalt; air thin and chill . . . Sleep was fitful, painful, slashed by auto headlights and brayed by truck engines.

In Cincinnati, Bill hoped to revisit native haunts—for Ira's benefit, of course, so he would get a true picture of the locale he was writing about. "Maybe your ambition'll come back," Bill suggested. He also wanted to visit the one surviving relative he knew he had in Cincinnati, his aunt Carrie Haug. She was the wife of his uncle by marriage, Zack, the one who had bragged to the magistrate when called up for sentence that he could steal a locomotive, "piece b' piece." Carrie was still alive at last report, Bill qualified his optimism somewhat, though she must be getting along in years. In Cincinnati, too, in the bureau of vital statistics in city hall, the record of Bill's birthday was kept. He hoped to obtain the date; more than hoped, it soon became apparent: he was eager to find out. He didn't know how old he was. "I figger I must be somewhere in my forties," he conjectured.

The little old Model A stuck sturdily to her job of putting highway behind her, at the rate of thirty-five miles per hour.

Ironically, all that would remain in memory of the long two-day trip was the very route he regretted choosing: through the Appalachians with their quickly cooling air, as the sky grew limpid and yellow with dusk. The two reached Cincinnati without incident.

Came the search for cheap lodgings, where they could stay the several days Bill anticipated spending—by the week was cheapest ($25 for two rooms and alcove. Kitchenette. Gas and light extra. $2.00 gas, $1.80 light). Thus the ordeal would begin: repulsive lodgings at bargain prices, the recollection traced with horror: of basement rooms with ravaged furnishings, where giant water bugs or roaches traversed the floor at night with creaking gait, where windows opened at the level of a dismal, narrow yard across which noisy and noisome garbage cans stood in a row at the back door of a greasy-spoon diner. The atmosphere of the place, despite the lateness of the year, seemed humid and decomposing, traced with the mustiness of the cellar beneath, sunless and unclean. This was no adventure now, any of it, no slumming expedition, no quest for local color. This, or not too much better, was what life was to be like for him on his own—not quite, he hoped, no, not quite that bad! How ass-backwards he did everything; would it be less so later? The customary, the pro forma privations, he thought satirically, that the apprentice writer underwent for him were utterly reversed. After the achievement, privation; after acclaim, nonentity. Well, he had asked for it. What the hell was his kind of nitwit—inept, imprudent, impractical—going to do to rehabilitate himself? He would never get any smarter, but he might feel less unwholesome to himself. He had produced a creditable novel, yes, out of the trauma of a ghetto childhood. The experience could be embalmed in print, but the individual would decay, arrested in infantilism that way. He knew.

But frantic, adrift, dissociated, all but helpless in the throes of severance, he had counted on Bill's comradeship, sympathy, some consolation arising out of the debt that Ira felt Bill owed him for the use of Ira's car. What he hadn't counted on—the reality—was the greater and ever more onerous sway Bill exerted over him, domineering, often strident, absolute. Even in the course of two or three days, their roles had been completely reversed. If Ira had been Bill's mentor over a very limited area—literacy—Bill was Ira's mentor now, without limit. He assumed complete control, and Ira was subordinated to follower, nay, vassal. He had come out from under Edith's dominion only to be plunged directly under Bill's. He could only escape by means of the scant notes he jotted down, at infrequent intervals, which Bill looked upon—for Ira caught the other glaring more than once with undisguised suspicion and rancor. Ira's only escape from Bill's interminable CP tirades, now commingled with derogatory personal reference, was the little haphazard journal in which he attempted to record vicissitudes and states of mind. So powerful was Bill's personality, so overriding—and so weak Ira's—that he could almost be convinced of anything Bill asserted in that harsh, grating, overbearing tone of his: that black was white, to use the most commonplace, the most threadbare of clichés. The mind went numb before Bill's sheer overwhelming force: that Lenin and Marx and Engels and Stalin were all from the proletariat. The boojwasie couldn't do shit; the proletariat did it all, invented all, discovered all. Had the beating that Bill had suffered in a strike on the docks so deranged him—and Ira been so unaware of what had happened—that he still expected Bill to be the once warm, friendly, even deferential comrade he had been? He now ranted, ranted in monologue. And stunned, Ira listened.

"If I could write, I'd be a better writer than you," Bill raged. "Youze can only write about that soft crap is the boojwasie. I'd be writin' about the workin' class, the revolutionary workin' class, an' what they done for Russia, and what they're goin' to do for the world!"

And Ira could only agree: Bill's writing would be superior, not that Ira's agreement appeased Bill, any more than a sapling's bending with the storm abated its fury. Who the hell would have guessed this fanatic madman would emerge from that seemingly controlled exterior, the disciplined proletarian in whom Ira had idealistically believed—and sought to portray, endowed with rough, innate poetry. No wonder he could get no further. He was living, he was writing in a dreamworld, not about the bourgeoisie, as Bill accused, but about Bill, revolutionary hero. What had he gotten himself into? Ira strove to focus his bewilderment into tenable judgment. How many days to LA? Days and days away, days and days to endure in numb subservience. What did it mean? It was his insidious self-contempt that reduced him, as Bill gloated aloud, into "nothin' but putty in my hands."

Only once did Ira flare up: when Bill with a typical sideswipe cast aspersion on M (he had seen her, the one time Ira had brought her to Bill and Bea's apartment in New York). Proletarian women were strong and rugged, Bill averred, stout women who could do the work of building socialism and bear robust children to their working-class mates. "You can see it from their pitchers in the Soviet Union magazines. They're like Bea. I wouldn't go to no TB hospital to pick out a wife."

"Meaning?"

"I'm just sayin' I wouldn't go to no sanatorium to pick out a wife. I'd pick me out a strong, healthy woman." Bill's throat, thick and sagging, reddened.

"You mean M? What makes you think I found her in a sanatorium?"

"I'm not sayin' that. I'm sayin' she's no strong proletarian woman."

"Is that how you decide? Whether a woman is heavy enough? Not whether you need each other, you love each other? How'd you pick Bea?"

Bill's voice grated furiously. "I'm sayin' the boojwasie chooses the delicate and the flat-chested ones, the ones that can't work. That ain't what the proletariat chooses."

"Bullshit!" Ira stormed. "How do you know the flat-chested ones are weak, and how do you know they can't work? I knew a woman in Maine where I stayed; she was seventy years old—all rope and sinew. She could outwork most men."

"I didn't say they couldn't."

"You did! Just because M happens to be slender."

"It don't make a shittin' bit o' difference what they are."

"It did a minute ago. You said it did."

"I says the proletariat chooses one kind an' the boojwasie likes a differnt kind; that's what I said."

"How do you expect her to be big and beefy, if her life's given over to music and the piano. I'll betcha that's true in the Soviet Union, too."

"Christ, you're all wet! I said I wouldn't go to no sanatorium to pick out a wife."

"I didn't go to one either."

Returning to his native city filled Bill with enthusiasm. Nostalgia streamed from him as they sauntered about the center of town. Fountain Square, with its rays of water squirting from bronze hands on bronze figures below, awoke memories of the days he lolled there on the grass, tough kid taunting the well-groomed passersby, calling them sticks of candy. Pawnshops and their contents, glass eyes, stoves and miter saws and pry bars, stirred him with excitement.

Following directions given by a newsdealer, Ira drove to Bill's boyhood haunts. Though greatly changed, he said, he was still able to orient himself and to reconstruct the neighborhood as he remembered it. And keyed up as he was, he conveyed the boyhood reality to Ira as the two walked about: manure, flies, teamsters, and slaughterhouse stench. The brewery, with its malty aura here, the dairy there, the icehouse across the street, and the street itself paved with round cobblestones. Here Bill had seen the drover twist the tails of bellowing steers to goad them on, had watched cattle driven past the house, had seen pens of hogs hauled past the door in chain-driven trucks, hogs and red hogs, had heard the bleat of sheep. The Jews had their own slaughterer, who made the rounds of the slaughterhouses. In square skull cap, he drew the long-bladed knife across the steer's throat. Regular killing was preceded by polling the animal with a sledge, the dust exploding from under the hair, and the spasmodic kicking of the felled beast. With sheep, the head was bent back, and the steel plunged into the throat. Bill recalled how big the numbers on the wagons had seemed in boyhood. His father drove one, and would get free drinks for hauling the coal ashes from the beer saloons. "Jesse Pomeroy played at killin' hogs," Bill remarked casually. "He hung up three kids by the leg in one o' the stables here an' killed 'em."

In the neighborhood where Bill remembered his aunt had last lived, he reminisced tirelessly, avidly, redundantly, as he sought to identify Carrie's house. Grandma whipping him with a wet sheet for calling her a sonofabitch—which he refused to retract; the butcher who threw a pig's trotter at him for hanging around the doorway too long; the milk wagon Bill drove off to another street, after which, he and Dan, his brother, helped themselves to all the cream they could lug off. Composites of his life rose to the surface as he searched for some clue of recognition. He had asked Santa Claus on two successive Christmases for a small wagon, one he could hitch a goat to, and not getting his wish, said to hell with Santa.

Among run-down, two-story brick houses, Bill led the way, stopping now one elderly person, now another, to ask whether they knew Carrie Haug, asking with a peculiar eagerness, as if she were the last tie to his past, one that had come alive again here in Cincinnati. Once, they were invited into the kitchen of a bony, elderly woman, invited to sit down and have a cup of coffee. Bill recounted the early days of the neighborhood and described his aunt; his uncle had died years before. The elderly woman thought she knew the name Carrie Haug, but couldn't recall whether she had moved away or entered a nursing home. They thanked the lady for her hospitality, Bill so much more like the man Ira had first known, affable, expansive, unembittered. And once again, with Ira in tow, Bill took up the search.

Streets, and alleys between streets, something Ira had never seen before, not backyards, but alleys, mostly deserted, sometimes occupied by children at their games. "See the difference between here and New York," Bill exulted. "See the room?" He stopped to ask an alert, gray-haired woman scrubbing a windowsill whether she had ever heard of Carrie Haug. No, she hadn't. Had he looked in the city directory? No, he had looked in the phone book. He ought to look in the city directory, she advised. Some of the big stores in town had one, the library, city hall. Bill thanked her heartily.

They went on. Multitudes of fences crisscrossed on either hand. High-tension wires overhead scored the clear blue air of the October afternoon. Flowers, geraniums still bloomed in the rusty lard pails on windowsills. Suspended from window shades hung nostalgic little wooden beer barrel shade pulls. No one remembered Carrie Haug. They stepped into grocery stores and saloons, above whose lintels, the striped, frayed awnings of a bygone era were rolled up. Never heard of her. And once again in the narrow back alleys, where ivy withered on the fences, sulfurous, spent sunflowers drooped, shorn of petals, and grapevines twined (recalling to Bill the days of bold depredations). Shuttered windows and listing, abandoned outhouses with crescent moon and diamond ventilators. "No, I can't say I ever heard of her. Carrie Haug?" the gnarled old man rested his foot on the spade.

They returned to the Ford. "I don't think we're going to find her," Ira said.

"We'll keep lookin' for her tomorrow. It's fer you I'm tryin' to find her."

"For me?" At last he was becoming aware of the forms of Bill's subterfuges.

"Well, you's the one wanted to know all about how we lived. She could tell you a lot."

Ira nodded. "Yeah."

"Of course, I want to give her a little present, too, if we find her."

It was their third day in Cincinnati, and the morning quest for Carrie was as disappointing as before. "I guess we're outta luck," Bill surmised grimly. Ira had consulted the directory, without success, and then they walked a last time through the sunny, apathetic streets. Was the sadness immanent in the neglected neighborhood, or was it Ira's own depression reflecting itself in externals? Bill teemed with nostalgic memories. Here, in an alley, maybe it was this one, he used to go barefoot. "Best thing to do when you're bein' chased for stealin' something is to throw the stuff at the guy."

"I know. You told me."

"I never was much good at runnin'. So I had to learn how to fight. The average kid puts a chip on his shoulder, an' says, 'I dare you knock it off.' Hell, you bust him one on the chin. That knocks it off."

The more Ira heard him talk, the more he learned of his escapades, in this, his native environment, the more did the last remnants of romantic illusions about the worker depart. Why he should have had them to begin with, having spent the first twenty years of his life in ghetto and slum, he didn't know. Revolution transfigured the workers, he thought. And perhaps it did—some; perhaps it did Bill at one time. Would to God he had gotten that book over with, before the illusions turned rancid. Too late now. And beyond him, too, alas, if not the talent, the disposition, the temperament, to get down to the facts, to facts such as this, to create something out of the actualities of a character such as this. Not the lapidary prose Maxwell Perkins bought three years ago, but the truth, something approaching this violence, this delinquency, this psyche.

Bill had perceived Ira's complete disenchantment with him. He made no pretense of colorful mimicry any longer, either in speech or slant of motive, of editing, as it were, his past, furnishing the embellishment he discerned Ira sought. He no longer cared what Ira saw, or what he thought, knowing that Ira was almost completely in his power. It was all very strange: it had become far more than a mere change of roles, more than dialectical negation, so called; it had become outright rejection. How significant a foreshadowing of what the dictatorship of the proletariat would hold for the cultivated soft-ies of the petite bourgeoisie, the artist and intellectual, the dabbler, the dilettante and connoisseur, Ira dreaded to think.

Bill lay asleep in his underwear, unless he was feigning. The events of the day just spent returned to Ira. Most of the morning had been given over to a fruitless search for Carrie. And when they had gone full circle, repeating their steps in streets passed through already—Ira was beginning to recognize them—a man he could only describe as bloated, pitifully obese, who sat like a human toad in a wheelchair, waved to them as they approached. "I seen you before," he said. "And I heard about you. You once lived here." His smile seemed to rise through depths of puffy flesh.

"Yeah, I once did. I'm lookin' fer my aunt now."

"They told me. You're lookin' for Carrie Haug."

"That's right." Bill thrust his artificial hand deeper into his pocket, and fixed the guy with his relentless blue eyes.

"You musta passed her house a couple o' times: 12 Cedar Lane. She lived there all her life."

"I didn't exactly remember."

"She's dead. Died about a year ago. Thirty-seven. Been a widow a long time. Lived on a Spanish-American War pension. Yep, Carrie Haug. She wasn't very heavy, wasn't very big."

"No."

"She used to say, 'No good Christian should smoke.' But it was all right to boom a little snuff under your lip, because you spit it out. That was no sin. She was all gums."

"Yeah?"

"She's dead."

"So she's dead?"

"That's right. Too bad. Good woman, too. She used to tithe the little she had for the church. There was somethin' went wrong with her innards."

"Yeah? Well. Thanks fer tellin' me."

The obese man nodded. Faintest condolence floated on his blubbery features.

"Bye." Bill became implacably impassive.

"Bye. Good luck."

They went on their way. "You don't think he's shittin' me?" Bill asked.

"No. Not that old man."

"I didn't think so. That settles it."

The alley in which they had stopped stretched lonely in the dusk, sunset permeating the dusty air. "That was a tannery over there, them closed doors. An' that was a packin' house. See the gate swingin' open? That's where they penned up small herds." His steel hook rested in the bend of Ira's elbow. "So Carrie's gone. My mother's sister; she was the last o' the old people." His hook gleamed, merged from gesture of dismissal to arc indicating the center of town. "No use lookin' no more. Let's drive over there to that city hall."

The certain tidings of Carrie's death was the first blow Bill suffered that day. The second came in the afternoon, when they inquired his date of birth in the office of the bureau of vital statistics in city hall. The fee for the service was fifty cents, and Ira paid it. They sat on the old-fashioned oak bench in the buff-and-white-walled office, while the middle-aged clerk, still wearing garters on the arms of his striped shirt, took Bill's name—not Loem, but Brenning—back into the files. He returned in a surprisingly short time with the information: Bill was born in March of 1888.

"How old does that make me?" Bill asked.

The clerk lifted his eyes to Bill's face, then sidelong to Ira's. "You're fifty," he said. "You became fifty in March of this year." His lips protruded.

"Fifty?" If Bill could show consternation, it was then. "I didn't think I was that old."

The clerk slid the penciled slip of paper on the counter toward Bill. "Those your parents?"

Bill made a show of scanning the writing. "Hilda an' Fred Brenning."

"That's your date of birth. Born on 22 Crescent Court."

Outdoors again, at the top of the city hall steps, he asked Ira to corroborate the clerk's finding: "Read that out once."

Ira read the date on the slip of paper, his parents' name, place of birth, date of birth.

"An' that makes me fifty?" He took back the slip of paper, even as he scrutinized Ira's face.

"Right. Eighty-eight to thirty-eight. You wonder how they can find it so fast. You were off by at least three years."

"Fifty." He pushed back his visored chauffeur's cap, the kind of cap Lenin wore in photos addressing a Russian crowd, exposing to full afternoon sunlight his coarse, rough visage, his scarred brow. "Christ, who'da thought it?" He found a pocket for the slip of paper in his dull white shirt.

And now, in the certainty of Carrie's death, in the certainty of his age, they made for the car.

"All right to have a couple o' boiled eggs and boiled spuds for supper?" Ira asked.

"You're always thinkin' o' your gut," he growled.

"I'm not always thinking of my gut. What else is safe to prepare in that dump? You've got an ulcer."

"I c'n eat anything. Don't worry about me. You're eggin' us to death."

"I don't know what else—" Ira began to reiterate, then shut up. Let him vent his bitterness.

"We'll get the hell outta here tomorrow. No use hangin' around here."

"Okay. That's only four days of the seven I paid for, but they can have the rest."

They reached the car, parked in the shopping street of the quarter—and suddenly Bill declaimed with such voice and such timbre that he drew the attention of the two men coming out of the café. "It don't make a shittin' bit o' difference how old you are. Brave men dies in struggle. They dies fightin' the system, fightin' the boss, the rulin' class." He seemed to embrace the thought physically, exultantly. "They dies like Chapayev. He couldn't read neither, but he showed 'em how to die. They'll never git Chapayev! Brave men dies like that, with machine-gun bullets spittin' in the water all around him. They dies on the barricades. They don't give up; they sells it out!"

They would be leaving the wretched premises tomorrow, reason in itself for rejoicing, deliverance, a day nearer LA. Ira got into the car. Things ought to be easier from now on, Ira thought.

They cleaned up the dishes after supper, and then they went for a last stroll to Fountain Square. Under a trefoil of an ornamental lamppost, a short distance away, a very small gathering of people like a fluctuating atoll, surrounded an even smaller group of Negro gospel singers, women wearing uniform gray garb and singing to the accompaniment of tambourines. "Down by the river," Ira heard the words of the hymn as they drew closer. They stopped at the outer fringe of the audience. Tune and tambourine held their variously pitched voices together. "Down by the river . . ." The spiritual ended, and testimonials commencing, they moved on. And then it began to happen—it seemed to Ira's incredulous ears to happen over an extended period of time, like the crumbling of a dike or seawall:

Bill's voice started to break. Harsh and grating at first, it dissolved into sobs.

He wept. Wonderment on Ira's part gave place to dismay—what was happening? What unbelievable thing was happening? Dismay gave way to sneaking elation: so this was the iron man, the steeled revolutionary—no different from anybody else, flesh and blood breaking down in the presence of religious appeal, undone by a band of Negro women singing "Down by the River." Ira kept respectful silence, fearful that speech would betray his dissembled feelings.

He was "teched," he wept; he was teched, not by the song but by memories of his boyhood on the banks of the Ohio and the canal; by memories of his grandmother washing clothes for something to eat; by all the misery the working class had to suffer. Ira assured him that he understood.

Ira was to pay for his understanding. As if guessing his exultation at the disclosure of his all too human weakness, Bill rode him mercilessly after he recovered, as much as blamed him for his breakdown, accused him of callousness at the plight of the poor and oppressed. Then he took to baiting him, harping on his petit bourgeois status: "They's rich ants and poor ants," he taunted, "and the rich ants hires the poor ants fer doormen. That's your kind." Ira found himself placed in the same position he had often placed Edith—in the ranks of the petite bourgeoisie.

Bill was asleep now. If Ira had thought before that this was no slumming expedition, no search for local color, not the least iota of that remained.

All during the time Ira had written his one and only novel, the specter of retribution would arise: he would have to pay for this ease, this secluded, comfortable study he was in, he had felt, the cocktails before dinner, this English tweed jacket he was wearing. So here was the first installment: horror—embodied in the giant water bugs he

74

heard creaking on the floor, the garbage cans under the stark back-door light of the beanery across the narrow yard, and the musty reek of the cellar that came up through the warped floorboards.

Anyone would have thought that a trip this long would have been filled with discussion of the current crisis in Europe, Chamberlain's appeasement policy, the sellout of the Czechs at Munich and what it presaged, the intensifying persecution of Jews by the Nazis—not at all. Ira's reading of articles or news items about international affairs from the local newspaper produced a loud yawn. Both to him were suspect, or contaminated: the newspaper and the reader. Still, Ira doubted if he were to read aloud articles or commentary out of the *Daily Worker*, whether his reaction would be any different. It would be the same story: Ira would be displaying his superiority, even in this one thing, literacy, something not to be tolerated. After a year of trying to learn to read, Bill had made no effort to continue, and easily rationalized it. Sometimes Ira wondered whether it wasn't a vast uncertainty that made him so domineering, and yet Ira had to confess that he was right most of the time, or at least partly right. He accused Ira of being tight, penny-pinching, and of being completely self-seeking—familiar accusations that Ira could scarcely deny. He either talked or slept; and when awake, often worked himself up into a passion of two hours' duration, as though he were rehearsing a harangue of vindication of himself. Apparently, he had been charged by members of the Party with behaving like a dictator, and of losing his head during a crisis.

The innumerable frays he had been in, the countless beatings he had administered, underwent an alteration of meaning, the obverse side of the coin: not the native American individual pitted heroically against the evils in society, but a semiparanoid avenging personal slights—often triggered by the very barbs and slurs Bill himself was guilty of. Likely as not, it was vengeance that took its toll eventually: his right hand shredded when machinery whose gears he was assigned to clean during the noon break was mysteriously, surreptitiously, turned on, though a monitor was always posted at the main switch.

They tarried another day and night in Cincinnati. There was no more for them to do actually, but they stayed on, which made the last day there seem like an anticlimactic cap on futility. On pretext, by now threadbare, of helping furnish Ira with further material for his writing, Bill seemed intent on separating himself from his nostalgias, of reconciling himself to his own and the city's changes. So they rambled through the main shopping thoroughfares, without goal. He was more relaxed now, easier. He sang "Casey Jones," he sang "The Old Gray Mare." And in the evening, finally, he had Ira drive them up to Price Hill, once an area of palatial estates, now shabby and rundown. Dusk settled over the city, as they sat on a wall on the bluff overlooking the river, the Ohio, flowing southerly dark and calm. Across it on the eastern bank, tiny automobiles negotiated tiny streets among miniature houses.

The future of the working class would be glorious, Bill expatiated. The time would come when machinery would do most of the work, men less and less, after capitalist exploitation was abolished. He was in a mellow mood, all too infrequent—perhaps the scene below affected him. "An' if the time comes when all we does is push a button to git the job done, then that's all we does. Then nobody works."

A youth came up and sat down beside them. He wore glasses, was delicate in feature and well-spoken. They talked awhile about the beautiful scene; and after he left, Bill and Ira argued amiably about what the art and culture of the future would be like, whether they would be delicate excrescences of society like that youth, or what. Art and culture would be plain, Bill decreed: it wouldn't be fancy and incomprehensible, as pleased the bourgeoisie. It would be plain and strong, the way the working class would appreciate it.

"But what if there were no working class left?" Ira hedged. "What if you just pushed a button as you said, and nobody worked?"

"They'd be Communist artists," was Bill's rejoinder. "They'd be natcherly Communist. Like breathin'. Nobody'd have to tell 'em they was supposed to do this or that, so the people liked it. They'd work natcherly so the people liked it—not just what the rulin' class liked."

The next morning they repacked all their belongings in the car, and in clear sunlight the Model A chugged up the long sweep of road across the bridge over the Ohio and into the sky above the bluff, leaving behind Cincinnati and memory of the ordeal.

In an ascension of cheerfulness, now that only a few days separated them from LA, Ira hummed the "Marseillaise." In rough, yet not unpleasant, voice, and carrying the tune well, Bill countered with the "Internationale." Some dozen days had now come to an end. Ira had begun this journey quoting mentally one of the first stanzas of the "Ancient Mariner." As it drew to a close, facetiousness wouldn't be the only thing served, if he concluded by borrowing from Coleridge again: those lines about the Pilot's boy, who now doth crazy go.

CHAPTER 6

That afternoon he had had a troublesome stiff neck, alleviated somewhat by the nap he had just aroused from in the furnished rooms Bill had temporarily rented in a dusty part of LA, while they waited for the "Investigator" in a larger cabin in the Florence Motor Court, where Bea and the children had been living. Their bus ride out to the coast had been long and tiresome, but presumably free from the irritant that was Bill.

The old woman who owned the rooming house, a two-story frame building, still retained what must have been the mannerisms of her youth, a coquettish, soubrettish expressiveness. In a stagy, aged voice, she described herself as a widow too poor to own a car, and hardly able to afford the sixty dollars needed to reshingle the roof before it began leaking seriously. The interior of the house, whose floors had a perceptible list, was spotless, the linoleum scrubbed daily and sedulously. In the living room hung a large period photograph of a pretty, curly-haired young girl in a sailor suit, one of her hands resting on the head of a solemn Saint Bernard.

The neighborhood had something of the barren quality of *The Waste Land*, the deserted neighborhood "round behind the gashouse," where the poet fishes in the dull canal. Opposite the house, and occupying an entire square block, was the Salvage Department of the City Waterworks. Here, piled behind the wire fence in orderly fashion, were water mains of various sizes, giant shutoff valves, hydrants, and innumerable lengths of galvanized pipe, all eloquent of water supply, though the terrain was arid. Through the open doors of the large repair shop issued the rushing noise of machinery, like a parching wind. Train bells sounded from the small locomotive in the yard.

With the infant Foster in the folding pram, which had been carted in the Ford all the way from the East Coast, Bill walked by the house as the elderly landlady was sweeping the porch. "Don't sweep on us," he snarled. "There's germs in that dust."

"I wasn't sweeping on you," she protested. "I didn't see you."

"You didn't stop when we was comin', an' you was lookin' right at us."

"I'm sorry."

"You're sorry. If you was a man, I'd come up there, an' teach you a lesson."

"You're not very polite," she countered, with remarkable self-possession.

How surreal the exchange seemed, set in a relativist landscape where time had slowed down, unseen machinery soughed, and the shrunken self was stranded among waterworks. Bill would not retreat afterward from his insistence that the old woman had deliberately swept on them because of her aversion for Bill's "Commonist ideology." His stubbornness was foolish beyond imagination, but at other times had helped him survive.

Sometimes Ira wondered whether he had come all these three thousand miles just to get a room of his own? He might have done that in New York, merely moved a dozen or so blocks away from Waverly Place and thus achieved his purpose. On the other hand, it was satisfying to arise in the morning, even in a furnished room such as this, sit down and write a few paragraphs after breakfast, and feel, at least during the writing, responsible to no one, unburdened by cares, obligated only to the writing itself. The journal as a literary form appealed to him, though this was not how he proposed to spend the bulk of his time here.

He was continually torn by contrary impulses. Having written a novel, he wanted, first and foremost, to write another. At the same time, he was without economic independence, without the means to write a long piece of work, and was able to do so before only through Edith's bounty. That source was removed—unless he wished to renege on his own aspirations toward achieving adult independence. Nor was there any guarantee, or indication, that a return to his dependent status, to a ménage à trois with Dalton, would yield better results than had the past four years since he had completed his last opus. That brought up the question of self-support, getting a job. But a job would unquestionably prevent him from writing, impede him greatly, given the kind of writer he was, toilsome and contemplative and dilatory. He had been thinking of Hollywood and of writing to Lynn R, who knew his way around Hollywood, having worked there for several years, alternating with his writing of plays. But Ira was afraid to, literally afraid to, not because Hollywood had a reputation of corrupting the artist—he wondered what, if anything, was left of him—but of Lynn himself or of himself in relation to him. He had always been fond of him, admired his verbal nimbleness, his witticisms—but not the way he had exhibited his affection for Ira, which had become obvious the last time Lynn had been in New York, when he had imbibed too much. These womanless days since leaving Edith and M, Ira had become, as it were, inert, nervously spent, perhaps because overwrought without being aware; libido seemed to have gone into hibernation, its instrument become, as Petronius Arbiter phrased it, an inch of useless leather. But who knew? Ruminations about Bill and his domination over Ira seemed to imply a reciprocal role—he was troubled enough without writing Lynn R.

———

A week later, a two-bedroom cabin at the Florence Motor Court was approved by the Home Relief Bureau investigator, and Bill and Bea and the two children moved there. To all intents and purposes, they had settled down. Driving back to lodgings from a visit to Bill's cabin, in part his advocate, in part his prosecutor, Ira mulled over things argued about at supper. At the very beginning of the meal Bill declaimed, "All I ever think about is the Revolution. That's what I want, the Revolution!" As Ira managed the car through the reduced traffic on the dull streets of midevening, he recalled Bill's telling him of the rebuke he had received from Israel Amter, high CP functionary: that Trotskyism was working in him. And Bill's rebellious, unspoken response, made to Ira afterward: "He's a shit, too."

Bill and Bea had been "bumping" lately, Bea admitted, when she and Ira had the chance for a word alone together. The atmosphere between them of late seemed highly charged, higher even than that between Bill and Ira. Ira had thought at first it was little Foster's wailing that put their nerves on edge: the child had what appeared to be a stiff neck, but turned out to be an "eyetooth" breaking through the gums. Now that the infant was quiet, they still disputed about the least thing in tones vociferous, harsh, and unsettling. Ira had witnessed some of that in New York, before they had left, but nothing like this. She advised him that the door was always open, and that she got along better the two weeks he was away. They argued over his roughshod methods of reinstating himself with the Home Relief Bureau, his belligerent dragging out of documents to prove that the Home Relief Bureau was cheating him—as a result of which, Bea claimed, the bureau cut Bill off from payments for another four weeks. It was something he never told Ira, but as usual presented himself in the light of the persecuted but unflinching mili-

tant. He roared at her that all workers ought to do that, fight capitalism uncompromisingly.

This brought them into another dispute: whether the workers were dumb or not. She asserted that she could show him in the
words of Marx and Lenin that they were. He raged that she couldn't.
Workers are backward or misled, but not dumb. As the argument
became more furious, new eruptions took place, volcanic side eruptions, as it were. She took him to task for the difference in the way
he treated little Foster and his treatment of Dian, Bea's child by Bill's
brother, Dan. Bill denied this vehemently: he treated them both alike,
he averred. Which was patently untrue, as Ira had had occasion to
observe: his difference in concern of the two children was unmistak-
able; it was flagrantly unequal. She accused him of speaking to her
like a foreman calling a gang of men. He flung back, "Well, don't act
like a first mate on a freighter."

Three letters from three women in New York were on the table
beside Ira as he made these reflections: M's optimistic and buoyant
one; Edith's letter, full of lamentation and anguish; and Mrs. Emily
R's, the Boston and Long Island socialite whose children Ira had
tutored. Her letter was spirited, instilled with the courage of her
American forebears. She denounced the betrayal of the Czechs by
Chamberlain, urged resistance by the democracies against the growing menace of Nazi Germany.

Ira drove over to the Y, whose gym his New York membership entitled him to use, and on his way, he passed the Methodist
church where streamers in front of the building proclaimed, "This
church, together with all Christians, prays for the persecuted Jews of
Europe." It was interesting that Bill rarely dwelled on this, despite
his professed empathy, although Ira didn't either.

Always belated, insecure in his political insights, fearful of her-
esy or error, as in everything else, his thoughts wavering, Ira drove
into the rooming house parking lot, switched off the engine, got out,

and climbed the flight of stairs to his room. On his writing table next to the window still lay the three letters. He opened Edith's. The page was dark, not for lack of light, but dark with compactness, dark print. The lines were single-spaced, presenting a page of solid typescript. Ira began rereading her letter for the third time, her imprecations sounding as dire and desperate as they did in person in New York.

Dear Ira:

I am trying to tell you truths, Ira, though perhaps too violently, not vindictively, if you'll read this through. Perhaps it does no good, but sometimes it does do a person good to be faced with himself, whom he has dodged all his life—at least I've found that to be true of me.

Put yourself into a novel and perhaps you'll realize something of what you are. You are first and foremost a completely self-engrossed individualist, to whom communism, the proletariat, or your friends and intimates have meant nothing, except what you could feed on. You have no emotional imagination about anyone on earth but yourself. And you have been far more immoral, to my mind, and would be to that of others if they knew, in acting as you have, than any of the liberal left, people you so frequently criticize. I'm very tired of your rationalizations based on society, or your own pain, or your need to grow to maturity.

I do not believe one word about what you say are your reasons for going out there to LA, except that once more they are rationalizations of an escape from obligations of every kind—toward me, toward M. None of your psuedo-Marxian explanations, or your explanations of higher states of being, are anything but funny to me. And I know, now, that there's no reason to suppose you won't be just as selfish with another woman as you

*were with me. And just as cruel and blind—given the time to
get over your romantic illusion.*

*You can say all you like about growing pains, but I believe
nothing of it until I see that you've grown. I've spent about $200
on this trip of yours so far, between Bill and Bea and Doris and
you, and you knew I could not afford it. You got your money
from your mother, yes, but the Loems got theirs from me and
dropped Doris on me, too. I don't resent the Loems at all and
am fond of them, but at this time in my life you should not
have asked me to be responsible for them. I have been far from
well. I do not know and won't for another week whether or not
I'm pregnant. But except to legalize a child, I'd have nothing
more to do with you, if that were so, and I'm not sure whether
I'd want to have even that much to do with you. In any case,
I've not been able to pay $20 for another test, and have simply
waited the required time to really know. You gave me such a
shock that something happened to make me miserably unwell. I
wonder if you will ever dare tell M that you lived with me till
the last minute.*

*You might at least have cleared out before I got back to New
York, but no. Oh, doubtlessly you thought you were doing the
best you could by me, but you were doing the worst thing possible. We all make mistakes, and certainly I made my share of
them in allowing you to treat me as you did for so long a time.
I never would have done so, I suppose, had I not been badly
hurt in childhood myself. You probably think you have been
badly hurt, too. But so far as I can see the trouble with you is
that, unlike your sister, you were given too much, first by your
mother, and then by me. If now you blamed yourself, not society, not me, I'd see some hope for you.*

*You've taken far more from me—even if only the important
years of life—than I have from you, whatever way you may*

84

assign responsibility for allowing this to happen. And as any sort of man you should have known this. You were not a man, and you are not yet—as far as I can judge. I've always said that you should function through your art and live by it, but I begin to feel sure that your art will be no good until you come to some sense of what is reality in this world—the mere business of trying to make a living, through your writing or through some other means that properly fit in with your writing. Others have done it. You could have found some way. I always hoped you would find that you had to get to work, and when you did, you would consider your responsibility to me, but no. However, because I've fostered this thing so long, and because you think you can work your way through by your writing, I am sending this check.

Edith

Various people called at Bea and Bill's during Ira's visits there. One was a wizened comrade named Avery, with two moles on his chin, who arrived with a pint of California port wine under his shirt. He told of selling fifty dollars worth of CP literature a month. His "outfit," composed of some twenty-two members, later increased to twenty-eight, and then, because of transfers, again reduced to twenty-two, was a "legal" outfit. It could hire halls and hold a few street meetings, something the LA Red Squad wouldn't permit the illegal outfits to do. According to him, the masses, whom he terms hoodlums, half in earnest, half in jest, gave every indication of voting against their own interests on Proposition One, which has to do with the timing of rent-relief payments by the city. Listening to him speak, Ira was struck by the difference between Avery, someone representative of the usual Party member, and Bill: The one focused on the concrete issues of immediate interest to the masses; the other dwelled almost solely on the vast, dramatic storms he wishfully foresaw gathering in the nebulous future. It went without saying, unfortunately, that the latter appealed to Ira, and not the former: the color, the swirl, the clash, the immense upheaval. What was mere rent relief by comparison?

Avery, it seemed from Bea's account later, had been a carpenter by trade. He left his wife in Chicago, got a job in California, and spent all his spare time building a home there. He also had a paramour in Chicago. His letters to his paramour were intercepted by her mother, who sent them to his wife in Chicago. She divorced him—only to marry a scoundrel a short time later who put her in a brothel. Comrade Avery scarcely breathed a sober breath for a year thereafter.

Later that evening, after the departure of Comrade Avery, Ira broached a tentative plan of leaving LA in the direction of San Diego, close to the Mexican border. There, Ira knew no one; there, he thought, he might slough off what he was. Without reproof, but with reasoned disagreement, Bill pointed out how a single trained teacher could teach many comrades to write, to write of their experiences in life, as William Z. Foster had done, to write stories and articles. Ira was a writer as well as a teacher. Why didn't he do his part for the Revolution by getting a paid job in the Party for two or three nights a week, right there in LA. He'd earn enough to get by that way, and at the same time perform a needed service for the working class. And Ira was again torn by what was just and ethical, by the obligatory on the one hand, and by his inveterate shirking on the other. And undoubtedly, the hidden reason for his obduracy was his confidence in remaining in his class, that in the end necessity could be staved off. As a last resort, in fine, there was always Edith, with her all-too-ready purse.

The upshot was that the impulse to break away from Bill was canceled by Bill himself, and once again Ira was resigned to staying in LA, and close to him. Ira marveled helplessly at the man's unswerving purposiveness, which decided Ira's future for him, enlisting in his cause Ira's own milksop resolve. In spite of everything, nevertheless, in spite of himself, too, something was accruing, accruing to character, oddly enough, an enhancement of comprehension, or so Ira fancied, a minute seasoning of the personality. He was learning to forget Edith, his mother, even publishers, retaining only M's image, like an icon to calm his disquiet. Otherwise, Ira knew nothing better to do in the meantime but to rely on Bill's guidance and precept; perhaps they would bear fruit in the form of self-support and a measure of independence, as he suggested.

Spaghetti was for supper the next night, which Bill reminded Ira that he ate like a horse does hay. He and Bea had spent a good part of the afternoon in a fruitless search for a furnished or partly furnished house, one in which they could all live together. It's just as well, Ira thought, for all the economies he might make living with them, that they hadn't found such a place. The rooming house Ira lived in was beginning to fill up (Ira had been the first tenant there). The other roomers offered some needed distraction, and at the same time, all went to work in the morning, giving him as much privacy as he could ask for six days a week.

Bea and Ira went shopping before supper, for groceries and utensils for her as well as for himself. She had qualms about going into Woolworth's five-and-ten, having been apprehended there for shoplifting when she was a girl. And she hoped above all things not to run into her mother (the first time she had ever mentioned her folks, or even her California origins), saying she'd shit a brick if she did chance to meet her mother. They shopped at Woolworth's without incident, stored everything into the Ford, and returned to the cabin, where they were met by Bill: pallid, and bristling with hostility. He said nothing. The thought crossed Ira's mind that he might be suffering severe ulcer pains. Ira went outdoors and began cleaning the Model A, while supper cooked. He came in when Bea called.

At issue was a matter that Ira had confided to Bea (and almost immediately regretted): his having written to Edith asking her this once to defray his room rent. His gut turned over, Bill told Ira, when he heard about Ira's contemptible sponging on the woman he had deserted. Stung, Ira retorted mockingly that he hoped his gut was now back in place. Without explicitly likening Ira to a pimp, Bill drew analogies that came perilously close. He declared that Ira should have rejoined the Movement months and months ago, tied up with a CP writers' group, but since he couldn't get him to stir in that direction, he ought at least to take the first steps toward the Struggle: begin earning his own living. And then he drew another egregious analogy: of the Irish longshoreman he had tried to recruit into the Party by giving the other a number of free meals at noon, only to discover the Irishman accepted the handouts cynically, without the least intention of joining the Party. "The bastard thought only about his own gut," Bill rasped. Setting polemic to one side, his words carried a lasting sting. Ira's position was morally reprehensible: to turn to Edith for financial assistance, while at the same time writing to M about the depth of his affection for her and sounding out hers for him.

CHAPTER 7

Ira had had no luck whatever with respect to Hollywood, with regard to a position of scriptwriter in a movie studio; this will-o'-the-wisp aspiration, which presumably had drawn him out to LA, was now thoroughly squashed. Lynn R, whom Ira had hoped—and feared—to turn to for introductions, was back in Oklahoma and, according to Edith, had acquired a new friend, a folksinger, gifted in presence as well as voice. How well Ira recalled Lynn on his visits to New York, strumming a guitar and singing cowboy songs in his hotel room after tall Tom and Jerrys and an elegant lunch.

The theatrical agency, whose name Ira had chosen from the phone book, and where he had left his novel as evidence (he hoped) of screen-writing potential, was warm and rich in decor, liberal in fabric and leather, impressive in open-grained, massive desks. Ira was greeted cordially by two partners, both Jewish, one tall, one short, both nattily attired in lustrous tweed. What a fine glow new and fashionable raiment gave off: it was almost impossible to discern the individual wearing it. Ira thought they were both homely, but couldn't take a Bible oath on it, such was the alchemy of expensive garb. They were cordial, especially when Ira mentioned that he was a friend of Lynn R, but—and who could blame them—their cordiality was restrained, awaiting the event, which would come the

following week, when Ira would call again to hear their pronounce-
ment, and incidentally, retrieve his novel.

On the appointed day, Ira called at the office again. And now
his reception was stripped of all punctilio; it was Jewish, or squea-
mish, or both. They wanted nothing to do with the book and could
scarcely conceal their aversion. They both seemed pained, almost
stiff with alarm, as if their interests were threatened by the book
on the elaborately bracketed desk. They wanted the taint removed
as soon as possible. Ira could only remember one thing similar in
nature, though completely different in circumstances: a scene from
The Informer, when the Irish traitor, played by Victor McLaglin (the
only good thing that crude he-man ever did, thanks to the magnificent direction of John Ford) is paid his blood money by the British
officer. The latter disdains to touch the money, but, using his swag-
ger stick like a croupier, shoves the money away from him toward its
wretched recipient. So did they, almost, and with Ira's book! Utterly
crestfallen, he picked up his novel and departed. That was to be his
first and last try at Hollywood. Trial would be a better word. Ira
refused to risk such humiliation a second time.

What did he feel now, thus defeated and isolated by rejection?
He could reply to Edith's letter, praising her liberality and understanding: You write a very considerate letter. My life is in your hands;
please wire more money. (Did Bill now regard himself as a legitimate competitor for Edith's largesse? What a thought!) However,
Ira felt more worn-out than satiric, more shattered than anything
else. He could imagine Bill's saying, were Ira to admit defeat and
take his leave for New York: If youze don't do right by our Nell, I'll
come out there and knock you off.

What to do? Devote as much time as he could to writing his
new novel. Combat his doubts and indolence. Work. Hope that life
would proffer a solution.

The earth having been dug away from around its roots, the tree in the adjoining yard outside Ira's window lay on the ground. His dandruff fell glimmering from his fingers clawing through his hair. Now, with rhythmic rip and scrape, crosscut saw with a man at each end, bit into the tree trunk. Eucalyptus logs are tawny in hue . . .

M's letter, postmarked November 27, scolded him gently for his irrepressible tendency to justify himself, and because her words coincided so with Edith's oft-repeated reproach, Ira felt physically cold and lit the small gas stove. For lunch he had buttermilk and raisin bread, Bill having borrowed a dollar of his last five the evening before, allegedly to spend it on food for the family. Bea had seen Ira to the door and pressed a note into his hand as he stepped outside: Ira read it when he reached home. Could Ira please give her two dollars so she could buy Christmas gifts for the kids?

The next day, Ira walked over to the stationery store on Baxter Boulevard. On the way, the street he passed through bent into a pretty curve to the west. The trim frame houses seemed in harmony with their surroundings, the tufted palm trees, the plumed palm trees, the mock-orange trees with their acorn-sized orange fruit. He passed a garden in which a solitary rose still bloomed. Sunlight splayed out in the neat alleys. Pepper trees bowed in the breeze. He had awakened early this morning and seen the candy-striped dawn, watched it slowly strip down as if to be ready for the strife of day. Sauntering along thus in a zone of quiet charm, Ira forgot his despond.

The owner of the stationery store was Jewish. "How's the fight against Fascism coming?" Ira asked.

"Not fast enough," he answered. He showed him some pages in the *Reader's Digest*, an article on the alarming growth of American Fascism. "*Unser* America," he remarks. "These American Nazis scare me worse than the German ones."

"That's exactly the way I feel. I feel a growing dread, if you know what I mean," Ira replied.

The owner offered Ira a cigar.

Back at his writing table, Ira interrupted his work. He was continually aware of the hectic hollowness of what he set down, a paucity of substance, a dearth of that vibrance that resounded in his first novel. Probably hopeless all this he was doing, without depth or viability. And surrendering to hopelessness, he gave up and brooded for a while.

Outdoors in the next yard he watched a young woman prop up a sagging, heavily loaded clothesline with a rake, and he found relief in speculating on an invention he could patent: a pole with a fork at one end and a ball swivel at the other.

The young woman, who also aired her terrier in the yard, was married to a Japanese. She was Nordic, slender, chic, wore a blue flannel bathrobe, a tight-fitting one. She always looked up at Ira's window while she hung clothes on the line: silk stockings, towels, teddies, men's shirts. Curious, how bleak and depleted Ira felt. While he was writing his first novel, he was plagued by sexual urge—every minute, it seemed. And now, he was as if devastated, sexually vitiated. Strange phenomenon.

Her brother-in-law, from what Ira could judge, was the one who cut down the eucalyptus tree, and apparently would supervise the building of a small cottage in the yard. The first step in clearing the ground was to cut down the tree, and now that it was felled, he hacked away at the limbs, evoking in Ira a sensation of sorrow as he watched. Immediately afterward, he stretched guidelines on the ground, where Ira presumed ditches would be dug for foundations. The Japanese husband lifted his eyes, curved them delicately at Ira. He needed have little fear.

That night, feeling jaded, empty, too forlorn and lonely to stay home, Ira drove to the Mexican district. He parked close to the Mexican street, Oliveras, the oldest street in LA, with square brick or tile surfacing over the gutter. Gasoline mantle lamps, soft and like the lighting of a stage setting, lit the many stands lining the curbs, some selling food, some knickknacks of ceramic. Here and there, on stairs or on stools next to shops, in native costume, Mexicans serenaded the throng. White folk stood in numbers about the stands where enchiladas were frying in grease; the whites guffawed as they ate, expelled breath in boisterous hoo-hoos to cool their palates singed by the hot chili. Other places sold airy-fairy spun sugar, also dyed and painted gourds, strings of varnished beans, and gaily-colored enameled Mexican scenes on tiles. Graphologists alternated with portrait painters between small restaurants and cafés. Hungry for human company, Ira stood and watched, sadder by the minute.

So he stepped into a Japanese-owned barroom and ordered a glass of claret, which promptly soured his innards. A few minutes passed while he morosely reviewed his verbal tiltings with Bill, Ira's spinelessness, Bill's machinations. Then, all at once his attention was wrested away from self to the 150outside. He became a spectator of a brawl between two men: one of them, a Mexican of average height, the other, also Mexican, but an exceptionally big fellow. Both drunk, they began lambasting each other. All the patrons seemed fairly calm about it, but when too big a crowd gathered in the doorway, the little Japanese proprietor went outside and blew a long blast on a whistle that trilled like a postman's.

"Break it up!" some of the patrons yelled. The fight stopped, and the crowd dispersed. The little Japanese came in smiling. The altercation over, the two contestants talked to each other in Spanish, not too excitedly, seeming to comment by word and gesture about the cause of the fracas. The big fellow had a deep cut on his cheek. Someone said they were friends. And suddenly the fight started again in earnest. The big fellow seized the smaller guy and knocked him down with a single blow; a woman, evidently the fallen man's companion, sprang at his stalwart adversary and gouged his cheeks. He shoved her away. She grabbed what looked like a heavy lemon squeezer out of her shopping bag and banged him over the head with it. He knocked her sprawling to the floor, the lemon squeezer flying into a corner. Squalling, she got to her feet and seized a beer bottle. With no time to whistle for help, the little Japanese proprietor threw himself between the bottle-brandishing woman and the big fellow. Now her companion joined in, but this time to prevent her from going any further; he pinned her arms to her side and, holding her with a encircled arm, tore the bottle from her grip. She still tried to grab it from him again. He blocked her in the lunge and dragged her out of the bar; then he came back, sought and found the lemon squeezer in the corner. No one seemed too agitated. Ira had another five-cent glass of claret.

Soured though his stomach was, he came away satisfied, almost at peace for a change, feeling as if the scene had freed him of his dread isolation, his dread loneliness, as if Ira had been permitted to share at least some emotion not his own, some emotion in common with others. He drove back to his room and discovered a new letter from Edith.

Dear Ira,

It must be perfectly obvious that I care for you terribly or I would not bother to argue any of this—you wouldn't be worth it. But I am not doing this with any hope for myself in you, Ira, with any idea that you can ever again be even what you were to me, and certainly no idea from the letters you write that you can be any better or finer person. If you have to have your vanities through another woman, take them. Perhaps we all need our vanities. And you have so largely destroyed mine that I can't even find them in my work, which you mocked and ignored for years. You even left behind you my book of poems that I had dedicated to you, and until you know how these things hurt, you'll never know anything. My entire energies were directed into transforming you into a decent character, but you have turned ugly and weak before my eyes. Now, because I've been so wrong in identifying with you, my energies should be turned to making something of myself. But because I'm sick, and because you destroyed my chief store of energy, my only spiritual force, restoring myself will be a pretty hard job. I could take those thirteen years together as a rich experience, had you not both cheapend me and myself in my own eyes. I should be very glad if you could arouse any pride I had in you. It might make me feel that not all my life with you was a rank-smelling thing.

I'll let you know if there is anything in this business of my having a child. The doctor thinks either that it is true, or that the shock you gave me has so completely, has so adversely affected my health that it has brought about an abrupt stoppage of menstrual functioning. I've been very much under the weather, and having to work very hard in the face of it. And again, because you have a robust body, you will never be able to know what this kind of thing means. But pregnant or not, child or not, I'd never turn to you, except perhaps for a formal ceremony to be broken immediately by law or by a suit for divorce, since you care no more for me than for some plank you may have stepped on to get somewhere else. I'm not going to write again, unless I'm pregnant, or unless something comes up of a formal nature that needs attention. I'm not sure, but I'm inclined to think I'd have been wiser and more prudent in not writing these last two letters. I can do very little for you financially. You knew this when you left and struck at me this way when I was poorest. I don't have Dalton to borrow from, though he did say he'd be willing to help you in his own way, if you wished.

But I have nothing to do with that. He thinks I made you what you are. I don't! I think you were what you are still always, and I had no strength to influence you or to tell you, though I knew, nor to act on my knowledge of what you were. All this because you were so much more violent a person than I, and because you were confused—that much I can grant you—no other grace, Ira. We can all be confused and blind, and still be forgiven if we don't stick in it.

Edith

With no new remittance from Edith, Ira was forced to sell his Model A, to a Texan. Christmas had come and gone, and it was now January 1939. Horton, his fellow lodger, and Ira had agreed previously to run a joint notice in the LA morning paper, advertising their cars for sale. Horton's was a sleek, trim Willys Knight sports car, sparkling, red-painted, and clean; Ira's a worn, weathered, drab little Model A coupe. Horton's asking price was $150, Ira's $75. The two vehicles stood parked side by side in the empty lot adjoining the lodging house. Only two prospective buyers answered the ad. The first, fairly tall, rakish and assured, Jewish, and his shorter Jewish companion arrived on foot to inspect the offerings. By their manner, Ira felt sure they were some kind of Hollywood hangers-on, or small-time operators of some other type, successful, crass, and cocksure. The taller of the two, evidently the purchaser and leader, grimaced contemptuously when he glanced at the Model A. "Your heap?" he asked.

"Yeah," Ira said meekly.

He turned away in distaste, then smiled approvingly at Horton's snappy little Willys Knight; got in, with his friend, confidently put the car through a few routine paces, got out, and bought it at the asking price. And minutes later, his elbow in the open window, his friend complacently in the passenger's seat, he drove with casual assurance out of the empty lot. Ira went upstairs to his room and flung himself on his bed.

Royer, Ira's landlord, called up from downstairs: somebody to look at his car.

In light gray topcoat, Stetson hat, a Texan was with his son, a college student. The son was diffident, friendly; the father sported an oversized yellow pencil in his jacket pocket and had large, grease-ingrained palms. He offered $55 for the car. In vain Ira pleaded that he was hard up, that he had to live on the proceeds; would he split the difference; would he make it $5, even $2.50 more? The Texan was like flint. He set the price, as if Ira didn't exist. He set the price, and Ira's pleas rolled off him like dew off granite. In his nervelessness Ira couldn't get the car started, until he realized he hadn't inserted the ignition key far enough. $55. It was sold. He could just imagine the young collegian saying, "Gee, Dad, thanks. That's swell, Dad. Just what I want." Filial gratitude, paternal pride, pride that was armor-plated in dealings with others, seamless and armor-plated.

It was growing late as Ira climbed the stairs to his room. The wish to die increased in intensity. The day's events, the vacuity of self—or was it the selling of the car, like severing a major link to all he was, to the last vestige of definite identity?—numbed every-thing within him. If one could only die without noticing it, or being noticed. Yes, cease to exist without any awareness, interior or exte-rior. And now he had a—a prompting, yes, a curious prompting, never manifested before, never pushing into consciousness: Put this aside, these notes, and write Lynn R a letter. Say, I would like to come out to Oklahoma, where you're staying. I hope your friend won't mind. I can't bear this void of myself any longer. I am ready to give up, simply give up. Anything would be better than this break-down of all I was that has taken place within me, anything that remotely offered a chance at reintegration into a unified person. Please write me, Lynn.

Where would Ira get Lynn's address? From Edith. Then write Edith an urgent note asking for Lynn R's present address—under guise of making contacts with Hollywood scenario writers.

Almost beside himself with desolation, Ira brooded. He wished he had never known Edith, never written a novel, never gone to Yaddo, met M, his only hold on hope of restoration, but becoming at this distance ever more tenuous, untenable.

Why the hell would he write Edith for Lynn's address? God-damn dope. He made for the trolley stop on the corner. All he had to do was send the letter to his agents, French and Co., and write, Please Forward. What the hell was the matter with him?

He couldn't write, he couldn't write, because of remorse, because the thought of how he had cut Bea over the phone kept coming back and coming back. She meant to be nice to you, he told him-self: You didn't have to say that—Oh, the hell, he thought, every time they call, it's a touch. Every time I go to see them in that squalid cabin, it's a touch for money. I know they're broke, but god-damn it, so am I, and I can't afford it. But you didn't have to say that, the adversary thought held its ground: She meant to be kind to you. Maybe all she had in mind was to ask you over for a little supper. Maybe that story about her kid in Sacramento—her other kid—having a tumor is true. Maybe she wasn't going to scrounge for train fare; maybe all she meant was to be nice to you. But Jesus, how in hell could he be sure? He recalled Dolly's admonition: "Don't give them any money. Bea's all right, but Bill ain't, and she does what he tells her. Instead o' buyin' a secondhand bed for little Dian, they bought a new crib for Foster out of relief money." A dollar when he was there last, a dollar yesterday when Bill called at the rooming house—the nerve of the guy. And this afternoon Bea called up. Christ, I'm down to where I'll have to borrow bus fare back to New York, if I want to ride back. But maybe all she meant was to be nice to you.

Oh, forget it. She'll get over it, forget it. He couldn't forget it, and he couldn't write. Oh, the hell with it. He opened the blank pages of the same notebook in which he was writing, took out the letter to Lynn, addressed it to French and Co. But nothing more, no street or street number. Go down to skid row. Blow the stink off you. Call the telephone operator for the phone number, and they'll give you the address: There's a French and Co. theater agents on such and such an address. Is that the party? That's it, that's it. On Eighty-eighth Street. Broadway. That's it.

He had his dungarees on, his blue work shirt, his ankle-high work shoes. He had better clothes than that, but there wasn't any point in wearing better clothes to skid row. He was wearing the kind of clothes that skid row accepted and understood, the kind of clothes the hobos and the down-and-outers wore.

So, he put on his old jacket and slipped the letter to Lynn in his breast pocket, and went out into LA's damp, misty-gray night air. It was twenty-five long blocks to skid row, counting the blocks over to Main Street. His work shoes, which needed repair, were worn to frazzled circles on the second sole. It cost seven cents to ride the trolley, and he needed the exercise anyway. And passing the brightly lit used-car lot on Ferguson, again the thought assailed him: All she meant was to be nice to you. She said, "Did you eat your supper yet?" And he said, "No." Then she told him about little Louise in Sacramento. Dan wouldn't send her to the hospital for treatment; the kid needed a doctor. And Ira said, "What the hell can I do about it?" And that's when she fell silent. And that's when Ira felt as if he had cut her across the mouth with a lash as long as the telephone line between her and him, and that's when Ira pictured her leaning against the wall of the phone booth, trying to catch her breath, though he couldn't see her.

He turned east at Figueroa and Pico, angling toward Main Street, where the lights beckoned, where human faces passed and stores displayed their wares, where the tawdry arcades housed the shooting galleries and the handgrip tester and the lung testers, and the dummy Oriental princess, in green velvet and turbans, pivoted creakily when you dropped a nickel in the slot and picked out your fortune card; where the hockshops were, and the sailors sauntered, and the whores waited. There were other streets and avenues in LA with better faces and deportment, and better clothes, but the faces on Main Street were at his level now, the faces and the pace, and that was what he preferred. I'll walk by the Union Mission, he thought, and I'll go in and get coffee and doughnuts for a nickel, and I'll talk to some of the hobos.

I'm a sonofabitch, I'm hungry already. I had two potatoes, carrots, and four strips of bacon for supper, and I'm hungry already.

He had reached Broadway, and merged with the moving crowd along the brightly lit sidewalk. Let's see: What have I got in my pocket? And without taking the coins out, he tried to feel whether one of the three coins he fingered was a nickel—a nickel with which to call the telephone operator and ask for information. Either he had thirty-six cents or sixteen cents. No, he wouldn't have to ask the druggist for change to make the call. It was a nickel. Two bucks and sixteen cents was all he had.

Bea had meant, maybe she knew Ira would enjoy a home-cooked meal instead of goddamn pancakes for breakfast, beginning to taste like a rubber doormat. And boiled potatoes and maybe butter and beans and canned mackerel. All that in the hope of working himself free of dependency on the pervasive, prevailing, everlasting Older Woman, giving him bed and board and body. And now look what he'd come to, Oh, Jesus Christ, with a letter in his pocket to mail, a charming homo, embraced him drunk, pressed his soft, full lips against Ira's. Where the hell was that drugstore, the one with the phone booth?

Ahead of him the double entrance to two shops gaped its incandescence, the drugstore on one side, the photographer's gallery on the other. And against the motley photos in the photographer's window, a young tart, pretty, bold, brunette, accosted two callow youths as Ira slowed his gait. "Hi, y'all. Where y'all goin'?"

"You a whore?" asked one of the youths with ineffable, callow candor.

"Y'all lookin' for one?" she asked.

"No," they guffawed at each other, and walked on.

"Y'all hurry back." She called after them, laughing. It seemed the most natural thing in the world.

He paused in the doorway on the drugstore side, waiting, waiting to be solicited, just for the sake of being spoken to. I've got two bucks in my pocket; how much for just talking to me? Oblivious of him, she looked the other way, around the corner of the photo shop instead.

I'm dead, he thought. He walked past the pharmacy without entering. Even she can sense I'm dead. And in reality I ought to be. M, M, so far away, I'm so screwed up now, what good will I be to you? No self-control, no center to my life, my life just a smear. So I cut the heart out of a woman who's known only privations all her days, and wanted to give me a feed. And I said, what the hell can I do? See what I am, darling, my cool, aloof, lesbian-seeming darling at the black Steinway grand, see what I am? "What's the matter with Bill?" Ira said. "Has he lost his wits? He ought to know how to deal with those things better than I do. After all, Dan's his own brother." And the silence, the silence that said to him: You might as well hang up the phone, and go upstairs to your room. You haven't got a gun, but you've got a jackknife. And the silence. "All right," she said at last, "but I thought—"

"Well, I don't want to be hard-boiled about it, call me again," Ira said. "Call me some other time." Dead. Dead for a ducat, as Hamlet said. Not even the broad for hire would give you a tumble, the bimbo loitering in the photo gallery, four snapshots for a dime.

He walked on, leaving the lights of Main Street behind him, circled about randomly toward Tenth Street. The fluorescents shone on the Hearst printing presses within the great square plate-glass windows of the Examiner Building, flooding the corner. He paused, the anguish within him seeking to cleave to anything, whether purposive, fatuous, anything. Slowly, the great, black machines behind the plate-glass window started moving, reeling out a Sunday comic sheet, in colors, so slow he could read the title. It was the comic sheet, Jiggs—he recognized it—Jiggs and Maggie, Jiggs and Maggie sliding along, ambling from roller to roller, dipping from level to level. The banal, improbable Irishman, hankering for his old haunts, despite his newly accumulated wealth, despite his top hat and spats, still longing for corned beef and cabbage, still longing to hobnob with former cronies at Clancy's saloon; while his social-register-smitten wife strained in the opposite direction, peered through her fancy lorgnette, put on all manner of false airs.

A press hand kept leaning over the comic sheet. Troubled evidently by its dilatoriness, he looked up and toward the interior of the building, as if expecting someone to come to his assistance. Assistance arrived in the form of a close-cropped, bullet-headed man wearing eyeglasses and a young fellow, evidently the older man's helper, in streaked overalls and carrying a metal toolbox.

They tinkered, made adjustments; the pressman wiped away grease on the press with a comic sheet. The repairman nodded, and he and his helper stepped into the aisle beside the press. Now a humming filtered through the plate-glass window. Inside, the three men watched, and on the outside, Ira, too.

The humming increased. The press speeded up: Jiggs and Maggie, Jiggs and Maggie, Jiggs and Maggie spewed out of semblance, barely Jiggs and Maggie, scarcely Jiggs and Maggie. Accelerating, they flew past, swifter still and swifter, until gone were Jiggs and Maggie, lost in a multihued ribbon of paper and a high-pitched hum. And banality was gone, triviality was gone, gone the comic strip's silly postures and problems. All had become a freshet of blended color, diving downward and leaping upward in strict angle, and again, as if the artist's palette had become a cataract.

What the hell did it mean? Rainbow-colored mush. What did Shelley say? Life is a dome of many-colored glass. Jiggs and Maggie. What the hell am I doing? He turned away, again trudged along the darkening sidewalk, while he felt inside his breast pocket for the letter: save the stamp anyway.

CHAPTER 8

Coming into view, a dilapidated, old rattletrap rolled toward Ira on the other side of the street. A genuine jalopy, if there ever was one, it chuffed and smoked and rattled with every yard of motion. And just as it reached the corner—pop! The front tire blew, the car lurched, stopped by sudden jammed-on brakes, lunged forward as if the chassis would leave its frame.

A middle-aged Mexican got out, came around to the front end, surveyed the utterly flat tire, and removed his broad felt hat. With both hands he lifted his hat from his iron-gray poll; so expressive his swarthy face, so unbearably comic his anguished attitude, so excruciating, it pierced Ira through and through. The poor man could stand no more. His half-grown kids got out of the car, and looked at the bald, blown tire with sheepish, embarrassed grins, and then looked at their father with his hat in both hands. The kids got the jack and the tire irons out of the trunk and rolled out a spare that thumped on the pavement as bald as a baloney.

"So he took off his hat with both hands," said Bill with his customary snort of quiet satisfaction when Ira told him about the incident he had witnessed waiting for the trolley. "Took it off with both hands." He couldn't get enough of the recounting of the incident. He handed Foster over to Bea.

"Yeah, he lifted it up off the top of his head." Ira had come over in remorse after being so harsh with Bea, but also to tell them his new idea.

"What does that mean to you?" Bill asked.

"To me? What can it mean?" Ira challenged. And yet he knew Bill had probed exactly to the difference between them. Ira saw himself reflected in the Mexican, his growing desperation, the apprehension devouring Ira, which was the reason he had taken the trolley to visit Bill in the first place. Bea came in from the bedroom, after placing Foster back in his crib. "We were talking about a Mexican I saw, the way he took his hat off when his front tire blew out. He looked like he'd reached the end of his rope."

Blue-eyed, so girlishly fresh-cheeked and full-bodied, incongruously out of place in this setting, living with Bill, a one-handed man and fifty years old, Bea seemed to be trying to sense the mood of their colloquy.

"Bill asks me what it means," Ira clarified.

"Damn right. The petty boojwa don't understand what it means."

"No? I'll tell you something else. There's many a Communist Party member doesn't understand it either."

"The hell they don't. That shows you what misery the masses is goin' through."

"It shows you more than that, a lot more. But you have to be more than a Communist to see it. You haven't got that through your head."

"The rest is bullshit. I know what you're goin' t' tell me." His fingers curled in ridiculously dainty fashion. "You have to have the little cherry on top o' the ice cream sundae. An' we don't. An' that's what you see, an' we don't."

"Okay. Have it your way."

"What'd you see?" Bea asked.

"That's it. I can hardly tell you. That little brown kid of his, holding his papa's hand and looking up at him. If he were marble, he'd look like Laocoön's son. Now who the hell is Laocoön? Abraham Laocoön. So forget it."

"Will you have some coffee?" Bea offered.

"I would, thanks."

"Let's all have some java," Bill shifted to his joshing tone. "It's only twenty cents a pound."

And while they waited for Bea to brew the coffee, Ira began. "I'll tell you why I came down. It's kinda hard—I mean," he shook his head. "I want to go back to New York."

And impassive as ever at such times, Bill studied him. Bea came away from the gas range to join them. It was she who asked, "When?"

"As soon as I can get my stuff together. I don't know. Soon." Ira shrugged heavily. "You know how it is."

"How're you goin'?" Bill asked.

"I'd go by bus. I can just about make the fare, I think."

"They won't take all your stuff," said Bill. "Less'n you pay extra."

"They won't?"

"All them big books you brought." He meant Ira's unabridged Latin and Greek dictionaries that he had picked up secondhand in a Fourth Avenue bookstore, and rebound in prime green oilcloth by himself, and brought to LA in the Model A. And his other dictionaries, the Italian, the French, the German, legacy of his humanist, "disciplined" days prior to writing his novel. He needn't have brought them. He could have left them in Brooklyn, with his parents, but there stood his father in the way, with that terrible quarrel between them. "Yeah."

"If we both chipped in together, and got one o' them panel trucks, we could all go back."

"What!"

"Them Model T panel trucks is dirt cheap."

"I can't drive a Model T."

"I can. That's all I drove all my life."

"My God!" Ira said. "We can't stack all that stuff, yours and mine, and three grown-ups and two kids in a Model T. Where the hell you gonna put 'em?" Ira looked up at Bea bringing the coffee. Whatever her feelings were, she gave no sign.

"We don't have to travel fast, as long as we git there. An' we'll git there. I've traveled that way before, an' with kids. You're better off with kids. An' with this hand gone," he displayed his hook, "people're good for anything you ask 'em, gas or a handout, or a place to sleep. I could get on Home Relief in New York. I'd show you how to get on Home Relief, too. Let's go out to a used-car lot." And at Ira's hesitation, "You got nothin' to lose."

So once again, steered by him where Ira didn't want to go, he went. Bill led the way to the Strate-Deal used-car lot, and there, among the dozens of dubious clunkers, he stopped before a Model T panel truck, vintage '26, antediluvian in aspect—a bona fide *katerenke*, a hand organ, Mom used to call them, with their crank handles dangling in front (though this one had a self-starter). The sticker price on the windshield was $31.90.

"Let's try it out," said Bill. And with the keys obtained from the little Jewish dealer in the shanty, and with Ira's heart full of foreboding, they chugged out of the lot onto the highway. Bill manipulated the controls adeptly, his feet sliding on and off the iron pedals like those of a trained organist, his good left hand manipulating spark and gas confidently, the steel hook on his right arm secured in one of the spokes of the big steering wheel. They tested the vehicle, or Bill did, negotiated a five-mile stretch on the boulevard and rolled into the used-car lot just as the gas gave out. Ira had warned him not to drive too far, but the experience was too exhilarating for Bill's prudence to govern. The engine died.

"Can we get our deposit back later if we change our minds?" Bill asked the dealer.

He nodded.

"Why don't you lay a two-dollar deposit on it?" Bill suggested, and obediently, Ira did. So the car was secured, but not before Bill delivered himself of one of his compendious talks on the Communist Party, how it was the only force squarely committed to the fight against Fascism and Nazism. "Of course, right now we ain't lookin' to carry out a full revolutionary program," Bill explained. "We're backin' liberal policies; that means we're supportin' the interests o' small business, an' Jews."

Between the two-dollar deposit, Ira calculated silently as they headed back to the cabin, his rent payment, victuals, and inevitable contribution to the Loems, he had spent the ruinous sum of ten dollars in a single week. He now had only thirty dollars left from the sale of the Model A.

CHAPTER 9

A *telegram from M arrived* in February, conveying birthday greetings, but cryptic in tone; too soon for her to have received Ira's ambivalent letter to her, and yet, as if they were in phase, responding telepathically to his mood. It was his thirty-third year. He was awakened by Royer, his landlord, who brought him the cabled message, and Ira told him of the plans Bill and he were considering. He disapproved of the scheme, strenuously, instantaneously, and entirely; so spontaneous, in fact, was his reaction that Ira ruled out all thought of self-interest on his part in losing Ira's regular four dollars per week in room rent. "Blizzards" was the first word he uttered: the blizzards they could expect to encounter in the Midwest, the frigid weather to which they would be exposing two small children. Coupled with Ira's own doubts, his feeling of having been coerced by Bill into doing something he was averse to doing, Ira resolved to do everything he could to get out of the project.

Angry at first for having allowed himself to be cajoled even this far, saving humor prevailed once more. As he walked to the Auto Club, amusement grew at his antic and incorrigible bent for getting himself into predicaments. It was up to him somehow to find a way of reneging from commitment without seeming to. Meanwhile he might as well enjoy the walk. The route from the rooming house to the Auto Club lay through a neighborhood of once elegant private homes, with gables and cupolas, many elaborate façades in which curved bay windows projected, almost all of them fronted by palm trees. The homes were currently occupied by Greek letter fraternities, and college youth lolled in the sunshine beside their fine cars, college youth, some stereotypically cartoon tubby, with horn-rimmed spectacles on snub, sharp noses.

Arriving at the Auto Club office, Ira got a map. The clerk who waited on him red-penciled the best route from LA to New York. Never before had it been Ira's pleasure to encounter such a gratifyingly calamitous clerk! He warned Ira of the hazards of cold weather and snow-blocked roads, and the disasters they posed for adults, let alone small children traveling in a dilapidated car. "A Model T Ford! Mister, the life's gone out of a Model T long ago!"

On the heels of irrelevancy followed another talk with Royer at the garbage incinerator. He reminded Ira that the route red-penciled by the clerk would entail an additional expenditure of $10 to $12 in tolls they would have to pay traveling over certain roads and crossing certain bridges. So over to Bill's with the map—and the dire tidings. Ira made a strong case against undertaking so long a journey in wintry weather and in a rattletrap vehicle with two young children. Bea was very much alarmed, but Bill, undaunted, said he and his father had survived worse: walked twelve miles home through a blizzard from a snow-stalled car. They would survive, too, and continued in that vein despite Bea's protests—until Hendy, the construction worker, dropped in and corroborated everything Ira had repeated of Royer's warnings and those of the Auto Club clerk. Adding further disconcerting data of his own, Hendy predicted that they'd get at most sixteen miles to the gallon, and would have to use a quart of oil every hundred miles, if he knew anything about a Model T Ford of that vintage. That would amount to a cash outlay of more than sixty-five dollars for the trip, not counting repairs.

Hendy left. And thanks to him, Bill slowly, painfully revised his timetable for the prospective departure. They had better wait a month. "Maybe we'll save up a little more, too. That'd make it easier."

"We'll never save any money," Bea countered. "It slips through our fingers like sand."

"And I can't wait either," Ira seconded. "My reserves are drying up fast."

"All right, let's put Foster in the baby carriage, an' go look at auto trailers anyway," said Bill. "It won't hurt to know what they gits for 'em, even if we don't go."

Ira accompanied him. He was certain they could find nothing in any secondhand trailer-sales lot that they could even remotely afford. And they couldn't. It was difficult for Ira to hide his glee: he had actually won a round, for the first time. It was dizzying. Mustering all the staunch Communist optimism that a joyful cynicism was capable of, Ira parted with Bill at the trolley stop. Maybe he was beginning to use his head, at last.

And afterward, back at the rooming house, Ira joined a couple of fellow lodgers in the hallway, Fred Skelsey and John Davis, in amiable conversation.

"I've got a pot roast goin' I started yesterday," Skelsey said to Ira when the other had left. "Why don't you boil up a few spuds, and we'll share it—unless you've got something else."

"I haven't. But that's no fair trade."

"We'll make it up some other time."

Ira went into his room, peeled four spuds, and set them on a fairly high gas flame to boil. A minute later Skelsey knocked at the door. Everything about the man was efficient, with nothing to spare for ostentation or pretense: a tall, spare body, nothing prominent, nothing distinguished; quiet, observant brown eyes, dark, straight hair, regular features, all matching, all in proportion, as if the purpose of the whole were functional and nothing else. His gaze took in

Ira's room effortlessly, without scrutiny, and yet Ira felt certain that
nothing—writing table, books, and appurtenances of authorship—
escaped him. "Why don't you come into my room while the spuds
are boiling, and we'll shoot the breeze."

Skelsey yawned after supper, of the frequency and kind that recalled
to Ira the way he would yawn when at his aunt Mamie's house, trying to conceal his designs on his cousin Stella. He yawned and said
that the LA city employees had a three-day holiday coming due on
Lincoln's birthday; he was thinking of driving to Frisco to see his
mother. Ira expressed pro forma congratulations at the pleasure in
store for him. He yawned again, and asked whether Ira would care
to make the trip with him and share the expense of a night in a hotel
room? His impulse was to say yes, but intuition warned him not
to, and Ira excused himself on the pretext of his writing, which he
explained had not been coming along well, but might, if he perse-
vered over the holidays.

Ira was in a panic when he got back to his room. His first reaction was to pack up his belongings and flee from the rooming house.
The man was obviously a homosexual who had singled Ira out, and
his best bet was to quit the premises, change lodgings, anything,
escape. The horror of that rusty-clothed, lanky stiff, who lured Ira
at age ten on a trolley car ride to the woods of Fort Tryon Park,
and there masturbated against a tree with one hand, while his other
hand gripped Ira's buttock, came back with full force. Fred Skelsey
was another and more devious kind. Ira broke out into a sweat. He
tried to invoke common sense, clinging to it, wrestling with it to
come to his aid.

Panting, he thought of Jacob and the angel and, little by little,
calmed down. He had nothing to fear as long as he gave Fred no
opportunity, no occasion: Be circumspect about that drinking bout

he had invited Ira to join him on the tenth, when he got his paycheck. He'd better decamp on that day and spend it with Bill. And thinking back: Fred's vicious description of the striptease dancer in the nightclub where his ex-brother-in-law was a musician in a "combo," the loathing in Fred's voice as he said she was practically fucking some big guy there. And his manifest devotion to his mother—that proved it! And his running away from home at the age of twelve because of his father.

But when the summons came, Ira's loneliness conquered his fear, and he responded to Fred's invitation to a drinking bout. First, they consumed three half-pint bottles of whiskey between them in Skelsey's room. Then they drove over to the nightclub owned and run by Skelsey's friend Billy Green, corpulent, gray, and professionally convivial, and there they downed a few more bourbons. Vocalist as well as entertainer, Billy had a repertoire consisting of "old time favorites," veritable patsies of sentiment: "East Side, West Side," "Sweet Rosie O'Grady," "She's the Daughter of Rosie O'Grady," sung with the sway and lilt of Pat Rooney, but without the tap dance.

Ira and Fred had begun drinking in his room, while the beef stew, which Ira had been invited to share, simmered on the gas stove. After a couple of drinks, tongues were loosened, confessions began. Fred remarked that he had deferred driving to Frisco because of storm warnings and report of heavy fog along the coastal road. But contrary to all travelers' advisories, the day was warm and bright, and according to radio announcements clear all the way up the coast. "I could have kicked myself for not going," he said.

Without recourse to particulars, Ira told him about the suspension of plans to "drive East with a friend and his family," and sounded him out on his opinion of beating one's way east by freight this time of year. Skelsey had done so from El Paso to St. Louis one February, but it was miserable: a tramp had frozen to death hiding behind the water tender. It wasn't advisable. It would be a great experience if Ira tried it, but he should expect great hardship.

The beef stew was done, and Ira went back to his room to fetch his warmed-up canned string beans, and a half-pound stick of butter he had filched. Returning to Fred's room, Ira placed his contribution to the meal on the card table Fred had opened up, and was now setting the brass table lamp on. He stood for a moment next to the little pantry talking: He was still on probation at his accounting job with the city, and would be for another three months. Ira quipped from an A. E. Robinson movie in which one of the characters brags, "They can't fire us; we're civil servants."

To Ira's surprise, Fred replied that he intended to keep the job, which was no inferior one, only until he could find another "racket to go into." One had to go outside the law, he had long ago determined, to make any money. He couldn't stand the idea of growing into a crusty, old accountant supervisor. He saw the others in the office, bookkeepers and clerks alike: "At five o'clock they put on their scarves, get into their topcoats, and set out to make the five-thirty train to wherever, because Margy is waiting supper. I can't take that. I'd go bugs."

"Well, maybe that's what your little Margy might prevent, because you knew she was there. Someone cares for you. A loyal woman," Ira suggested. "Maybe that's what you're missing. There's Royer downstairs and his wife. The two get along together fine."

"Oh, marriage is all right—for somebody else, but not for me. I tried it," Fred said. "And my dice came up snake eyes. You know what I mean?"

"Yes, but so have others. Royer himself. But that doesn't rule out marriage." Ira thought of his faraway M and gesticulated impulsively. "The need two people have for each other; the attachment they form—"

"Oh, no, that's the worst part of it."

"What do you mean? That's the best part of it!"

"Oh, no."

"How can it be? Why am I dying to go back to a woman I love, who loves me, you know, not to be sentimental. In fact, I think that's why I have to go back. I'm beginning to die."

"That's where we're different. I get tougher."

"You get barren!" Ira exclaimed. "Don't take offense. That nightclub you took me to. What kind of a life is that? Sterile, you know what I mean? Garish. I don't know what the hell to call it. Jesus, Fred, it's empty."

"That's the way I want it."

"You do?"

"That's why I tell you I want no part of marriage. It gets in the way of all your operations. Whenever you made a move, you'd have to think of where the other person would be, and how you could protect her."

"Boy. Make a move. Protect her. All kinds of wild thoughts go through my mind."

"You're getting the idea," he said. He emptied his glass, lit a cigarette.

"Fred," Ira rested fork on plate. "Were you ever inclined toward homosexuality?"

He didn't seem to comprehend, and at Ira's questioning look he stopped eating. "No, in my business, with so damned many women around and so many women part of it, that's all I ever saw—all I ever took."

Ira explained that he thought perhaps Fred was, and that was why Ira had given his writing as an excuse for declining to go to Frisco with him.

Fred's lean features took on barest stain of color, and his head skewed about. It was the first time Ira had seen him lose the least

115

composure. "Why, hell, no! I thought you didn't want to go because you didn't have the money; you couldn't afford it. That was at least half-smart, telling me about your writing. I was about to say, all right, I'll pay for the hotel room. What would you have thought then?" He laughed shortly. "Locked me out, I guess, if we did go." He laughed again, but mirthlessly.

Ira apologized. "You never spoke about having anything to do with women," he explained.

"I have my girl. But I don't talk about her."

"No. I'm sorry." Ira apologized again. "Damned if I didn't patch together all kinds of damned things."

He told Ira about the time he was a punk kid. His father was a private detective, and always bragging about being on his own feet from the age of ten, and he had a bad temper, too. So the kid ran away from home at the age of twelve. And by fourteen he was doing a man's job in the wheat fields of South Dakota, and working along-side a Swede. Fred had a cheap cotton blanket for cover, and the Swede two Hudson Bay blankets, four pelt stripes of quality on each. When the two bedded down in the straw of the barn, he lent Fred one. "Pretty soon, along in the night, someone was feeling me," said Fred. "I fought him off." Fred paddled the air with his long arms. "And the Swede said, 'I just wanted to see if you're a man.'" Fred fell asleep again; and was again awakened. The Swede offered to suck his prick. "I'd heard of cocksuckers," said Fred, "but I never run into 'em before. I went so goddamn crazy mad, scared, and disgusted, I pulled a knife. I backed that Swede clean outta the barn. I jumped the job the next morning without collectin' my pay, but I had his two blankets and his gold watch."

Ira's faux pas burned into him and made him mute with shame. At the end of the meal, Fred remarked on his silence. "Have another drink," he invited. "May get you talking again."

"No thanks, there's no percentage in it after such a fine feed."

He laughed. "You can hold on to an edge, you try hard enough."

"I envy you," Ira said.

"You mean being able to hold liquor? Anybody can do it after a while—"

"No, no! I envy you your flight from home at the age of twelve. And precisely at the age of twelve I wish I had done the same. I wish I had had the guts to do the same!" Ira's vehemence excited his interest. "Who knows, I might have gotten killed; I'd certainly have broken my poor Mom's heart. If I'd survived, though, I'd have been somebody."

"You're not a bad guy. Why are you making such a point about twelve? That just happened to be how old I was when I beat it."

"Well, it's too complicated, and too deeply buried."

"Is that why you stopped talking before?" He was evidently sorting among hypotheses of his own. Inordinately cagey, able to concentrate without hindrance of feeling. That's what Caesar must have been like: formed his plans, and once formed, they stayed formed, and he slept soundly.

"No," Ira said.

"No?"

"That I should have made such a mistake in sizing you up, such a glaring mistake."

"Oh, hell," he laughed. "I don't take it personally. I just think it's funny."

"I'm glad you do. The serious side is its meaning for me."

"For you?" Again his thoughts seemed to revolve from Ira to his own conjecture. His sinewy finger pressed an ear lobe. "I'm not bragging. But I've been able to figure out some real shrewd operators. But you, I guess I never met your kind before. You take me for a fag, and then you take it to heart. You worry about it. Say, you know I think I'm beginning to get the idea. You don't just keep trying to figure out whether some new angle you want to put over is going to

117

work. You don't hunt for every hitch you can find. You—something else bothers you—you've got your mind on something else. That's it, isn't it?"

"Something like that. And you? Never?"

"What you're doing? You're the first one that ever gave me a clue."

Ira and Fred continued drinking. They discussed the question of getting even, the anatomy of vengeance. Fred could see why other people, or trusted partners, might betray him, but he still believed if a guy was goddamn fool enough to double-cross him, he'd have to pay for it. He spoke of a Swede partner.

"That's the second Swede tonight," Ira commented.

"There are a lot of 'em out here. This one was regular."

"That's a relief."

The Swede owned a powerboat, and Fred owned a powerboat, and the two teamed up. There were three brothers, in the same racket, who competed with Fred and his Swedish partner. They catered to a lower-class clientele, while Fred, through a city council-man connection, catered to a higher-class one. A case of bourbon in Canada cost $25 and was resold in Washington just across the border for $120. The three brothers decided they'd muscle in on the higher-class trade. And one day, the Swede, Fred's partner, was found shot dead on the beach, and his boat gone. When it was picked up adrift a few days later, its load of liquor was gone. The Feds were already closing in, and the game was getting hot. So Fred sold all his gear, packed his belongings in his car, and began driving toward the Mex-ican border. (His mien and voice became tense nearing the conclu-sion of his account.) On his way south, he heard the report over the radio: The three brothers had been found shot to death on an island. (That must have been why he had once hinted to Ira before about a scare the Feds had once given him.)

Supper over, Ira's dishes were reclaimed, and Fred's left where they were, except the beef stew transferred to a bowl and placed in the cupboard. The unfinished pint of whiskey taken along, Fred proposed they go out on the town. Ira acquiesced. And on the way downstairs to his car, Fred said, "I suppose I ought to get sore about the fairy end of it. Another time I might have."

"I was lucky. I picked the right time. Writer's intuition, you know."

"What the hell got into you to think I was a fag?"

Ira trailed him through the gloomy mist over the dim parking lot. "That's the terrible part of it," he said, when they got to the car.

"What do you mean?"

"I'm not sure yet. Or maybe I am."

"You've certainly given me something to think about, something I never thought about before. Maybe I oughtn't think about. It's not just that fag idea. It's something else you stirred up I never knew was there. And I still don't know."

"Sobering, isn't it? In fact, I think it's undone most of the bourbon."

He laughed. "I don't know why I like you." He started the engine. "But I do." He drove toward the parking lot ramp in the curb. "I have to admit I admire the way you can keep yourself at work at your desk, but I think you're leading too closed in a life. I couldn't do it. I have to act."

"For me this is action," Ira said. "I ran away from home at age thirty-two."

"Thirty-two. Is it doing you any good?"

"You can see what good it's doing me."

"I guess I get a feeling of what you're going through. I don't understand it, but I feel something. I got an inkling from you about it, something different. I—" He raised the thumb of the hand on the wheel. "I don't even know what to call it. Do you? The way you size things up?"

"Yes, I guess I do." Ira felt impelled to chuckle, and yet reticent, too. "Would it do you any good? That's the point."

"You never know. I don't think so. It might get in my way something awful. You see, when I ran away, everything I did after that made me tougher and sharper. I could figure better, I could size up people, I could see through propositions. Can that help, the way you size up life?"

"No."

"That's what I thought."

"Trouble is I didn't run away at twelve."

"There goes that twelve." He laughed.

"Like those Swedes."

"Yeah. Ever shoot craps?"

"A little. Never had any luck at it—once when I was a kid. I just mean—what the hell do I mean? I've said it already, Fred. I mean, if you run away at thirty-two, it's like taking down the partitions inside yourself, the partitions, the studs, the rafters, the joists. I don't know what the hell they are. You didn't run away because you wanted to get tougher, but you did. I ran away because I was falling apart."

They drove through nighttime LA, toward the center of town. Fred dwelled again on the limitations of legitimate business pursuits. Ira mentioned the 1870s, the days of the robber barons, who trod the line between legitimacy in enterprise and crookedness.

"That's where I belong," Fred said. "Those days are over. What do you do in that case?"

"I have another friend—you met him. He came to the rooming house once, has a hook. He's a dyed-in-the-wool individualist like yourself; but he finally saw you couldn't go it alone."

"You can't, if you're all muscle. From what you told me about him, and what I saw, that's what he is. I don't make a move without planning; I never take a step without planning. I don't wait, the way you told me he does, to call off a job because my sidekick's hand begins to shake; I figure the man out ahead of time."

"You know, being with Bill so long, I've became crazy enough to think I could use a gun myself."

"Why didn't you tell me? We could go in together."

"You'd trust me that much?"

"You couldn't stand up to a third degree. I wouldn't expect you to. But you wouldn't double-cross me."

"Thanks," Ira said. "I'm at loose ends enough to try anything."

"You might think it over," said Fred. "No stickups. I don't go in for that."

And this was Ira, riding through some lamp-lit boulevard in nocturnal LA, and not feeling tipsy, though he had drunk much more than ever before. Rather, as if the consumption of so large a quantity of alcohol had separated the psyche, ruinously separated or divided it, one part Edith's former protégé, the promising novelist, the other an extension of the predatory adolescent, the punk who stole the silver-filigreed fountain pen from a classmate in Stuyvesant High School and was expelled.

To Billy Green's nightclub, where Fred went off to talk to someone at the other end of the bar, while Billy sang, with touching affect, "Silver Threads among the Gold." The two with whom Fred held parley looked sinister, clean-shaven, and pallid as alabaster. He rejoined Ira and told him he had been offered a vice-presidency in a newly formed racket. One of the pair was an idea man; he knew how to pick ripe ones. And he had the prettiest little Swedish girl in town.

"Not again!" Ira erupted.

"Come along, we'll get you one," said Fred.

From Billy's, after a couple of drinks, they drove over to the Mexican joint, the place Ira had told Fred he had witnessed so much excitement. Wine and beer only were purveyed, "No hodlickah," said the Japanese bartender. They settled for a glass of beer. Patrons were entirely male.

A Mexican on Ira's exposed flank began talking to him. He was a barber, he said, and displayed clean, pink palms, the creases in them like a network of roads on a map. He was half drunk. "My hometown is San Diego," he informed Ira. "I get thrown into jail every time I show up in LA."

"Yes?"

"I don't know why. What is there about me? Five minutes ago the bouncer here was gonna throw me outta this place. You see anything wrong?"

"No. I can't imagine," Ira said.

On Fred's exposed side, a peculiar-looking character sidled up; he wore tinted driving goggles held together where they met the bridge of his nose with a soiled armature of adhesive tape. Ira heard him tell Fred he was an Eskimo. "Are you a bachelor?" he asked Fred.

"Yes."

"You live alone?"

"Yes."

"Do you know what nice boys do?"

"I know what nice girls do."

"Nice boys do it better."

"I don't think so." Fred remained his casual, razor-edged self. "You're an Eskimo. You come from a noble race. You ought to be ashamed of yourself."

The goggled Eskimo boy moved elsewhere.

Ira couldn't go any more beer. His barber neighbor suggested a mixture of beer and muscatel. "I can't go any more," Ira assured him. "Beer or muscatel, or beer and muscatel." It was closing time. The

Japanese owner switched off some of the lights by way of advance notice. They vamoosed.

"Did you hear the Eskimo boy proposition me?" Fred asked as they drove back to lodgings.

"I did, yes."

"I must be slipping." Cigarette smoke rising raggedly from his hand on the steering wheel, Fred gazed meditatively ahead at the deserted, lamp-lit highway. "I can't say I like it."

"Are you going to take that vice-presidency in the new racket. Or shouldn't I ask?"

"No. That's why I wanted you to go in with me. You're the only kind of a guy I'd want to ask me questions like that."

"Thanks."

"I'll have to think about it some more."

CHAPTER 10

The next week, Ira began packing, in a kind of desultory, provisional way, stuffing his belongings into satchel and cartons, with no clear notion of what to send by Railway Express and what to leave at Bill's for later shipment. Ira knew in general that he ought to separate out his clothes and papers and to send those on ahead. Bulkier books, thesaurus, dictionaries, he ought to leave behind. He had decided to thumb his way east across the continent. He would save money that way, and with luck might arrive in New York with a few dollars to his name. He had turned down Bill's advice that he get it all over with by buying a bus ticket and pay the extra charge for the overweight baggage he would take along. Ira didn't have enough for the bus ticket, let alone to pay the extra charge. Borrow some from your friends back east, Bill suggested, adding, "What about M?" No. He needed to show himself he could do it. Fred Skelsey understood; still, he offered to lend Ira the fare, or at least the difference between the cash Ira had on hand, twenty-two dollars, and the cost of getting everything to New York, including himself. Ira was tempted to accept his generosity, but declined. Mad compulsion: to expunge, expiate what he was by this, this exploit.

Ira went downstairs for a newspaper and a package of Granger smoking tobacco, and met his fellow lodger John Davis on the way to the store. Davis was older than Ira had thought when he first met him. Thirty-one, but with his bland features, fair hair, blue eyes, he looked more like twenty-five—which was a source of great irritation to his roommate, Lang, of the same age as Davis, because when both applied for similar jobs, Davis was chosen as the younger man.

He had a slight head cold, had taken the day off, and invited Ira to accompany him on an excursion to the beach. Ira was glad to go, though the cloud that hung over him impregnated his every act with uneasiness and vague dolor. On the drive, Davis gave him a lecture on sex, telling him that nine out of ten men knew nothing about sex and that he had made it his business to learn all about it.

"I do that about anything I'm interested in," he affirmed, "and that includes cooking."

He wasn't hung very heavy, he admitted, but he made up for the shortage by superior techniques. He was so good at it that the woman in the next house where he once roomed, whose husband was too large, used to peer into his window to see whether he was home. In addition to the use of Vaseline, he recommended planting the soles of his feet against the bedstead and lunging from there: "You get a jump out of it that way."

They walked out on the sunny wharf to watch the anglers at their pastime. Here, the brown mountains sloped down to the very margin of the ocean, and as one looked seaward, one saw a hazy landmass in the distance jutting into the Pacific. The fishermen baited their hooks with black mussels, which were hacked off the moss-covered piers below the wharf by the bait vendors, men in rowboats, their wares still embedded in moss and seaweed. Because fishing was dull, one man devoted himself to starfishing. Using a three-clawed grapnel, he hauled in a starfish with rays almost as wide from tip to tip as his shoulders. While he grapneled for another, Ira discoursed learnedly to a small, but gratifyingly astonished, group on the feeding habits of the starfish, how by dint of the remorseless suckers on its rays, it wearied the retractor muscles of a bivalve, until it opened. His audience must have been midwestern, for one woman inquired where the starfish's head was located. Zoologist manqué that Ira once was, and now novelist manqué, he explained that it seemed to function very well without one, refraining from adding, like many of us.

On the way back, Davis described at length the cold and grime of Chicago, pointing at the freshly painted white houses they drove by, saying, "You'll never see anything like that in Chicago."

"Not in New York either," Ira informed him gloomily.

"Why don't you stay here, and ask her to come out?"

"I don't know. I have to go back and start all over again, I think."

"Start what all over again?"

"Yeah." Ira had no answer. Indeed, what was there to start over? What was left of him to start over? A bundle of anxiety and despair.

They returned to the rooming house, where Davis invited Ira to have lunch in his room, egg sandwich, stewed prunes, and coffee. He talked about Hemingway, whom Davis had known in Chicago, as not really being the hard guy he made himself out to be. But he had guts. Davis related an incident in which some eighteen-year-olds rushed in on Hemingway yelling, "This is a stickup!" Hemingway threw an ax at one of them, just barely missing him. The same guy and his friends, said Davis, laid Ernie's sister.

Then he accompanied Ira to his room, where his haphazard packing was much in evidence. And of his own accord he offered to convey Ira and his satchel and cartons over to Bill's to continue the work of sorting out after Ira relinquished his room, which would be in a few more days. They loaded Ira's belongings in Davis's car and drove to Bill's.

There, talk focused at once on money. Bill was in good humor, jubilant, jesting about how small the bars were between him and the money in the bank teller's cage, and how big the bars in the jailhouse were afterward. Conversation shifted to the hazards of freight-train travel. Davis reminisced about almost freezing to death on a freight traveling through a Texas "norther." He and the other hobos would surely have frozen stiff if they hadn't built a fire out of the freight-train walls, moving the blaze from place to place as the floor caught fire. "What time of year was that?" Ira asked.

"About now," he answered, "the month of February."

Davis told about the brakeman, the "shacky" (caboose dweller), who ordered Davis "to hit the grit," with the freight traveling at sixty miles an hour. Davis refused. The shacky drew his foot back to kick, and Davis pulled out his knife. It was a Mexican standoff.

The day was inclement, winds blustery, dust clouds glittering as they swirled. Bill hinted, with that vagueness of mien and tone he adopted at such times, a form of deprecation, that "they" had enough money to get through the rest of the month. Promising more next month, and pleading pressing debts, Edith had sent them twenty dollars. Twenty dollars! That, plus what cash Ira still had, would buy him a bus ticket to New York. Yet it wasn't for that reason Ira found himself resenting their "borrowing" from Edith, sponging on her without scruple, as Bill had obviously been doing. This symbolic exchanging of roles, this displacement of himself by Bill, had awakened—he thought—something protective in Ira with regard to Edith, perhaps because of a sharp objectification of his own former parasitism, and he meant to call Bill to account for it, but didn't. In whatever other way this five-month ordeal had benefited him, besides forcing him in some degree to confront reality, to reorder his views, to try to reinterpret his perceptions, it had dispelled the last mists of his romanticism about the heroic working class—not legitimate sympathy for them, but the last distorting vapors of romanticism. At the same time, Ira felt confident that the bond with Edith had been irreparably broken. He had moved, or they both had moved, reciprocally, out of each other's primary concern. Would the same thing have happened, the same termination occurred, if Ira had moved twoscore city blocks away, instead of two thousand miles, and begun living with M? But one had to be ready to take that step, one had to be conditioned; custom had to be attenuated, self-indulgence beyond reach.

And so, with his thirty-third birthday past, Ira's final hours on the West Coast wore out. *En la trentième an* (and a little more) *de mon âge, quand toutes mes hontes j'ai bu . . .*

On February 19, Fred Skelsey drove Ira to the motor court, where he was to stay for a couple of days before beginning to beat his way east. The kids were eating ice cream when they got there, Bea feeding Foster, and Dian in the third day of measles. No sooner did they settle down than Bill opened fire with homey broadsides of Marxism—or Bill's own brand of proletarianism (interrupted by his irritated injunctions, directed at Dian, that she leave the cabin door alone). The superintendent of the National Biscuit Company could go off on a yacht, and stay drunk for a week straight, but the bakers would still be turning out cookies. Fred listened, indulgent and relaxed, almost compliant in his astute way—the lean, wiry matador in front of the charging bull—artfully deflecting Bill's revolutionary rank-and-file harangues with soft-spoken demurral. He told Bill that there would always be leadership, because that same rank and file looked to leadership for guidance and in the long run was helpless without it. "You can see them turning to leaders all over Europe: Germany, Italy, Russia. It doesn't make much difference."

At which Bill again charged in to the assault: "Youz must see that Nazism and Fascism didn't come outta Hitler's or Mussolini's block—" Bill tapped his head. "It's social. It come outta that state o' society."

"Well, did Russian Communism come out of Lenin's block, or Stalin's block?"

"No, 'course it didn't."

"But they all needed leaders, and you've got the biggest one in Russia."

Bill was outraged. "Don't youz see the difference between 'em? Capitalism can't maintain itself no more in Germany, except by dictatorship. That's why you get a Hitler."

"What have you got in Russia but a dictatorship?"

"Sure, the USSR is a dictatorship! But it's a dictatorship of the majority! It's a dictatorship o' the workin' class!"

"I don't know how often you go to the movies," said Skelsey. "If you take a look at the mobs yelling, Heil Hitler, you'd say it was a majority, too."

"Yeah, but they ain't the majority o' workers."

"How do you know what they are?"

"The Party put the analysis to it. Them you sees there is the agents of monopoly capitalism, the petty boojwasie. Sure, there might be some workers dumb enough to be there. We know that. Them's lumpen proletarians, bum proletarians. We got 'em here."

"All I can say is, if you take everything away from anybody who's got anything, except the bureaucrats, you take everything away from anybody who's had the ambition and the brains to make it, your best farmers, your best manufacturers, financiers, you're bound to have a majority of workers. What else have you got left— except bureaucrats?"

"They ain't bureaucrats," Bill's raised voice and forward thrust of steel hook combined in menacing earnestness. "The leadership is workers jes' like the rest. Every shop an' factory an' collective farm elects its own soviet to hash over an' vote on the quotas what's been set for 'em to produce."

"Who sets the quotas?"

"The Party, nachelly, all the Party members, high rankin' and low rankin'. They puts the analysis to how far we've gone an' how fast we're gettin' there. An' if we're goin' straight or not, followin' the Party line or not. An' then they sets the quotas."

"That's where I want to be then." Skelsey made no effort to conceal his cynicism. "I want to set the quotas. I want to be with the bureaucrats, the leading comrades, whatever you call 'em. They're the ones who'll have more of everything, whether the rest fill the quotas or not. They have special stores for them, don't they? I'll tell you, Bill, you still got to show me there's anywhere near as much democracy in Russia as there is right here. And as long as there isn't, that's what I want to do: be with the boys who set the quotas. Wouldn't you?"

Bill swiveled sideways in his chair and shook his head. Seconds passed, and he still said nothing. Puzzled by his rare—and strangely ominous—silence, Ira turned to look at Skelsey. Cool, inscrutable, his gaze was fixed with ruthless appraisal on Bill's averted face.

Ira asked Fred as a last favor to drive him over to the used-car lot in hope he'd be refunded his two dollars. Ira stepped into the little shanty where the pockmarked Jewish dealer was seated at a table playing solitaire. Ira said he was sorry they couldn't buy the Model T. He said he was, too. Ira told him the straits he was in, and that he was going to try to hitchhike east or go by freight train if he had to. The dealer lifted his head from the cards, and looked up at him, looked into his face hard for several seconds. "You the one who made the deposit?" he asked.

"Yes," Ira said hopefully.

He uttered not a word more, but shifted his attention to cards on the table and resumed his game. Ira left and got back into the car with Fred.

"So that two bucks is gone. Boy, am I stupid." And as Fred glanced at Ira while he started the car, "And the guy just mooched twenty bucks from the woman I used to live with. Meanwhile the kids are eating ice cream. Not that I begrudge them it."

"I'll lend you the money. I said so before. Not for the reasons you think." Fred chuckled briefly.

"No. I don't deserve it."

"That's what I like about you, I guess. You judge things on whether you deserve them. If you don't, you make hardships for yourself." He laughed freely. "I never heard of that. Not till the other night when we went out. With me, it's can I get away with it. That's where my time goes, taking all that into account. If you'd stayed, I almost think I could have used you for a partner. You might have taught me something: I mean the way a certain kind of people think, really believe. And at least one guy I'd be sure they couldn't buy. They could scare him maybe, but they couldn't buy him."

"It's awful," Ira said.

"Well, what do you think of me?"

"The way I feel now, it's as though what really counts—or the one who really counts—is the guy who can cope. You understand? The guy who can make his own way. I almost don't care how the hell he does it." His dejection was close to overpowering. "I don't know what it's all about. Just what I'm not."

Fred gave no sign. Ira stood at the threshold of an easy bus ride home. He wouldn't repeat his offer of assistance, Ira knew, but all he had to do was ask. They reached the door of the cabin, where Fred stopped, and they shook hands.

"Good luck," Fred said.

Ira got his bag of groceries out of the car and gazed at the lean, dark face through the windshield as he backed the car. "Thanks," Ira called. With a wave of farewell, he drove out of the auto court.

Ira could think of nothing to do afterward to ease his nervousness over the imminent unknown he was soon to embark on, no way to withstand Bill's flights of tense gaiety—which Ira was sure

was his reaction to Ira's own fears—than to take the empty bottle of
Oxhead whiskey to the open-air market a few blocks away and get it
filled with bulk wine out of a barrel.

Catering to Ira's fondness for the dish, Bea cooked spaghetti.
After dishwashing was over, and the two children tucked into bed,
Bill and Bea went to the movies, the first time they had done so
in the five months Ira had been there. Ice cream. Movies. Thought
limped with a kind of lassitude, or as if struggling through a figura-
tive canebrake of apprehension: Let the stricken deer go weep, the
hart ungalled play . . . they were flush. If Ira was in dubious cir-
cumstance, it was his fault; when wasn't it? Foster woke, diaper wet.
While Ira searched for a dry replacement, conscious of the hack-
neyed stock situation of the tyro confronted with the task, little Dian
broke into a fit of coughing. New trepidations. Foster was wearing
anti-thumb-sucking armlets, and these being a novelty, even after
Ira successfully performed the change of diapers, without punctur-
ing him with safety pins, he was wakeful, and began a loud wailing,
which awoke Dian, who broke into a fresh fit of coughing. At wits'
end, Ira removed the armlets and let Foster suck his thumbs to his
heart's content, whereat he promptly fell asleep, and Dian, too.

When Bill and Bea returned from the movies, Ira told them of
his alarms, and that he had tried Bill's device of standing beside the
crib to reassure Foster, but only made him yell the louder, because he
evidently recognized that Ira wasn't his father.

Bill beamed.

They all sat down to cocoa and the doughnuts they had brought
home, glazed, raised doughnuts, which they knew Ira had a particular fondness for. "Now tell me that again," Bill prompted. "How did
you stand next to his crib?"

Ira had to repeat the story at least twice.

They awoke to Foster's reveille. The slight headaches, which all of the adults complained of, and attributed to the wine, passed after they had breakfasted on bacon and eggs, Bill not quite so heartily as Ira did. Bill's stomach was off again. How tenderly, despite his own evident distress, he waited on the infant Foster and fed him his Farina. Ira concealed his relief when Bill and Bea informed him that they intended to stay on in LA until they could scrape together enough cash to buy a reliable car. Only too conscious of the altered timbre in his voice, as a result of his ulterior motives, Ira urged them to do just that, and suggested in addition that they move out of the motor court and into the outskirts of town, for the sake of the children's health. Which won from Bill the approving remark that "certain of the petty boojwasie understands the workin' class better'n lots o' workers." He followed Ira's silence at his rare compliment with inquiry about "the Madam," the Long Island socialite Mrs. Emily R, whose children Ira had once tutored: whether he could get his job back, and begin earning again. (His deviousness contended with Ira's own.) Ira was dubious. The two girls had already made their debuts, and young Ian, whom Ira had doted on, was at Groton. "What about M?" Bill probed. "Will she be able to find work bein' a musician?"

"It's hard to say."

"I do my revolutionary work, no matter where I'm at. It don't make no differnce. LA, New York."

"I know," Ira agreed. And in a moment of enlightenment, Ira seemed to see clearly how neatly his rank-and-filism balanced Ira's petit bourgeois outlook. Bea placed a hand fondly on Bill's shoulder. He drew away. She censured him for his he-man behavior. "Conditions made me like that," he justified his show of unyielding masculinity. But not to be deterred, as Bea passed him, she gripped his knee.

Breakfast over, Bill set Foster in the pram, and they strolled out in balmy LA weather in the direction of the railway freight office, where Ira went inside to ask the rates charged for shipping freight from LA to New York. $6.11 for hundred pounds, and only $10 insurance coverage, as against shipping by Railway Express, which charged 12 cents per pound and covered the shipment with an automatic $50 insurance. Debating relative advantages, they walked from there to the yard nearby in which used, wooden packing boxes were sold. Ira bought a large crate, a dollar-sized one. And resting it on Foster's pram, Foster having conveniently fallen asleep meanwhile, with the crate precariously shining in the sunlight between palm trees and houses, they trundled both crate and child back to the motor court. John Davis was in the cabin waiting for them.

And now there were three men to wrangle over the best and most economical way to ship Ira's possessions. To his surprise, John recommended shipping via marine. Why? Ira demanded. "Because you can replace everything you own if it was lost for a few bucks. Maybe not more than it would cost to ship by Railway Express."

"The hell I can," Ira said. "My books, papers, clothes. I could never replace some of that stuff."

It was amusing to see Bill squirm silently with impatience. Crafty as always, he suggested Bea prepare some lunch, and sent John out for a loaf of bread. With John gone, Bill bore down on Ira with the full powers of his persuasion: Ship the stuff he valued most by Railway Express, and what he valued least, leave behind in Bill's safekeeping. And already it was clear, if Ira followed his advice, the stuff he would leave behind was his prized dictionaries and thesaurus and, above all, his cherished Marxist classics, the very ones Bill had asked to circulate around through the Party.

Cold cuts, salami, spiced beef, in sandwiches for lunch, with a side dish of warmed-over spaghetti, and with Davis and Bill arguing throughout the meal. "You get seawater in your stuff you ship by steamer," Bill maintained.

And John just as stubbornly rejoined, "They bang the hell outa the crates you ship by freight. And sometimes on purpose, to see what's inside."

The meal over, Davis left. Ira began sorting out his most valued belongings, those that he would ship by Railway Express, separating them from the pile of possessions he would leave behind. Bill watched him. And in a voice strange for him in its reasonableness, he said, "You could get it all over with if you sent to M fer enough dough to take it with you by bus."

But committed to the role of hard guy, Ira dissented.

The box packed and nailed down, Ira went outside to call up the Railway Express office to arrange for their picking up his shipment the next morning. The motor court would be their first stop; they would be there early, no later than eight o'clock. That was fine with him. Ira had agreed with his landlord, Royer, to rendezvous with him at nine-thirty in the morning on his way to a walnut ranch he wanted to inspect. Ira would thus oversee the safe dispatch of his shipment and leave the cabin with plenty of time to meet Royer. His lift of about 125 miles in the direction of El Centro, where Ira hoped he could get a ride to Yuma in Arizona, would be a good beginning toward the long journey home.

And coming back from the phone booth, Ira ran into Bill's neighbor Dolly—Dolly and Mrs. Roche, a wadded, middle-aged woman with a green-pored nose and eyeglasses. She lived with a lethargic, semi-invalid, wheelchair-bound husband across the court. The two women had been drinking wine in the bar across the trolley tracks from the court. They were pleased with themselves, in fact, quite gleeful: an hour before, they had presented themselves as new customers at the Bi-Mor Supermarket, which entitled them to three glass tumblers apiece.

They proposed that Ira treat them to a beer. He escorted them across the street again, Dolly hanging onto his arm, immodestly, full-breasted contour of womanliness sending his wits pitching about in confusion, scaring into animation the long dormant, as they crossed the trolley tracks toward the half-curtained beer parlor on the other side of the mean street in the open air of afternoon.

They had beers. Dolly told with flagrant gaiety how often she had two-timed George, the last when he was employed out of town for two weeks. The neighbor across the bathroom had minded the kids while Dolly worked as a barmaid—the swell tips she received, the swell dates she made. Applauding Dolly's every disclosure, and encouraging her to further revelation, Mrs. Roche kept up a running patter about how dumb George was. "Just imagine a man going off to the movies and thinking his wife was going to stay home by herself."

"Did he?" Ira was aware that his thumb was scoring his index finger.

"Oh, he'd want me to go along with him sometimes. But he knew I wouldn't go. Twenty-five cents each: we wouldn't have enough to get through to the next relief check. So I let him have his fun, and I had mine."

"And saved a quarter," said Dolly.

"An' got more'n that," said Mrs. Roche.

At which they had a good laugh. Dolly wanted to know, with some asperity, why the Loems were entitled to a three-room cabin, with no more kids than she had, while she was allowed only a two-room cabin. "I'm gonna clip that relief investigator on the chin," she avowed. "She promised me some children's clothes, an' never gave me any. Bea's kids have 'em, an' I don't know why." Talk gyrated even more with the second beer. Ira could scarcely—and cared scarcely—attend to what was being said: to and by the bartender about what he could do with his ice-chilled hands; Mrs. Roche's long account about Mabel, her neighbor, who was suspected of being a thief, because a ten-dollar bill had disappeared after one of her visits.

"Was she the one who swiped Bill's broom?" Ira asked.

"She's the one all right. I couldn't find a fifty-cent piece after she left. But Dolly told me to shake my dress, and out it fell right out of the hem."

"I'd have choked the heifer, if we didn't find it," said Dolly, all this time distracting Ira by bumping his legs with hers, squeezing his thigh, fondling his kneecap. Mrs. Roche wanted to dance. Ira begged off. They left after the second beer. In the street again, the barber in front of his shop next to the beer parlor ogled Dolly with all the rapture of one glimpsing Paradise. He kissed his fingertips, and with an arm about his spiraling barber pole, said something rhapsodic about the beautiful ladies. Dolly told Ira that the barber's wife had died recently and that he wasn't the least unhappy about it. "But he's got too much pomade on him. An' I draw the line on them tight magician's mustaches."

"He might drill you with 'em!" Mrs. Roche squealed.

While they were in the bar, Dolly had tried to dissuade Ira from leaving LA the next day. Once again, when they stepped into the Roche cabin, Dolly importuned him not to leave for New York, enlisting the aid of Mrs. Roche, who insisted Ira had promised to take them both to a dance the next night, which he denied in strongest terms. Bloated and inebriate Mr. Roche, with an almost empty gallon of red wine beside him, listened with glazed eyes to what was being said, laughed vacantly with hanging jaw, mumbled that he had just given Dolly's kids an apple apiece and a graham cracker, and offered Ira a glass of wine. He declined. It was now five o'clock, and when Mrs. Roche went to the stove, saying it was time to prepare supper, Ira arose to go. Dolly and her two children, who had come in meanwhile, left with him. They crossed the court. Ira accompanied her to her door, and there, with the gloaming settling on the shabby wooden huts and the drab courtyard, she invited him in; he accepted the invitation. Squalor distilled a shimmering essence at once enticing and scary: a blond Ozark Circe in a light dress. Two glasses of beer. The dissembling twilight. The enticement: to come in and see the kind of rustic chairs the hillbillies nailed together in Arkansas. Once inside, she told the kids to put on their coats and go outdoors, which the two little girls did, with a kind of knowing obedience. Alone together, she threw herself at Ira; he seized her wrists: "Cut it out!" In the same instant balking, in the same instant inflaming: herself, him. They swayed in the dimness. She was fair, feminine, strong; glint of defiant, blue eyes in the gloom, her thigh led, bold against his long dormant, growing stalk. "Cut it out!"

"You can't make me."

"Cut it out. I'm a ho—I'm a fag!"

Her ringing laugh construed his words as part of the sport, redoubling provocation. "Ain't you the fine one, with that down there."

"I am!"

"You ain't neither." She made a playful thrust with her thigh. "Pos-sum-m-m."

"Cut it out! I can't help it."

Bold, she swung both hands behind her, his wrists following to her rump. He let go of her wrists. Argus-eyed Ira's hands sought the mounds of her: her melony breasts, mons, billowy rear.

"You been lookin' at me. I been lookin' at you, an' we ain't done nothin' but look. An' now we got a chance to do more'n look." Fingers plied fly buttons. "That feels nice, don't it? Say you won't go home tomorrow."

"Oh, Jesus." Fred Skelsey's lean visage swam before Ira's eyes: he had a proposition. Reality split into crooked fissures, like crazed china—

"Say you won't go tomorrow."

"No. I'm a cocksucker, I tell you!"

"I could love you, you possum."

"I'm not—Let go!"

"Yo' sullin' ain't foolin' me." She bloomed—in the waning light—in terrible gravity, enticing, entreating. "She can wait, honey. You know she can wait. I'm here, honey, an' yo' here. Come on, honey. You need me."

"Bitch. Oh, God! Oh, Chris' sake."

So free her smile, blue eyes lambent in the dimness, sportive the female pressure of her body. "Come on, honey. You can't let go any more'n I can—"

And then the cabin door flew open on courtyard twilight, and in darted the older girl. "Daddy's coming!" she said. And because they stood motionless, riveted—"Daddy's coming!" the child yelled even louder. And still not to be denied, though they separated, in panicky haste recomposing themselves, she refused to be misunderstood: "George is coming!"

"All right, Jeanie," said Dolly.

Ira sat down on the rustic chair. The three waited; and together with the younger child, George entered. Dolly switched on the floor lamp. Fortunately, fortunately, Ira had met him the night before, and told him he would step in to say good-bye before he left. Which now explained his having dropped in, Ira hoped. He was highly amused at his wife's being half lit, laughed in his soughing, uproarious way. Consummate in dissembling, she reminded him it was his turn to cook the mashed potatoes and gravy for supper. She patted his shoulder as she spoke, never casting a single glance at Ira. Only the kids, Ira thought as he stood up to leave, betrayed a childish, pixie mien at the funny secret they kept.

You're all right, Ira exulted crossing the dark court. Jesus, you're all right.

They celebrated Foster's first birthday that night. Margie, from across the bathroom passageway, was invited to participate. The strains of

139

her Victrola record's "Hamhocks and butter beans; that's what I like about the South" mingled with their "Happy Birthday, dear Foster!" Bea lit the tiny candle on the gaudy little birthday cake. "Candles is superstition," Bill orated. "When a candle is lit, the ghost walks."

"They ain't," Bea countered. "You light 'em, and the kids makes a wish."

Margie left. More of Bill's yarning during supper and afterward. Then a sudden manic gust that swept him with fits of mirth. He told about the prostitute in Cincinnati who was heard lamenting when the fireman threw her smoldering bed and mattress out the window, "There goes my old workbench." And the banker viewing the hole cut out of the plate-glass bank front by the robbers to gain entrance to his bank: "I never liked that damned glass anyway." In gruffest guttural Bill played the big Indian chief for Dian. Bea warned him he'd scare the child out of her wits; she was already terrified of the dark.

The evening, Ira's last one there, wore on with a graphic description of Bill's own and his father's tapeworm (his father could feel the head of the revolting creature rear up in his throat). And once again, like a spasm, the mental tic that never left him: reversion to the gun. His cold, blue eyes boring into Ira's, Bill sat there, the fingers of his sound hand curled on the table beside his steel hook, curling around the butt of a Colt .45. And so vivid the pantomime, it almost restored to the leather-sleeved stump its lost, lopped-off hand holding the other Colt .45 he once owned. Try to fix all this in mind against future erosion, Ira thought: the two kids sleeping in the bedroom, their plump, young, harassed mother, the dull shabbiness of surroundings, the bare, unpainted wood of the cabin walls, the scarred floors dragged over by worn furniture, the grim, indomitable face of the man sitting with forearms resting on the bare table as if he were gripping the butts of two guns.

After supper, they repaired to Margie's cabin so Ira could bid her farewell. Her cabin was similar in construction to the Loems', only smaller: walls of brown wooden boards, the studding exposed. Instead of portraits of Marx, Stalin, and William Z. Foster on the dreary walls, Margie had hand-painted plaster English setters pointing at hand-painted plaster pheasants on small gilded shelves. She put on her latest record, a plaintive song:

> *I don't know how it happened*
> *but it happened somehow.*
> *I don't worry*
> *'cause it makes no difference now.*

In the morning, his shipment to New York taken care of, and the balance of his belongings left with Bill for safekeeping, Bea sewed Ira's remaining funds, fifteen dollars, except for the dollar and some change in his pocket, under the lining of his jacket. Until such time and clime called for him to wear it, Ira prepared to carry over his arm his old hybrid topcoat-raincoat, unlined, of canvas weave and reversible. In the pockets he had stowed some items he had listed in the back of his pocket notebook:

1. Safety razor
2. Shaving cream
3. Soap
4. Socks
5. Eyeglass case

Also listed in the same notebook: directions where to meet Royer, and, in case someone among his acquaintances had clothing of Bill's size they wanted to give away to a deserving party, Bill's measurements: chest 44", waist 40", crotch inseam 30".

Came time to leave. Ira kissed the children, was hugged strongly by Bea, whom he thanked. And accompanied by Bill, he left the auto court, passing Dolly's cabin at the entrance, Dolly, he was sure, behind the curtain.

It was a bland California morning, pleasant and calm. After a few blocks Bill stopped. Ira did, too. They faced each other in farewell. "I wish you good luck, Berry," he said, using Ira's CP name. And Ira said, "Thanks." His eyes held steady before the gimlets of Bill's blue-eyed scrutiny. They shook hands, Bill's left hand in Ira's right. Ira walked another half block, and turned around to see Bill still standing where they had parted, his steel hook plunged deep into the pocket of his shapeless pants, watching Ira. Ira waved—a last time—and went on.

CHAPTER 11

The miles slipped by all too quickly, covering only the merest jot of the great journey stretching before Ira, the great journey he would soon have to undertake unassisted, unbefriended, and in ignorance.

After a little while, Ira and Royer shook hands. Royer let him off where Ira's highway, a road frequented by hitchhikers, forked toward El Centro. Ira stood a minute looking after the dwindling vehicle, loath to surrender his last connection to companionship, to someone concerned, but the car lurched ahead and then disappeared around a curve in the road.

Undoubtedly Ira was too reticent, undoubtedly he was too shy. For all his tentative thumbing, the waggling and waving of arms, he got only as far as the next town, and by then the winter sun was already low in the west. A fellow hitchhiker offered to guide him to the place he was going to stay: it was something better than a flophouse, he said, but not much.

About a mile hike brought them to the place, and it fitted his description—not much better than a flophouse on the Bowery, the chief difference being the absence of drunks standing, drooping and tattered, in the doorway. Evidently aimed at a clientele of transients like Ira, it went by the improbable name of the Dew Drop Inn and cost fifty cents a night per cubicle. Furnished with only a bed and a light, it was innocent of heat at night, with no showers in evidence, only lavatories and crappers. Ira was counseled by the occupant of the neighboring cubicle, a little wiseacre with a mustache, to make for Holtville, rather than the route that looked shortest, because it was better traveled and better for picking up rides.

It was a cinch to Holtville—the wise guy with the mustache was right. Effortlessly, Ira parlayed one ride into another and reached Holtville early in the afternoon. And there he stuck. And not only he—a whole file of hitchhikers, ludicrous in their numbers, compared with the trickle of traffic going their way. The reason for the scarcity of vehicles wasn't hard to find: from Holtville to Yuma, Arizona, next leg of the journey, lay a stretch of road, fifty miles or more, through desert, devoid of towns. Not only did few autos and trucks make the trip, but for hitchhikers only the whole trip was of any use. Otherwise, they'd be marooned in the middle of nowhere, in or between hamlets without names, tiny blank circles on a map. Though some trucks did pass by, truckers were enjoined by their insurance companies or by their employers not to pick up riders. The driver of the very infrequent passenger car that went all the way, who might have wished to give someone a lift, seeing that long file strung out along the highway, must have feared that he would be mobbed if he stopped for anyone.

The hours went by; so did the cars and trucks, but Ira advanced not a yard toward Yuma. And, as far as he could see, neither did anyone else, though most of them must have marched at least five miles back and forth in the hope of finding a more propitious station whereon to stab the air with their thumbs: futile Jack Horners were they. One heard the flinty jests of desperation: some guys had been here for three days (Ira could well believe it); some had applied for resident status. Many hitchhikers, Ira could see, having abandoned all hope of getting out of town eastward, had crossed the highway and were thumbing their way back west—and with far greater success. Anything to get out of Holtville, Ira thought. But then he learned that their aim was to backtrack to a railroad junction and hop a freight from there. To hell with the highways, they said.

Ira felt the same way. But, at a loss, he continued to stab the air with his thumb. Then he struck up with a short-statured wise guy. Ira thought for a moment that he was the one he had met in the flophouse the evening before, who had advised Holtville as the best bet. But he wasn't. This wise guy had no mustache. Nor would he ever have blown his last fifty cents for a flop, as Ira soon discovered.

He was as brash a guy as ever Ira had met; his story was that he drove new automobiles from Detroit to California, which somehow enabled the dealer to avoid paying an entry tax. Now and then, he drove a "hot" car, a stolen car, from one state to another. In between, he sold used cars. He had been on a drunk for days. Now he was penniless. He had eaten nothing since yesterday; he was beating his way back to Texarkana, his hometown. He knew all the ropes, all modes of travel, both highway—which he damned with heartfelt anathema—and freights. If only he could get to Yuma and the freight yards, wouldn't he show the rest of these lugs how to move? Acting with all the due circumspection of one who has only a few dimes on his person, after great deliberation Ira invited him into one of the truck stops for coffee and doughnuts. Ira now had a buddy. His name was Johnny Graham.

They thumbed in tandem now, buddies, but to no avail. Seeking luckier spots, they passed and passed again the prominent sign on the road that read, "Soliciting Rides Liable to Chain Gang."

"I'm gonna steal that goddamn sign," Johnny threatened.

But night came, and, lit up by approaching headlights that never slowed down, the sign was still there. So were they. At last, miraculously, their symbiosis paid off. Because Ira treated him to

145

another round of doughnuts and coffee in the truck stop, he and Ira were free to solicit drivers, their fellow diners, directly. Ira's polite entreaties got him only "Sorry, bud, it's my job." For all his brazen importunings, his truck-driver cant, his bold familiarity, Johnny didn't fare any better. A few times, truck drivers seemed on the point of yielding, but thought better of it. Then, at 2:15 A.M., Johnny's tactics paid off: "All right, you win," the trucker said.

In the back of the cab, behind the driver and his helper, was a concealed bunk, and that was to be their hidden roost for the next fifty miles. The truck butted through the freezing, thin night air, the treads of the heavy tires crooning to the highway asphalt. Through the bunk's portholes, single stars kept pace with them for long distances, steady as icy rivets. The truck slowed down, came to a stop. In the cold void, they heard a woman's voice, though they could see no one, a young woman's voice, cheery and clear, in greeting. And then the cab door opened, slammed shut; again the heavy vehicle lumbered into speed. Johnny and Ira merely looked at each other. All that mattered was that they were rolling toward Yuma. Perhaps another quarter to a half hour passed, and then the truck came to a stop. They heard the driver get out: "Far as I can take you, fellas." He opened the bunk door. "Just can't take you into town."

"Sure! Sure!" They understood. They sprang from the bunk down to the highway. "Thanks, Mister. Thanks, pal. Thanks a million."

The truck stayed there, and they soon walked out of range of its dimmed headlights. Incurious, they did not turn at the sound of the truck door opening, thudding closed. With hope renewed, they walked briskly toward the east, toward a horizon still seamless with night, starry, in quiet, keen air, and made out the first city lights about a half mile away: Yuma. And soon they were treading sidewalk.

The gleam of a diner pried into the dark street, promising

warmth, food, coffee, against the inhospitable desert gloom behind them. "Coffee an'?" Ira invited.

"Sure would." Sheer animal hunger sounded in his plea.

They entered, into humid comfort, found stools, ordered—coffee and two doughnuts apiece (at a cost of ten cents each) and, asking the waitress to hold it a sec, took turns in the lavatory.

And now, refreshed, another brisk walk, to the freight yards, as the night sky streaked into abrasion of dawn. Johnny spoke to other hobos moving along the gravel lanes between freights, and they found a boxcar and clambered aboard. They congratulated themselves on being alone, on having a private freight car. Alas, too soon. By the time the gray gravel between tracks shone in broad daylight, twenty more birds of passage had joined them. The door of the boxcar opened briefly on warm sunshine when a belated hobo climbed aboard, and rolled closed again. And finally, after those rumblings and bumpings, the mysterious joltings heralding the setting forth of freight trains, they clanked into motion, picked up speed, and were on their way. They rolled the door open to let in the sun. Some of them stretched out on the boxcar floor; some lay jackknifed against the walls; some sat. A gray-bearded old hobo, a "bindle stiff," Johnny labeled him, methodically unfurled various-sized rectangles of blanket and, sighing tranquilly, with hands locked together, reclined on his improvised couch, his head propped up by a stained knapsack.

Ira found a place next to Johnny. He hadn't slept in twenty-four hours. Awhile he watched in gratitude as the spectacular Arizona landscape whizzed past the open boxcar door—sunny butte and sloping sunlit mesa. And then overpowering drowsiness meshed everything together into a single clacking carrousel. Ah, what was more wonderful than traveling by freight!

The train made a stop in Tucson. How long it would stay there nobody knew. For an hour or so, Ira and Johnny joined the other hobos basking on the sun-warmed planks adjacent to the railroad street crossing. And then, bored, impatient, they strolled over to Main Street and, with the security of outcasts, studied the prosperous citizenry. A rodeo was due to be held that afternoon, so the town may have had more than its usual complement of visitors, and these and the notices of the coming diversion, and the air of anticipation engendered by it, beguiled them into loitering overlong. When they got back to the freight yard, their train had left.

Another was due in a little while, the hobos said. And, soon after, it thundered into the yard, slowing down, but only as if it meant to go on. Ira ran alongside at top speed, Johnny behind him. Ira had already been instructed never to grab the steel ladder at the end of a boxcar, but only the one at the beginning—in the direction the train was moving—because a miss on the rear ladder might mean plunging headlong under the wheels of the following car, while a miss on the front ladder would only send him slamming against the freight wall, and he would be hurled back, away from the train. So Ira made a grab for the front-end ladder, grasped, held on, climbed up to the catwalk atop the freight, knelt, clung to the catwalk—and the train suddenly stopped. Johnny howled with laughter.

"Jeez, that is funny," Ira said. "Risk your neck, and have the train stop."

"No. You're funny."

"Me?"

"You're hot shit, the way you grab a train on the fly." Johnny guffawed again. "If I ever saw anybody who couldn't make up his mind gettin' on a freight, it's you."

"Yeah? Why?"

"Chrissake, grab the goddamn ladder. It ain't gonna bite ye."

Chagrined at his ineptitude, Ira followed Johnny along the catwalk, leaping the gap from car to car. But chagrin was a luxury Ira couldn't afford here; even reflecting on it was inadmissible for somebody being whittled down to nobody, just another hobo, and an incompetent one at that. Pay attention. Watch what you're doing.

"Here's a reefer," Johnny said. He pulled up the rust-covered hatch and peered down. "Nobody in it."

In the dark refrigerator compartment, its length running the width of the freight, and little more than a yard wide, a steel ladder, affixed to the wall, led down to the bottom. They descended and looked back overhead, where the reefer hatch could be rigged ajar by an attached rod. Johnny climbed up a few rungs and set the rod.

"You got an extra handkerchief, right?"

"Yeah. What d'you want?"

"Gimme it, will ye?" And, taking the handkerchief, he wedged it under the supporting brackets of the tilted hatch. "That's so a brakey knows we're down here." He climbed down and explained: tramps asleep when the brakeman overhead locked the hatch in freezing weather—to protect the cargo—had been frozen to death when the car was left on a siding out of earshot.

"I get it."

The train began moving. They half sat, half reclined on the reefer floor. It was not a solid floor but a drainage floor: curved steel bars about a half-inch thick with two-inch spaces between them enabled the water of melting ice cakes in the summer to escape to a tray and the tracks beneath. The steel drainage scimitars pressed cruelly into Ira's buttocks.

Johnny soon fell asleep. Ira lit his pipe and watched smoke vent through the transom of the rigged hatch into the narrow dusk of day's end. The chill penetrated as the light faded. Soon, frigid dark roared into the confines of the empty ice compartment. How to pass the long night?

Long night awake . . . long night cold . . . long night on a freight, five days old . . . long night of *clackety-clack, clackety-clack* on wheels pounding eastward over the segmented tracks . . .

Howooo. Train whistled approaching a level crossing. What crossing? A crossing in Texas. How to pass the long cold night?

Why, writer manqué, are you not? Novelist manqué, no? Desperately balked of all the narratives that you tried, narratives that came to naught, no? Came to nort, all abort.

Why, sternly bring your faculties to a focus by composing an autobiography, freely associative . . . but governed by implicit rules of narration . . . augment suspense toward a climax . . . a climax that would exclude present distress. Hey, good ground rules: augment suspense toward a climax . . . that would exclude . . . the cold ache of legs as you lean against the swaying wall, the icy carving of the scimitar bars into butt . . . or shoulder . . . or flank, driving you upright again. Where would you begin? You already told them of your Lower East Side boyhood in one novel; what would you do, then?

No, what happens in this vision he had, in this early manhood, seemed to defy the ground rules he had just laid down. In this thundering crypt above the rails, Ira saw his life as pivoting about certain crucial, certain critical points, where the event determined the rest, the lamentable sequence that followed inexorably in its wake. *Clackety-clack. Clackety-clack.* The year was 1914. Here's the nub of the disaster: Zaida and Baba (grandfather, grandmother), two uncles, and two aunts, one skip ahead of the Great War, depart Galicia, sell—Zaida does—the little *gesheft*, the little store, in the little hamlet of Veljish (on no map at all), which pays for second-class passage to Amerikka, to New York. Now, were it not for that semi-Americanized whoremonger of a hotel waiter, Ira's uncle Saul, who looked down his snooty beak at the Lower East Side and persuaded the Galician pilgrims to settle in Harlem, ah, how different his history would have been, how different Ira. For Mom would have been content to remain on the East Side, in their lofty aerie overlooking the East River, on Avenue D and Ninth Street. And Ira would not have been plucked out of his Orthodox Yiddish mini-state like a what? Vegetable, or a mandrake in Blake's etching. Ira would have grown up in unquestioned Orthodoxy, tough little cocksure fisticuffian gamin, who had to hide under the bed when mothers came looking for him for having bloodied their kids' noses. Ira, alas, who in the course of a single year among the Irish on 119th Street in East Harlem went from a wiry kid to "Fat, fat, the water rat. Fifty bullets in your hat." Oh, don't blame the Irish.

Ira was outnumbered, and hung around Mom, even learning to embroider cloth between two hoops while he sat on the stoop beside her. Jewboy Achilles become Mama's boy, tied to her apron strings. Oh, don't blame the Irish. He should have fought, biffed and battled, for he was once good at it, and that was their language: biff and battle. Ira had nothing else to recommend him: poor eyes, maladroit, too, couldn't catch a ball and couldn't throw one, lousy at stickball. Who knew about such goyish sports on the East Side? Or marbles, or pitching pennies? But don't blame the Irish. A punch in the nose for a punch in the nose. Jew bastard! But oh, untroubled Ira had been in his milieu, amid jabbering Jews under the omnipotent sway of a Hebrew God. And then he was suddenly hurled into the alien and incomprehensible goyish maw of East Harlem. Wanna fight? No. So don't blame the Irish . . .

Go sit and brood, sit and brood, if you can rest your ass on serried scimitars.

But that was the first, that was the first switch in the tracks, Ira still insisted. First major fork in life's journey. And *clackety-clack* and *clackety-clack* all you damn please.

The movers stole Mom's red coral beads. Red coral beads, red coral beads, Mom's mourned-for cherry-red coral beads. They disappeared in transit to Harlem.

But I got no support, I got no support. What the hell do you expect of a kid who had a timid mouse of a father, frightened, panicky, whacked the daylights out of him when Mrs. True from upstairs accused him of pushing her kid to the sidewalk, which he hadn't done. She slapped him in front of Pop, and then he added a barbarous beating, so atrocious that dumpy, squat Mrs. Shapiro from the first floor intervened: "You'll destroy your own son for a goya?" And Mom arrived from shopping, frantic, hearing Ira's screams all the way through the hall, planting herself before Pop, the frenzied madman, and demanding of Mrs. True belligerently, "Vot you vant?"

Oh, Mother. How ugly, how lowering gloomy the kitchen setting. Oh, Mother. Beaten the hell out of, drubbed to a whimper, to a snivelling nullity—

Try rolling over to the other flank.

They had no right to pluck Ira out like a radish, like a beet, like a scallion, like a parsnip from among his own. And force him to grow hydroponically, a root crop like him, that adored the dirt and the din of the twoscore streets of his Jewish mini-state. The irony of it: Zaida, given name Ben Zion, Orthodox Jew with a beard, comes to these shores with his family and undoes Orthodoxy. He forgot the anticipation, the delirious anticipation of the June day, sitting two flights up in the new apartment prepared for them by Saul and Mamie, Ira's aunt, who lived across the street on 115th Street between Park and Madison, a nice *bitvinn* it was called. What did that little tyke imagine his newly arriving kinfolk would look like? Rich, generous, loving Jewish nobility come to rescue him from the unhappiness of the hostile goyish environment of 119th Street! Jewish nobility come to irradiate his unhappy home life! Empathetic, aye, opulent kinfolk, informed with novelty, with captivating fable, proffering handfuls of silver coins, endlessly doting, endlessly rejoicing in him.

Instead, getting out of the two taxicabs to the screams of hysterical Mamie from on high of "Tata, Tata! Oy, Mama, Mamaleh!" that drew the attention of all passersby within earshot on the street below were six ordinary, newly arrived, bewildered Jewish immigrants from Galicia in the erstwhile Austrian Empire.

With Saul overseeing the unloading of persons and baggage, amid commotion in the hall, the newcomers and their escorts ascended to the apartment. Everybody rushed in. Embraces ensued, resounding embraces. Under the supervision of Zaida, the newcomers were herded to the kitchen sink, and each rinsed his or her mouth with salt water. Ira swore, they rinsed it with something. Epsom salts? Nah. Go ask an Orthodox Jew. But that isn't the crux of the matter; the crux of the matter is, or was, that your dreams of noble permissiveness, openhanded, freehearted affection, contracted into a bearded, paunchy Jew who spoke such dense Yiddish you could scarce make way against it, contracted into a Slavic, snub-nosed, gentle, dear, depleted Baba, with little gold-rimmed eyeglasses, dam of a dozen offspring. The older of the two immigrant uncles looked like Baba, stocky, aged eighteen, with a head of thick, wavy chestnut hair, and the younger uncle, long-nosed and straight-haired, dazed into reticence, stood apart, gangly and tall. One aunt, the older, was composed and slow-spoken, while the other aunt was green-toothed, erratic, and noisy with excitement. Both homely. Ira shrank. Too much to absorb, all their lopsided gesticulations, shrugging, their grimaces and outcries: *"Oy, gewald un azoy, oy, gewald un azoy! Takeh emes? Un azoy! Oy ich khalesh un azoy!"*

With Mom's permission to leave, with a nickel to comfort him, but still dejected, Ira walked to Central Park and there climbed the granite outcrop atop the rowboat-dotted lake on 110th Street. And along a crease in the ground in a bosky grove where ran a little trickle of rainwater, Ira became the buckskinned and fringed American Scout, self-reliant, self-sufficient, in the pristine wilderness of America he knelt down and drank, in ritual, dim commitment. Sipping from the polluted rivulet in much trodden Central Park. That's not the crux; that's just a boyhood memory.

Oh, legs ache, ache standing. But sitting down is scant comfort on a seat of sabers.

The brain incandesces and fades, synapses glow and gutter out. You left Judaism, right? Right, ol' boy, ol' boy. Left Judaism, and damn glad to. You go with Zaida on a sleepy summer Shabbes to the shul, to the prayer-book musty tenement ground-floor synagogue, sit hour after hour and daven where shown, pray but not know what for, glibly match the right sounds to the printed letters, as you were taught to do on the East Side. And Zaida's proud of you, his old-est grandson, sure, sure, growing up devout. But the thing wears threadbare for a kid, is a hell of a bore—even though, ah, that was fun, at the Havdalah service—Havdalah, wasn't it? Half a dollah. To be made much of by the other bearded Jews, Shloymeh F., Zai-da's so dignified older brother, actually wore a shiny silk top hat on Shabbes, what a stereotype target for snowballs if he'd ever appeared in Ira's part of Harlem, among the juvenile scamps, Shloymeh with his forked gray beard and proud bearing and rich clearing of the throat. And the other pious congregants offering the only urchin at the Havdalah wine and lovely segments of salt herring, and— man, when that hit his palate the first time!—ripe wrinkled Greek olives.

All right, all right, sit down, if you can't stand up anymore. But the novelty wasn't enough to keep you coming regularly. So you shirked. And you and little Eddy, the Irish widow janitor's kid, became friends, and he showed you how to make tin-can telephones that stretched on a string from his flat on the ground floor to yours a flight up the worn stairs. And after many a fuzzy greeting, many a humming giggle and blurry message, you were well on the way to shedding your Judaism.

Ira stood up. Cold vacancy, interminable rattle and roar, his partner curled up in sleep, and a single blue star trailing like a dis-tant kite, in and out of view. Ira was tired of his yarn. The point was that he was here on this jigging jiggling freight. He had survived. He would wait the goddamn night out, surly and rancorous.

Weariness thrust in abeyance by the sudden thud on the roof of the freight car, Ira looked up: *thud*. Someone had leaped from one freight roof to another. The reefer hatch was lifted. Density of a person obliterating his shape of night sky, bowed, "Who down there?" under stars spreading all about him. "Hey, you—you down there?" A Negro voice.

"We are!" Ira yelled up. And alarmed: "Hey, Johnny!"

"Wha'?"

"How many you down there?"

Apprised in an instant, and instantly hostile: "There's two of us down here already. That's enough. We don't want no more."

The one overhead lingered for a moment and then withdrew.

"Boy, it's cold up there right out in the open. I hope he finds someplace to hide," Ira said.

"He's a nigger. He'll find a place to duck. I never worry about 'em." Arkansas spoke through Johnny.

"I wonder where the hell he's been? Come out all of a sudden that way."

"He should have stayed wherever he was, God damn him. I was sleepin' good. I mighta slept all the way to El Paso." He reached for his cap, massaged his glimmering features, yawned noisily, his teeth gleaming at the terminal grunt.

An hour later, Johnny's glimmering face tipped up toward the roof. "You hear that?"

"I think so."

"Is that the nigger again?"

"I don't know."

"It can't be a shacky."

"No? Why not?"

"If he was closin' up the reefers, we'da heard them other hatches slam."

"You mean closed against the cold?"

"Yeah. It's that black bastard."

Certainty grew, grew as swiftly as the distant thud of someone landing on the catwalk at the farther end of the freight became bounding footsteps approaching. Desperate hands raised the hatch overhead.

"Hey, I'm comin' down, man. I'm freezin'.'"

"There's two of us down here already. I told you. Stay out!"

"There's three, fo' in the others. There's five in one."

"Bullshit. Keep goin'."

"Been over the whole freight, man. There's only two o' you." The voice was young. "I'm comin' down."

"You try it! I'm tellin' you, boy. Two's enough down here."

The figure peering down from above didn't seem so much uncertain as restrained, trying to sense by instinct what the temper was below, the forces he had to brace himself to confront.

"For Christ sake, let him come down," Ira whispered.

"What for? Fuck's too lazy to go all the way up to the locomotive. There's lots o' reefers."

"That hatch cover! Jesus, if he locked us in—You crazy?"

"I'm comin' down, man."

Raised all the way, the hatch opened into a transom gorged with stars. Cascades of starlight poured through the gaping sluice above as he stooped, took his first step down, his booted foot seeking the rung below; and before he closed the hatch, stemming the flood of starlight above him, something—something metallic—glinted in the same hand. Down he came to the reefer bottom—woefully underclad, only a jacket over his shirt. With hands in pockets, "Man, I'm cold. Gettin' outta that wind like comin' to a stove."

"It's all right," Ira said.

Johnny moved silently to Ira's side of the compartment.

"I guess we got room," Ira said. "Where were you?"

"In a gondola. Layin' flat an' huggin' the bottom. Man, I like to freeze to death. I said I gotta get outta here, I gotta get outta here, 'fo' I freeze stiff. I tried ridin' behind a tank car. Too cold to live."

"You want a smoke?"

"Sleep. That's what I want, man." He took his hand out of his jacket pocket. "I 'fraid to go to sleep in that gondola. If I fall asleep in that gondola, they pick me up froze harder'n a rock. This is the first time I feel safe to sleep."

Drawing his knees up, his small hat jammed down on his head, he slipped to the reefer floor, and as he turned on his side he retrieved a short length of glinting metal from his jacket pocket, slid the hand holding the object between the curved steel bars of the drain, and deposited the glinting piece on the drip pan beneath. He was asleep in a minute—coughed himself awake; his hand groped between drainage bars, and, reassured, he stretched out his legs as far as he could, hat still jammed down on his small head, motionless, audibly, he fell asleep.

"He's got a knife," Johnny whispered.

"I guess so."

"Sonofabitch. That's why he come down. Two of us, he figured, an' he's got a knife."

"What the hell's the difference?" Ira hissed. "He's asleep, isn't he? That's all he wanted."

"How do you know?"

"Oh, bullshit." The pervasive shadowy Jew in the background flinched against myriad wounds suffered in centuries past. "Listen, Johnny, I'm not going to argue about it. It's a waste of time. You want to stretch out and go to sleep? Go ahead. I can't sleep. I'll—I'll watch."

"I'm not afraid of him. It ain't that. They're all yeller anyway. It's just that nobody else'd let him down, an' we did. Shit, they'd tell him there was six in the reefer."

An angry silence. Better keep quiet. Futile: you'll never penetrate that barrier; you don't even understand it, can't put it into words. Screwy. No more sense than a puppy dog chasing his tail. Think of something else.

Ira slid down to his end of the steel bars of the drainage floor. "Ow." Released from aching knees, he welcomed the few minutes of respite before the rigid scimitars against his buttocks supplanted old pain with new.

"I can see what he's got." Johnny settled beside him.

"You can?" Listlessly, "What?"

"Table knife, that's all. It's no goddamn razor."

"All right. I got a jackknife. How's that?"

"Better git it out an' keep it open. Just keep it open in your jacket pocket."

"Oh, for Christ sake." Peevishly, Ira rolled his rump away from the biting drainage bars, pulled the jackknife out of his back pocket, opened the three-inch Boy Scout blade, and exhibited it.

"You stab with it," Johnny said. "Go right for the belly. Know what I mean? You hold the blade down with your thumb and stab."

"Oh, nuts." Ira dropped the open jackknife into his jacket pocket.

"Yeah?"

"Yeah," Ira retorted angrily. "You know what I think? You got it ass backward. That poor colored guy is carrying that cheesy knife to protect himself. That's why. They wouldn't let him into any of the reefers. You can tell why he came down here. If he was going to fight for his life to keep from freezing, we were his best chance. Jesus, can't you see that? The guy's sleeping on that goddamn steel like a feather bed. Look at him. He hasn't moved an inch in all this time. Doesn't hear us. Anything. He's absolutely worn out."

"Worn out, my ass. He's used to it. You don't know these fuckin' niggers. They're tougher'n rawhide."

"Okay. I've had enough. I don't want to talk about it anymore."

Bang and jerk of freight-car coupling. Each time the car slacked its motion over flat Texas, Ira reflected, the locomotive had to jerk it onward. That goddamn boob had him sitting here with an open Boy Scout knife in his jacket pocket. Christ, absentminded as Ira was—and cold—he was apt to cut himself before he cut anybody else. He ought to snap the blade closed before he thrust his hand in his pocket to warm his fingers. Boy, that crazy Arkansas bastard. Wasn't he crazy?

"Want the tobacco?" Ira made a peace overture.

"Nah. . . . Thanks. I'm beginnin' to feel like a little shut-eye again."

"Yeah? Wish I could say the same. I feel it, but it doesn't do me any good."

"What're you gonna do? Be a watchman till light?"

"I don't know. It looks that way."

"Aw, let's have a smoke, if you're not going to sleep. Okay?" Ira brought out the can of Prince Albert. They rolled cigarettes, struck a match, lighting up the thin, jackknifed form sound asleep on the gleaming steel drainage bars. They smoked in silence.

Nothing to do. Lead the way. Pretend to sleep. Maybe the guy would follow suit, and they could drop the subject. Ira mashed the half-smoked cigarette against a drainage bar, curled on his side. Room enough for his shoes to the side of the sleeper's boots . . .

The stratagem worked. In a few minutes, when Ira cautiously lifted his head to peer, with arm pillowing face, Johnny's dark form lay bunched in sleep. Jesus, the archenemies, offset, end to end, nether to nether, like a what? Couldn't think of anything. Feet to feet. Two feet to feet. *Eine kleine Nachtmusik* . . . in a reefer . . .

That was sleep coming on, sleep. Ah, sleep, it is a precious thing, beloved from pole to pole . . . Oh, threshold, beautiful threshold of let go.

Utterly spent, Ira slept until after daybreak, until after morning light was framed in the rigged hatch overhead, unaware that his two fellow travelers were standing hunched over at opposite walls of the reefer, saying little. Ira awoke when the freight's tempo changed, the slowing down of motion allowing the distinct creak of car and train tracks beneath to emerge from the roar.

"We comin' to the yards," the young Negro said, slender and limber, now that Ira could see him—and chipper, too, in movement. He had apparently slept the night through from the minute he lay down.

"We're gittin' to El Paso," Johnny said. "C'mon, wake up. We got to get ready to get off her."

Dreary and stiff, Ira got to his feet.

"No bull ketch me climbin' down," the Negro youth announced confidently. "I'll run him a race on the roof to a gondola, an' then oveh the other side."

"Yeah? What if he pulls a gun?"

"I'll jump the other side of the freight, man, like I tol' you, 'fo' I let him pistol-whip me."

He seemed capable of it, too, lithe and agile. And as the train kept up its moderate, even rate of speed, he knelt down on one knee, slipped his brown flat wrist through the space between the drainage rails, and brought out the ordinary table knife they had seen him secrete there the night before. The streaked roughness of the crudely sharpened blade flashed a moment in daylight. He dropped it into his jacket pocket. Dully, Ira weighed his motives. Certainly he wouldn't dare—against a railroad bull, a man armed with a gun? In Texas? Jesus, he'd be lynched! Why had he waited until daylight to retrieve the weapon . . . to display it?

Johnny's warning interrupted Ira's foggy groping. His words came in a lowered voice and with a kind of worried severity, and, to Ira's surprise, were not about the Negro youth. "You see one, a big guy—"

"Who?"

"A railroad bull, for Chrissake. You gotta get down an' away fast. You woke up yet?"

"Yeah. What does he do? Wait for every freight that comes in?"

"No. But you never know when he's around. Loosen up. Stamp your feet, wave your arms. C'mon."

"Jesus, I had a helluva night."

"He won't give a shit about that. Loosen up." He moved his own arms in prompting, kept a steady gaze on the Negro youth.

Who smiled. "Yeah, man, y'gotta git ready to hightail it outta them yards. What if he Texas Slim?" He allowed himself a gleeful chuckle. "He fast on his feet."

The freight slowed, slowed, jarred, came to a clashing stop, though they still felt in motion. Already the Negro youth had mounted the ladder and was climbing. Speedy and sure, his arm thrust back the hatch. Another rung upward and he heaved himself into open air; he sprang into daylight and disappeared. By the time Ira mounted the lower rungs, he could hear him climbing down the outside. And up, Johnny crowding behind, Ira let the hatch fall back. Broad daylight. Blue dome of sky. Freight-car roofs in all directions. Ira had lived through it.

He jumped off the bottom rung down to the ground. But the Negro youth was tarrying there, and now Ira could guess, guess with a degree of certainty, at the same time oddly conscious that he felt no alarm. Standing between ramparts of brick-red and yellow freights, open gondolas, and tank cars, the brown youth in the small, earth-colored hat eyed them, Ira in particular, right hand in jacket pocket.

"Ah'm hungry, man."

"So're we," Johnny said.

"Sell you my boots, man." He pulled up his pants, bringing into view stockingless, lean brown shins above the edge of typical cow-

161

boy boots. "What y'all say? Sell 'em to you fo' just a little money."

The thoughts that scurry through the mind: the whole proposi-tion was preposterous. What the hell was he going to wear? And walk on this gravel? On streets? And in the cold? His wily eyes in his small head, watchful of every move, his wiry, quick body, ready for something, practiced, free and supple as a lynx. And a wickedly sharpened dinner knife hidden in his jacket pocket. And the two of them, yes, Johnny, shallow hard guy, and Ira, uncertain, untried, had to think of a way out of this, this emergency. Who the hell wanted his boots? He just wanted Ira to show some money. Forestall him somehow. Say okay, and ask him how much, ask him to take them off. "Listen," Ira said solicitously, "you need those boots. How're you gonna get around?"

"I need breakfast mo'n I need these boots right now."

"Well, that's different. You'd be crippled without boots. Wait a minute."

Large-eyed, askance, and as sidelong as a profile out of Egypt, he watched Ira, the knuckles of his left hand bulging out the thin cloth of the jacket pocket. Ira fished into his topcoat. He knew there was a dime among the change there. He didn't want to show any more money than that. But Ira had forgotten the open Boy Scout knife. It nicked him. Strange, strange: collapsed into unimaginable density as they say happened to a neutron star, all his history seemed in that instant, all its tenets, its dictates. Johnny beside him became tense, as Ira's fingers avoided the open blade and fished for the dime. "Here, keep your boots. Take this dime. Get yourself something to eat." Ira handed the youth the dime, conscious of Johnny's scowl.

"Thanks, man." Lissome again, he took the coin; or, rather, he accepted it, entirely without subservience or obligation, but with a short, triumphant laugh, turning, swiftly, strode jauntily away into the motley perspective between converging freights.

"What the hell'd you give him the dough for?" Johnny's tough visage grimaced. Under the visor of his cap his brow furrowed in a scowl; even his short body all but flapped in a spasm of wrath, so pronounced it gave one the impression of a ripple contrary to the wave, pulses contrary to his stride. They hurried toward a break in the double lines of freights. "We coulda took care of him."

Ira couldn't help grinning. "Maybe."

"What d'ye mean, maybe? I wouldn't let no nigger ride over me."

"I know." But Ira's mind seemed to be sifting out something worth a minute's consideration. A kind of insight: That wasn't the way—this was the important thing—a Negro was supposed to behave. That was it: not the cocksureness, no; then what? A sense of equality, independence. Sure, he had deliberately displayed the weapon to cow them. Or he would have grabbed the dough and run. And he was fast enough to get away. Okay. Whatever. Was Ira imagining things? Was it really a sign of change? A new stance of the Negro, a new attitude. "It's only a dime."

Johnny seemed to be going through some kind of parallel evaluation, but one that reached an entirely opposite judgment: "Sure it's only a dime. But you let him git the better of you, you let him git ahead of you."

"Oh, balls." Ira tossed his head. "Get into a fight with a guy with a knife. For a dime?"

"I told you we oughta git that cheese dagger away from him while he was asleep. You saw him."

"Well, we didn't. And now get your throat slashed for ten cents."

"He never would've. If we jumped him together, never. If he'd knowed you had a open jackknife, he never would've tried it."

"Well, it wasn't open."

"What for you got your finger scratched?"

"I don't know. Must have done it some other time." Johnny clawed the air in frustration.

"Jesus." Ira tried to shunt the conversation into other channels. "He turned out of sight about here, didn't he?" He leaned forward to squint ahead. "How come we can't find it?"

"We're comin' to it. There. I can see the snubbers at the end o' the tracks. Trouble is you northe'ners don't know niggers. You keep lettin' 'em git more an' more outa their place. They'll git us all down that way."

"Okay. I see it. Boy, look at those lines of freights behind us."

"It's El Paso. It's a big junction."

Grumpy with each other but trying to reach an accommodation of necessity, knowing that they had to, they let the subject drop. With Johnny leading the way, in silence, like a short bridge to the commonplace, they rounded the spring snubber at the end of a line of freights and tramped out of the yard up the incline to the blacktop highway at the edge. They were now off railroad property, out of danger, in the clear, a couple of grouchy, slouchy, seedy hobos walking by the run-down dwellings at the outskirts of El Paso.

CHAPTER 12

They had jumped off the freight.

And once again that tragicomic potential for error that seemed to swarm about him, ever ready to do its work, materialized. They were sick of freights, Johnny and he. The prospect of another night of horror, like the night in the steel-bottomed reefer, was too awful for Ira to contemplate. Anything was better.

Johnny led the way. As usual, he had a cousin in Dallas, sister city to Fort Worth, only some twenty miles away. The cousin owned a pool parlor. The twenty miles was a short stretch to hitchhike; and once the stretch was behind them, Johnny promised Ira a place to spend the night in the back room of the pool parlor. The next morning, bright and early, they would set forth on Highway 30 to Texarkana. With any kind of luck, an easy day's hitchhike, Texarkana, straddling the state lines between Texas and Arkansas. Home was almost in sight, at least Johnny's home, his ma's home, where Ira was welcome to spend a day or two. And then Johnny, the seasoned hobo, would guide Ira to the freight yards and see that he got aboard the right freight heading east. How enticing it all seemed. He had a bed to look forward to, a bed, a meal, a bath maybe, a toilet, a shave—and Johnny to put him on the right freight when the time came to go. The plan even offered a certain fringe literary benefit—

to see how Texarkansans lived, to spend a day or two in the home of a Texarkansan.

But with the twilight at their heels, in the seedy part of the trolley-clanging town, the two passed the shopwindow of an Auto Travel agency, the large placard behind the glass reading, "Detroit by Car $9." And Ira slackened pace, lingered before the placard. "Only nine bucks," he said longingly, "to Detroit."

Not lost on cagey Johnny: "You got it?"

The answer should have been "No"; the answer was "Yes," hedged by "I think so."

"Let's go in. Doesn't cost anything to find out." He was quick to see his advantage, a chance to shake his clog, all the more necessary when thumbing rides.

They went inside a nondescript place, a freckled Texan behind a desk, smoking a cigarette. A few chairs along the walls. Inquiry was made. Yes, a car was leaving tonight for Detroit. And as if the two belonged to some kind of clique or calling, the agency owner and Johnny engaged in guarded colloquy. Word and mien suggested familiarity with vocations: running cars through state lines to evade taxes. "We got room for one more," said the owner of the agency. And as Ira wavered—"Do I count you in? There's only one place left, and somebody else might come along."

Done. Agreed. He would go. Ira went outside the store with Johnny, and on the sidewalk bade him farewell—gave him a quarter. Contented, Johnny departed (Ira was certain) to the nearest barroom. There again, that moment, that dual, that liberating moment in the dark street: of betrayal, of Johnny expecting betrayal, expecting base treatment, as a way of life, meted out to him as he would mete it out, unexpectedly mitigated by the acquisition of two bits— and the sloughing off a burden. And in Ira's mind came the awareness that he had betrayed a pal, cast him off: they were buddies, after all, something above the mere consideration of coffee and doughnuts now and then. They had suffered the hardships of riding freights. Johnny had witnessed Ira's agony in the reefer, and extended rough comfort.

Hours passed before the full complement of passengers arrived. And during that time Ira sat, walked around outdoors, tried to chat with the owner and later, when the owner went for supper, with the owner's aloof, muted blond wife. Never, it seemed to Ira, had he encountered such flint-hard, ruthless personalities, man and wife, seamlessly unyielding everywhere, excluding least iota of friendliness. He felt misgivings: Were these the prevailing species of Texans? They couldn't all be that way. As a humanist and a Marxist (more or less), Ira thought he knew better. And yet, taken as a whole, they evoked in him a sudden strong identity with a downtrodden Mexican-American. They personified the character and temperament of those that wrested the land from its native inhabitants, indeed ruthlessly wrested his Ford for fifty bucks. In the tedious hours the random, cloudy procession of thought brought recollection of the Californians: Royer, how different, generous, and Skelsey, rumrunner and probably killer, generous, offering to make up the difference needed to buy a bus ticket home. But nothing like that here: without rift of sympathy, pity.

It was 10 P.M., six hours after he parted with Johnny, before the other passengers arrived. He was seated between two boozy, corpulent Texans, who each finished a pint of liquor before the night was over. The passenger who seemed most decent and, later on, even deprecating sat beside the owner of the agency, Harkivy, who did the driving. After perfunctory introductions, Harkivy collected two dollars from each passenger for the first leg of the trip.

And scarcely were they in their seats than the fatal question was put—by the ex-poultryman on Ira's right hand: Was he Jewish?

"Who, me?" A second longer to prolong the teetering before the plunge: "No, not me." And then followed the usual probes: What was he? He was a Greek Orthodox from the Carpathians. What was that? The religion of the Slovaks in Austria. So he was an Austrian. Yeah. But before it was over he was certain they were convinced he was a Jew. And now they had him where they wanted him: a Jewish non-Jew. With impunity, without risk of offense, they could harry him, assail and Jew-bait, capital sport that brought a smile to Harkivy's face, easing the tension of driving through the dangerous sleet that had begun to fall, glazing the windshield outside the sweep of the windshield wipers: Joo-oo . . . Joo-oo . . . Jew . . . Jew. "They're the goddamndest no-good skunks that ever walked the earth." With nothing visible to distract save the passing headlights through the portholes in the glaze.

As if in a vessel undersea, and himself clamped between a Texan ex-poultryman and a Texan auto-parts salesman. Helpless, hemmed-in, comfortably trapped, not writhing in agony on the freezing steel bars of a reefer, but warmed by the car heater, and with buttocks cushioned on a plush car seat. Joo-oo . . . Joo-oo . . . Jew . . . Jew, the windshield wipers droned against the clear semicircles of glass, the external quasi existence of sleet slanting out of the dark or out of passing headlights. Joo-oo . . . Joo-oo . . . Jew . . . Jew . . . filling up the spaces between stock virulence and vicious catchphrase. "The goddamn Jews own 74 percent of the country's wealth. That's right out o' *Liberty Magazine*," spewed out Mr. Haling, the beefy ex-poultryman. "The goddamn bastards, they'd sell their own grandmother if there was a dollar in it. You can't trust any of 'em." Joo . . . Joo . . . Jew . . . Jew. And from the port side, the matching venom of the auto-parts dealer: "What the hell do they do with their dough? The Christians don't see any of it, once the Jews get hold of it."

Ira sat tautly quiet. He was the nigger now. The colored guy who had forced his way down the reefer ladder hadn't suffered what he was suffering now, Ira thought in hyperbole—the silent corrosive humiliation of persecution. He hadn't been baited. Not then, anyway. Even Johnny with all his race hatred hadn't dared say anything overt. And the other had a weapon, homemade, but a weapon. And confident, assured he was safe, he had gone to sleep immediately. Jesus, the Jew was different. No, Ira was different. The colored guy couldn't hide—hide was right—that one couldn't; he couldn't deny his skin. Ira could, or thought he could, and hadn't, and thus invited this ordeal. Ordeal different from what the colored guy would have had to go through—say, if he were between two or three like Johnny in the reefer. How would he have suffered it? The windshield wiper had begun to sweep the glass with a different sound, rubbing on a drying surface. The sleet storm was abating. Harkivy turned off the wipers. For a while, the car rolled along over the wet nonreflecting night highway. Ira's two fellow passengers dozed off. Respite.

How would he have suffered it? Jesus, physical, mental, racial, social. This was political, wasn't it? Of a political nature, with political allusions, overtones—he didn't know how to formulate it, or even whether he was right or wrong. Probably wrong. The situation, his predicament had implications that were political, not only physical, psychological, not only social: All his life he had shunned politics, anything that had to do with political movements, parties, political action of any kind—and the joke was that he had joined the Communist Party, most activist of all. And therein lay his whole weakness, his passiveness, his inability to participate in a constructive way; therein lay the whole ludicrous inconsistency of his membership— the cause of his literary immobilization perhaps.

Who the hell knew? The two gross boors sleeping it off on either side of him, snoring, grunting, farting on either side of him, were American Nazis, Texas Hitlerites. That's what made this ordeal different. Then, how could you learn to become explicit about political matters and continue being an artist. How learn to become a partisan and continue being an artist? Impossible, wasn't it? Too much to ask. Change everything he was. Well, quit being an artist, that was all. Or the one he was, certainly: quit that one . . .

Somewhere in Oklahoma, Harkivy stopped the car, turned around in his seat to awaken the sleepers, and collected the two-dollar toll for the next leg of the journey. Nightmarish tedium came to an end in the bleary dawn, when the car was halted in the still-deserted business district of Kansas City, Kansas, and a breakfast stop was announced—for exactly a half hour.

The four went one way, toward the diner on the avenue. And Ira the other: "I need a little walk" was his excuse. And after a half dozen deviously zigzagged blocks, he separated himself from the car to such an extent that he was sure he could never have found it again, even if he tried.

So he hoofed it to the Y instead, got a room. And after brief debate with himself, whose outcome he knew beforehand, he walked to the nearest Western Union and sent M a telegram: "Please wire $25 money order bus fare home."

There was nothing for him to do except wait, have faith in the constancy of a tall girl in a city a thousand miles away, have faith in her faith, in their implicit pledge; listen to the accordion play-ing of the broken-nose street musician across the way, drowned out by trolley bell clanging now and then, watch pedestrians trample snow. He spent the day reflecting on his ordeal, and his inability to assimilate it. And what did that augur for him, his slow-witted, plodding mind? He'd have to see M, he'd have to ask her: Do you think there's a chance left? Of any kind of restoration? Lopped off, truncated, docked . . . any hope?

PART THREE

....

New York

CHAPTER 13

Ira's bus irrupted from the Holland Tubes into late-afternoon Manhattan from a six-month phantasmagoria of exile, into a city, alas, no longer his home. A sense of estrangement informed once familiar streets with a pale cast, a pale, forbidding cast. Never did he feel the estrangement more deeply than when the bus, rolling uptown along Seventh Avenue, passed the corner of Morton Street. Behind him fell the little service station where the illiterate Italian youth and he had overhauled the Model A Ford in which Bill and he had set out for California—the youth an illiterate, and Ira, in his way, even more so.

Ira caught a glimpse of Morton Street, so long lived in, where he had become a novelist, the older woman's lover, a literary figure. The street turned away from him as they sped by, separated by a discontinuity in the mind, more impassable than any physical gulf.

Ira's first mission was to M, feeling both the debt he owed her and the overwhelming desire for her, now that she was so close. He went with all haste to her furnished basement music studio. How tall and dear she looked, and she laughed a great deal and was overjoyed to see him. She had gained weight, a pound or two, and it became her.

173

They talked of ways and means of marrying, of Ira's getting a job, perhaps on WPA construction work. He seemed so tough in her eyes, and lean and manly. She wanted to be his baby, she said, which is what Ira so deeply wanted her to be, needed her to be in order to become the tough and manly person she wanted him to be. His big girl, her tears cool on his cheek.

Did Ira love her very much? she asked and asked again: Did he really love her? "Tell me you love me once more," she said.

And Ira said he did. And confessed that he felt like a babe in the woods before the vast uncertainties of the future. She admitted she felt that way, too. And she went on, in that dry tone she sometimes assumed, that she had thought until only a short time ago that her life was already fixed, settled, and determined; and now it was in flux again, all tentative and hazardous. Her tone of voice changed from the dry to the young girl's as she looked at him. They wondered how Ira had ever managed to break through her guard at Yaddo, and a quite formidable guard it was, a smooth, impervious surface. He could no longer remember how he had done it; he had been too crude to respect it, perhaps. Only now, when she put on her very flat, lesbian, brown tam before they went out for a walk, was he aware of the cool nobility of her features, and the aristocracy of her bearing. "You look like a blue blood." Ira remarked, when they left the house.

"I am," she said calmly.

They sauntered in the direction of Park Avenue, through the nipping night air, and the troughs of obscurity between street lamps. She laughed, and in a voice, tender, and imploring, said, "When will you have money enough, dear, so that we can feel just a little secure?"

"Yeah. When?" That was all Ira could say. Strange, he reflected as they walked, that this should be what he asked for, what he would have: the need of this kind of compulsion, this kind of dependency on him, that another was now his responsibility. All changed in less than a year's time. Who would ever have dreamed that in so short a space Ira would be prepared, nay, willing, to yield up his indolence, his artist's indolence and self-centered detachment, and actually seek out adult obligations, even those under capitalism.

"It's dawned on me that the maturity of a capitalist individual is better than none," Ira said. "It's better than the immaturity of a half-baked Marxist." She laughed.

Earlier, while she was cooking the meal they had had for supper, she had suspended preparations several times to listen to him, with small girls' brown-eyed, fixed attention, while Ira expatiated—over his drink—how necessary it had become for the artist to become a man: It was no longer possible to be an artist without becoming a man. Ira wasn't sure whether the process was dialectical or not, only that heretofore the artist had simply to refine his art, to intensify it, to enhance it. But now, it would seem that the very drive to enhance his art would drive him out of the realm of art altogether, and into that of experience. Why? Because he had nothing to work with anymore, only shriveled values, equivocal responses, rickety sentiments—even perceptions were ambivalent. He would have to learn from life what was true for him in the grip of necessity. Ira cited Leonard E at Yaddo. He cited someone similar, himself: someone who got all the breaks any creative writer could ask for, and yet was unable to create. Therefore he needed her, if he was ever to be an artist again; he needed her emotional dependence on him—which may have been flattering in one sense, though probably not in another.

She turned around from the electric hot plate where the pan of beef and vegetable stew was simmering. "Does the process have to be so very conscious?" she asked.

"I don't know. I'm trying to find words for what I've been through and going through," Ira said.

———

They walked as far as Madison Avenue, where she lingered before the windows displaying the latest in fashionable men's clothing; then they returned to her studio. She planned on going to Boston soon, to visit a friend, a fellow student of Madame Boulanger's, and intended to stay a couple of days. Because she would be absent from her apartment, they thought it best for Ira to take his manuscript out of her small trunk where she stored it for safekeeping. It was the manuscript of the novel he had begun, and failed to complete, in LA. She wanted him to read a page of it. Almost from the first sentence his voice seemed toneless to himself, toneless and flat, reflecting prose that was equally flat and insipid. Ira couldn't go on. And wrapping up the manuscript again, he muttered, "You're the only artist around here. I'm not."

She whimpered fondly at his dejection, kissed him with soft, pliant, cool lips. Ira went off feeling quite crushed. He should never have subjected her to this. She was all he had.

The following day, Ira turned his attention to material concerns. He had to get on Home Relief at the earliest. He had already learned that in order to do so, you rented a furnished room—and this he had already done, the dingiest of the dingy—and paid rent for a week or two. Then, on the verge of eviction, you became an emergency client, received emergency consideration, and were speedily placed on Home Relief rolls. So Ira was told. His small drab room faced the rear of the house, the back window looking out, not on the usual clothesline-crisscrossed backyard, but on a wide court, indicative of a formerly genteel neighborhood—or so the landlady, Mrs. Towb, told him—where sparrows twittered and mated, and carried bits of lint and strands of cotton in their beaks. The shrubs below were already quite green, the larger trees sprinkled with tiny leaves. His neighbor, unseen on the other side of the flimsy partition, bawled in his sleep;

his cries seemed loudest in the transition between sleep and waking, or between sessions of deepest slumber. The trains of the Second Avenue El roared unnervingly into his room, but he quickly grew accustomed to their tumult.

He was unaccustomed to a changed New York, changed in atmosphere and ways, as he was in spirit: Sections of the Sixth Avenue El were already gone, stumps of its pillars still in place on Third Street. Prelude, he had heard, to the eventual removal of all the elevated structures, landmarks that hung like grimy iron veils on street crossings.

A few nights after his return, Ira walked downtown to Sixteenth Street in search of Doris Brenning, Bill's daughter, in her large furnished room, to see whether he could glean word of Bill. She was out; at least, no one answered the bell.

When he thought of Doris, there was a quickening of desire, and a confusion between Doris and himself as real people and as characters in fiction. The intricate irony of it, and the inveteracy of the old self. His seeking out the latest news regarding Bill's movements in LA was also of the same ambivalent nature: a genuine desire to be informed about him, and a plausible screening of other motives, a furtherance of other motives. So confused were fable and actuality within him, he could almost rationalize to himself that seducing her would be an act performed merely to further his writing, or to render such an incident with greater fidelity in a story. Ira tried to delve into the source of the attraction, unearth its cause, not as literary symbol, but in his own psyche; and it occurred to him, aside from Doris's ungifted mind, freckled blandness, and buxomness, that sex, its bent, its route set by unspeakable parameters, its rut continued independently of his love for M, like gravity on a flying projectile. So with Doris, daughter of Bill, and Bill in the offing, ever stern CP proletarian mentor, looming and vengeful, the element of peril, element of guilt before paternal authority, even surrogate, threat of dire consequences reasserted themselves.

This did not stop him. A few nights later, at eight-thirty, Ira paid her another visit. She was in, and Ira heard from her a disjointed recital of Bill's latest acts and intentions. He proposed going to Arkansas with Bea and the two children. Why Arkansas? Doris didn't know. But she did know that he had made Bea write, yet again, to Edith for one hundred dollars to cover the expense of the trip.

"A hundred dollars!" Ira exclaimed.

"Yes. But Dalton won't let her send any money, until she finds out what it's all about."

Doris had been sending them money regularly, and now was being asked to send a lump sum of fifty dollars. "And I'm up to my neck in debt," she said, and added in the same breath that Bea had been cut off relief.

"It's impossible!" Ira said. "With two small children?"

"That's what she wrote."

"I think he's just trying to get together enough money to come east."

"But it's insane!" she protested.

"I agree."

All Ira could do was repeat that there wasn't any sense to Bill's coming here, but he had been with him until last February, in LA, and sometimes he seemed wild, even frenzied. Oh, the revelations, the witnesses people so often bore against themselves, if one waited long enough, even one as slow as he was, the insights, the reversals of character people sometimes provided, the revisions of interpretation-—and not only that, the unforeseen novelistic climaxes.

She was flushed with resentment, freckles coppery, facial down pale on reddish skin; and in almost hectic contrast, her lucid blue eyes stared out at Ira. "You never know what Dad's up to. You never knew what his whole family was up to. Grammaw two-timed his father when she was younger, and the whole family stole from each other."

"Yes? I left some books there I valued, and clothes. I don't care about the clothes. But the books cost so little to send. I offered to pay them back twice, three times—"

"You'll never see them."

"I guess not. I should have sent them parcel post, if I had had any brains."

"All I know is I'll be in the middle of doing something in the shop, in the street, talking to somebody, and all of a sudden I'll start answering Dad."

"Do I recognize that."

"You do it, too?"

"Not so much now. But every hour in Los Angeles."

"He drives me crazy. He'll drive me crazy if he comes here. I can't stand it." Tears began to well up in her eyes.

Ira stood up. "Listen, I don't want him here either." He approached and said earnestly. "You understand that, don't you?"

"Yeah, now I do. I don't know what I'll do if he comes." She wept.

"It's a long way still. It's still up in the air. And you've got a trade. You don't have to stay." He patted her shoulder, then let his hand rest there. It was deliberate and ulterior. Ira knew what he was inviting, and still did it, inviting it. And he was fortunate: She made no other response except to look up at him quiescent and grateful, Bill's blue eyes lifted in surrender, Bill's daughter, body slack and passive, face expectant, cork-hued and fuzzy, at his hip level as she sat at the edge of the bed. There was a kind of slavering that took place within the self. Oh, you know what it is, careened through the mind. You know what it is: you can't now. Ira moved away, sprung through and through with regret: Jesus, losing a chance like that.

Bill's scowl in the offing. The rake of risk, rapture of evil. Ineffable delirium: getting even.

"Let's keep in touch, right?" Ira said. "Maybe we can make things easier for ourselves."

"I'm glad you'll be here." The matter of fact reasserted itself in slight movement: straightening of fingers, scrape of her shoes on the floor, turn of head. She seemed to have second thoughts, too. She uttered a kind of neighing sound that threaded into a sigh, and with knuckles cornered, wiped away a tear. "You'll be here, anyway."

"Sure."

"Only you and Billy know what he's like."

"Oh, I know, all right . . . Okay?"

They moved on to other topics. Ira expected a winding down of discourse, but overshadowing all that had come before was the news he least expected to hear: that Edith and Dalton were now married.

Ira laughed—out of a silly and strange sense of relief.

"It's so soon," said Doris. "I didn't know it would be so soon. And I sure didn't expect it would be Dalton."

"Why not?"

"I thought he was married."

"He did behave that way," Ira agreed. "He is now." And with that, he left.

CHAPTER 14

Ira's first weeks back in New York passed quickly, an excited, confusing welter of encounters with old acquaintances, leavened by visits to M. Of course, money was a problem. Owing two weeks' back rent on his first room, and Home Relief not imminent, he had snuck off in the middle of the night for fear that the landlady would lock up his possessions while he was out one day.

He went over to Frank Green's, an old Irish friend he had met through Bill. The rich, navy-blue, camel's hair coat Edith had bought Ira was in the cleaners, and he would need fifty cents to get it out. He wanted to get it out of the cleaners in order to pawn it for a few dollars. The news of Edith's marriage kept recurring to him as he walked, recurring each time with mounting sorrow. It was a confused sorrow, preempting the glee with which he had first greeted the news. So that was the end, the irreversible end to the relationship with the woman with whom he had lived since undergraduate days, since 1927, a junior at CCNY. Raw, slum oaf that he had been, she had inculcated in him something of manners, self-confidence, social ease; she had supplied cultivated surroundings, supplied years of her earnings, her very self spent in nurturing the aspiring novelist. And now the end. Ira had gotten what he had sought. He couldn't have it both ways; and he didn't want it both ways either. There was no reconciliation between feelings and intellect, such as his were. By the time he reached Frank's place, he was deep in dolor.

Frank was out. So Ira walked along the Bowery to find a pawnshop where he could pawn his silver Omega watch. There were no pawnshops until Tenth Street, the others having turned into curio shops and swap shops. He was overwhelmed by the possibility, nay, probability of Bill's returning east, Edith's marriage, and by what at another time might have diverted him, but now seemed to culminate all past follies: that he should pawn his watch in order to get his coat, and then pawn the coat in order, among other things, to get the watch out of hock. Ira passed the first pawnshop. Loath to go in, to set a seal on his stupidity, he walked to the next pawnshop, which was not until Thirteenth Street. And there, the pawnbroker refused to take his watch in pawn—even for fifty cents, an Omega with a solid silver case. "We don't take them," he said. Disgusted with himself, praying for better luck in the first pawnshop, the one he had so ill-advisedly passed, he turned back downtown. For if he didn't pawn it in that one, he would have to hike all the way downtown to Bleecker Street, where the pawnshops were more numerous.

Ira had just reached Tenth Street when lo! coming toward him was his former landlady Mrs. Towb. At once, she began upbraiding him: a man she respected so much, an educated man, to sneak off without paying his rent.

"Let me explain." And Ira told her he had sneaked off with his clothing, when his Home Relief rent check hadn't arrived on time, for fear she would lock up his things, as so many landladies did when welfare tenants were in arrears. She protested: Never! She never would have, and that Ira knew she never would have. He knew she was telling the truth. Strange to say, though he was all prepared to lie his way out of the mess, he was suddenly seized by an uncontrollable desire to weep—and would have walked away from her, except she called him back. He could trust her, she said, because she also had a college-boy son. Even if he was short of money, he could have come to her—she didn't care about the three dollars Ira owed her.

He hadn't understood that, Ira said; he didn't understand much, but he was learning. And she asked him where he lived. "A hole in the wall," he said. "Uptown, to be near the girl I want to marry."

"So what're you doing here?"

"I came downtown to pawn my watch for fifty cents, so I can get my coat out of the cleaners."

She pinched apart the brass prongs of her purse. "Here." She proffered a large, bright half-dollar.

Ira protested.

"Don't be foolish. If I give, take it."

And then he did weep, with the fifty-cent piece in his pocket, walking to the cleaners. Wept and thought of Edith married.

The coat reclaimed and then hocked, in Ira's possession for only a few minutes, he spent the next two hours walking to his uncles' cafeteria on Seventy-first street and Columbus Avenue, under the El. The Model Cafeteria, it was called, and Max, Ira's "second uncle," was chef or short-order cook. Harry, Ira's youngest uncle, was counterman, and Max's wife, Rose, a waitress. Harry, now in his forties, already stooped and sour of visage, not helped by his long nose—and notable for his tactlessness—asked him on sight, before hello: Did Ira still have his girl?

"Yes."

"How old is she?" he asked.

"She's thirty-one, became thirty-one this month."

"Well, what's this I hear about you living with an old woman?" He meant Edith, of course, as Ira knew all the time.

"Where did you get the idea she was an old woman?" Ira countered.

"They told me she was an old woman."

"Oh, you mean the other one. She was only thirty-eight," Ira lied. "And I'm no spring chicken, you know. I'm thirty-three."

"Then you're not living with the same one?"

"No."

And after this further inquiry and rejoinder, Harry said, "I'll have to tell Ida about this. She'll be surprised."

Ira could already envisage the news vibrating along the family trunk lines.

"What are you going to eat?" asked Harry.

"Coffee," Ira said.

"Have something else."

"No, thanks," Ira said. "I'm not hungry." And he went on to explain that his only reason for dropping in was that he happened to be in the neighborhood visiting a friend. And linked lie with lie: that he had received seventy-five dollars for some ghostwriting he had done.

"Have something to eat," Harry urged.

"All right, I will. But only on condition you let me pay for it."

"Okay," he acquiesced (and for a moment Ira's heart sank). "Half price."

Ira ordered a hamburger steak, devoured all the bread in sight, and was brought another serving of bread, grinning. "I thought you said you weren't hungry."

"Well, I worked up an appetite."

After Ira had finished the repast, he went around the counter, back into the kitchen, where Max, in cook's uniform and with a large napkin about his neck, presided. He was closely knit, just under average height, with blue eyes and extremely thick, wavy, chestnut hair, now flecked with gray. The small kitchen was hot and close, the walls brown as a roach, and humid. Ira watched him while he filled a couple of orders, fingering the meatballs and positioning the pork chops on the plate. "What do you think they do at the Waldorf?" he replied to Ira's unspoken question. "Different?"

"Tell me about the time you were a sign painter," Ira said, as Max dispatched the plate through the pass-through window, and tinkled the bell. "I watched you once when I was a kid: You were putting a gold-leaf sign on a store window on Park Avenue—pushcart Park Avenue. About 112th Street."

He broke into a chuckle. "Once I had a big sign to put up on Thirty-second Street on a wooden house over Madam Fnyefnyeh's dress shop. The shop, you know, it was full of high-class robes, ladies' clothes. So the boss said, 'Drive these big nails into the sign and come right back. So I started to hammer in a nail. I hammer—Bong! I hear: Bong. Bongle! *Oy, gewald!* I drove the nail right through the big mirror she had in the middle of the wall inside. Broken to pieces! So what the hell did I know! The boss said, 'Hurry up and drive the nails in and come right back.' Bong! Bangle. It was a mirror the size of the wall, and I heard it break." He laughed. "I'll never forget. Madam Fnyefnyeh came out with those eyeglasses on a stick. I left the sign hanging from one nail, and I ran all the way to the shop. 'Bong!' I said to the boss—"

"Roast lamb, red cabbage, and beans. No gravy," Harry called through the serving window.

Smiling reminiscently, Max dished up the order. "Why does a sign painter get bald?" he asked, and answered, "Because he runs the gold-leaf brush through his hair."

"And where does he run it after he's bald?"

"On the back of his neck. Where else?"

The night man came in. Dour, Germanic, he listened awhile as Max went on to tell Ira about a date he had with a girl in Bridgeport, but being a greenhorn, he had gone to Harmon. And of another girl to whom he lied about all the property he owned. To impress her he spent $4.40 for theater tickets for each one every Saturday night, told her he owned apartment houses, owned restaurants. And when her father said, "I think it's a match," and asked Max to bring his parents to meet the girl's parents, her mother being an invalid, Max never showed up again, disappeared completely. The night man thereupon told Ira a story of a bragging sergeant in the German army who had lied to his company that he lived in a fine house with a stable of four black horses. A soldier in the company, passing through the town, decided to pay the sergeant a visit and discovered that the sergeant's family lived over a stable, and on its lintel was a picture of four black horses. "So it never pays to bullshit," the night man said, pulling up the trapdoor leading down to the cellar. "Like him." And descended out of sight.

"Well, why did you go into the restaurant business after you learned the sign painter's trade?" Ira asked.

"Because I wanted to eat," Max said vehemently. "To eat. To eat. To yeat! I never had enough to eat in my father's house. He kept all the food locked up."

"I know. Mom told me. Did you finally?"

"Get enough to eat?"

"Yes."

"I can't look at it. This—" he picked up his cigar, "is all I eat maybe the whole day."

Rose appeared in the doorway. "Breast of veal," she said. "Must be very hot. You hear? Corn and potatoes, must be very hot."

"I got only one breast of veal," said Max regretfully. "That's all I got left. It's fat."

"So I'll ask her," said Rose—and vanished.

"When I first went into the restaurant business in Queens," said Max, "I made eight thousand dollars the first year. Maybe it was just dumb luck. So I invested six thousand in real estate that didn't bring me a dime. It brought me a court judgment instead of a balance, the six thousand dollars didn't pay. If I had six thousand today, I'd what? I'd eat crap. I'd be rich with six thousand dollars—"

Rose was in the doorway again. "She says, all right, she says cut away the fat."

"I can't cut away the fat," Max frowned. "How'm I gonna cut away the fat? It's in the veal."

"So I'll ask her," said Rose—and vanished.

"The restaurant business is shot, that's all." Max picked up his cigar.

"The Depression?"

"What Depression? How can you make money when drugstores compete with you? Do you care where you get a cup of coffee, so long as it's a good cup of coffee, in a cafeteria or in a drugstore?"

"No, I guess not."

"So you see: drugstores ruined the restaurant business. We used to give them a ham sandwich between two slices of bread. Plain. Ten cents. Along comes the drugstore, and puts in a piece of lettuce between. So we have to go and put in a slice of tomato. So the drugstore adds two olives. So we add french fries. So shit. Where's the profit?"

"That's the trouble with this country," the night man lowered the trapdoor. "No law."

"No law?" Ira said, startled.

"No law," he reiterated. "In Yermany is a drugstore a drugstore. That's what Hitler do."

"Once we used to charge ten cents for a slice of raisin cake. Who ever heard of charging a nickel. We could get away with it, till the drugstores started to compete. Now—"

Rose stood in the doorway. "So all right. Give her roast veal with it. Must be very hot."

"I'll make it hot," Max fumed. "I'll—" He cut three substantial slices of roast veal, and placed them on the griddle to warm up. "No, what I always wanted was automotive. I was always looking for automotive."

"And now you're a cook," Ira said.

"Oh, I know when I'm licked. Some people don't know when they're licked, but I know when I'm licked."

"What do you mean by automotive?"

"Automotive," said Max. "Automotive. It doesn't have to be automobiles. It can be diesel engines, electric motors. That's what I should have been."

The night man grimaced in violent disbelief.

"Well, why weren't you?" Ira asked.

"Because I went to Cooper Union at night, and what did they teach me? Pencil and paper work. Mechanical drawing."

"That's strange. What course did you take?"

"Architectural engineering."

Like a mute in a play, or a mime, the night man contorted behind a shoulder as if warding off enormous prevarication.

Max removed the slices of veal from the griddle and arranged them on the plate with the vegetables. "But what I wanted was automotive." He rang the service bell. Rose appeared, took the plate off the counter, and disappeared.

"Well, why the hell did you take architectural engineering?" Ira demanded.

"A greenhorn, I heard them say engineer, engineer—"

But Rose was in the doorway again. "That ain't what she wanted," Rose complained. She gave the night man the plate.

"Didn't you say roast veal? Didn't she say roast veal?" he called on the night man and Ira to testify.

"I said, with roast veal!" Rose shouted. "I said breast of veal with roast veal."

"What kind of an order is that!" Max fumed at her. "Breast of

veal with roast veal. Who ever heard of such an order? You're gettin'
as crazy as she is!"

"You got any scallops?" Harry asked through the service window.

"See if we got any scallops," Max said to the night man. "She
wants roast veal because the breast of veal is fat," Rose explained
with patient desperation.

"So why don't she order roast veal?" Max countered.

"We got scallops," said the night man.

"Because she wants breast of veal, too," said Rose.

Wincing in extravagant travail, eyes clam-shut, the night man
seemed determined to tie himself into a knot as he handed Max
the platter of scallops. Max rang the service bell. "We got scallops,"
he announced through the service window. He cleared away two
slices of the disputed sliced veal from the plate, flopped the breast
of veal in their place, wiped the spatter of gravy from the plate's
rim with a napkin—and thumb—and rang the service bell. "You
don't think they do this at the Waldorf?" He picked up his cigar. "I
love machinery. Now this automatic french-fry potato fryer. That's
an invention! Before, you always had to watch so it wouldn't burn.
Now—you see why I love automotive? I can fix anything. I take one
look, and that's all."

The night man seemed too spent for protest. He had become
grim. And there was Rose in the doorway again. "She wants it hot!
I told you she wants it hot!"

"Gimme it!" Max made a grab for the plate. Rose scuttled out of
sight. "I'll make it hot!" Max said furiously. "Here's hot!" He hauled
up his privates. "Hot!" He ladled a little soup stock into a saucepan,
cast the shopworn breast of veal into the broth, and turned the gas
flame high. "I'll give them hot!"

"They're crazy!" said the night man. "They're all crazy."

"Chef's special," Harry called into the service window. "Where's
the scallops?"

"On the fire," said Max.

"Yeah, on the fire." Harry echoed in disbelief.

"All right, they're comin' up," Max compromised.

"Hamburger steak, mashed potatoes, and peas," Rose ordered at a discreet distance.

"A bowl," said Harry.

Rose placed a plate on the shelf next to the door: "Put a hamburger on it, well done." She bore off the hybrid veal.

"A bowl. That's two," said Harry.

Business was becoming brisk. Ira was in the way. He bade Max good-bye.

"Are you going?" asked Rose. "Don't forget to give your mother my regards."

"I will, thanks. So long, Max."

Out in the street again, he walked east to Central Park West, and there, across from the park, he turned south. It was now 7 P.M., and he was due for dinner at M's.

CHAPTER 15

The next day, Ira had an engagement with a Miss Virginia N, a literary agent recommended to him by Max Perkins, to discuss the feasibility of his converting or adapting the four aborted novels in his possession into short stories. What she told him was both naive and yet of serious consequence, and its effect on him was unsettling in the extreme. She recommended things so elementary, and for him so difficult, that he wondered whether he was capable of writing short stories at all. She stressed coming to the point and leaving sensibility out of the picture, neither of which Ira supposed he'd ever done. On the other hand, the question of the literary value of the piece of prose was never raised: that was extraneous. Her advice disconcerted him enough that he was loath even to reread the passages she proposed he work into yarns, let alone attempt to rewrite them. She discarded the life for the scheme. The scheme Ira had never mastered; he thought he had a sense of life. She advised him to keep the "I" out of it. Ira thought he had a certain prism, splaying undifferentiated light into a beguiling spectrum. So he thought of himself, flattered himself, and it seemed of no value in the writing game.

The next day was the first sultry day and night of the year, typical New York sultriness, unwelcome harbinger of the stifling summer he might have to spend in his small room. His regular stipend now that he was on Home Relief had stretched only as far as a slightly nicer room uptown.

He had spent into the small hours writing a piece aimed at *The New Yorker*, flattered that Virginia N should think that prestigious magazine was his best bet. Alas, and contrary to instructions, Ira had written it with himself as central character, so he discarded it. At three in the afternoon he began writing the story over again, sans self. And wrote with seeming success, until almost seven in the evening, at which time he was to meet M for dinner at Betty and John's, M's sister and brother-in-law. M had thought they would have steak, so it would behoove Ira to get there on time. But they had scallops, and John himself arrived late. A little more time spent on the piece might have seen it completed at a reasonable hour.

Ira felt in an optimistic mood when he suspended work, because it was going so well; and he lamented humorously at Betty and John's that he almost had a *New Yorker* sketch finished, except for keeping a dinner date—but he wouldn't miss scallops like these for anything.

Betty was determined to rent the penthouse atop the loft building on Twenty-third Street where she and John lived. The penthouse was built for an artist, and had a living room 35 feet by 25 feet, which would make an excellent studio for John to do his commercial photography. The place also had a terrace and extra bedrooms for M and Ira, if they wanted to move in with them and share expenses. Everyone joked about Ira's being the only Home Relief client who would be living in a penthouse.

They discussed M's letter from her mother, threatening to cut her off, and Ira expressed his relief that Betty and John had pioneered, so to speak, in marrying, despite parental disapproval (Mother had apparently disapproved, though not so vehemently, of the marriage of M's two older brothers). John teased M about looking so superior and mature when he and Betty were married, as if they were kids.

"I had a pretty good surface once, didn't I?" M asked, almost penitently.

They said Mother's letter to M was mild, compared with the ones Betty received in opposition to her marriage to him. "Vicious" was the word they used to describe Mother's missives; Father, too, was set against them—he was scarcely on speaking terms with John. John was thin, tall, blond, and delicately built, delicate in health, too: he had had mastoid operations. On the date that his and Betty's marriage was first planned, he was hospitalized with pneumonia. He was extremely quick in his movements, deft about photographic equipment and appliances in general, and a craftsman in the use of tools—enviably so. Nor did it ever seem to occur to him to be reticent or self-conscious, but he was thoroughly at home in the world: not bold, simply without doubts. He was anything but handsome, with an angular face and prominent nose, in contrast to Betty, who was pretty and shapely.

On important family occasions, Betty said, Father always found reason to stay late at the office. And he had stayed at the office until three-thirty in the afternoon, with the wedding ceremony set at four. Their parents' room was being used as a cloakroom, though few guests had been invited; and perhaps because the minister and his wife were in the bedroom at the moment, Father, who was changing clothes in the walk-in closet just off the bedroom, chose not to meet the minister, but exited through the door in the dressing room that hadn't been used for years; in fact, it had a bureau against it on the other side, and opened on the room that had been set aside for the bride. She was there, talking to John, when who should shove the bureau away, enter unceremoniously, and depart without a word to either bride or groom, but Father.

"Why?" Ira asked John. "You're first-rate native American stock. Your father is an engineer—at Bell Labs, isn't it?"

"And his mother comes from the Gideons, famous American editors of the Bible," said Betty, who had already anticipated his question.

"All the more reason," Ira argued. "So what was the objection?"

Betty laughed throatily—she was a heavy smoker. "John didn't wear a hat."

"Aw, c'mon."

"He refused to be conventional."

"And worst of all, I didn't have money in sufficient amounts to make Mother overlook my other faults," said John. "That's the one thing that counts with Mother. She would have forgiven me everything, if I had been a millionaire."

"My God," Ira groaned. "Conventional? Money? What am I gonna do? I'll have to defend myself when they come here."

"Oh, no, you're so far outside the pale, they won't know what to do," said John. "You're better off than we were."

"Yeah? What if I can have something to show them in *The New Yorker*. Or at least get it accepted, so I can tell 'em about it?" He addressed M.

"That would be fine," she smiled.

"Oh, that would impress Mother," John seconded. "Anything as swanky as *The New Yorker*." John was almost compulsively garrulous, with a curious, and harmless, way of nagging, or better said, overseeing and commenting on his wife's domesticity—and other occupations as well—to which she responded according to her mood and inclination, with the result that their marriage seemed like a loom between them on which they wove a tapestry of talk. Ira stayed late into the night, though he and M were due in Brooklyn the next morning—he had promised his mother that they would come for brunch, so she could meet M.

———

To save money the next morning, Ira skimped on paying the extra fare on the BMT, and took the Lexington Avenue subway intending to go to Broadway, but instead they went to South Ferry and had to retrace their steps. Then they got on a Flatbush train, and had to get off at Atlantic Avenue and change for a New Lots train, and didn't reach Mom's place until after eleven. But M had not a word of complaint, despite the long roundabout way Ira led her in making connections on subway lines, and afterward through block after block of sunny, warm, Jewish East New York. She was not taught to complain, she told him.

Mom was greatly relieved when Ira and M arrived. She had been worried they wouldn't come. And seeing the two women together for the first time, his beloved, tall and fair in her brown dress, ascendant Anglo-Saxon American in bearing and speech and countenance; and Mom, short of stature and heavy in her red-figured housedress, with gray and coarse bobbed hair, and only obscure sorrow lending something of distinction to her fleshy features, speaking with thick immigrant accent still, and moving about ponderously on swollen ankles. The contrast was more than perception was willing to accept.

The table was set for two, the oblong kitchen table, and Mom seated M and Ira at opposite ends, an absurd distance from each other, and served them all manner of Jewish smoked-fish delicacies— gold-skinned whitefish, lox, a chunk of smoked sturgeon—together with irregular slabs of home-sliced rye bread rife with caraway seeds, all of which M genuinely relished, always welcoming substantial new textures, new savors, favoring the homey against the stylish. While she served them, Mom also fed her frowzy, mongrel poodle a bit of white chicken meat, which she had to pretend to tread on, in order to arouse the wizened, old cur's appetite. Otherwise, he wouldn't eat, Mom explained.

Afterward, the meal over, they sat on the convertible couch in the living room. Did they love each other? Mom asked Ira and M. And M kissed him.

"She's comely," Mom said in Yiddish; and essaying her English again, said for M's benefit that Ira was no fool, for after all, he had exchanged the old and jaded for the new and fresher.

They borrowed a table setting before leaving, a few pieces of cutlery. Mom chided Ira for acting so estranged, that he must come more often—and when Pop was home. He would be generous to Ira now that he brought a prospective wife with him, a kind and lovely one. "And you know without my telling you," she added dryly in Yiddish, "he and you are both a little crazy."

The ample luncheon over, she kissed M when they left. "Jews immediately include the whole world—the whole world of feeling anyway—in what you'd call a homey social discourse," Ira remarked as they walked back to the subway station.

"I like it," said M.

CHAPTER 16

W*alking back to the rooming* house from the Home Relief
Bureau, where Ira was told to return in a week, the earliest day he
could see his investigator, he stopped to view an odd spectacle at
Forty-fourth Street and Second Avenue. The El structure was lowest
at that intersection because of a rise in the ground. The sign under
the El trestle warned "12' 6" Clearance." A truck had broken down,
but in a very peculiar way. It was an old truck, daubed and smeared
whitish gray, evidently because of the use it was put to, for it carried
a load of mortar-mixing trays, water drums, scaffolding, trestles,
planks, wheelbarrows, the paraphernalia of masonry.

The truck had come to a halt directly beneath the El, in the
bus lane. When Ira first drew near, he thought that one of the
truck's wheels had broken through the pavement—he had seen
such accidents before—but no, it wasn't that at all. What had happened was that the frame of the truck, the pair of longitudinal
steel beams underneath, had snapped in half neatly; and the truck,
being overloaded at the tailboard, had folded into two parts: the
loaded rear end tilted up; the cab and engine tilted down. It was a
'28 Chevrolet.

The driver, a Negro, was standing beside the wreck, and with him two or three curiosity mongers, examining the break in the frame. Pedestrians stopped at the curb to look and to wisecrack. The driver came back to the curb. He seemed to be in his midforties, strongly built, though not tall, self-possessed and collected, with only a hint of the strain of the fix he was in troubling his eyes, like a passing shadow. He was asked what he was going to do.

"Well, I called up my cousin in Brooklyn," he replied calmly. "He said he'd be here in an hour."

"What time did you break down?"

"Oh, 'bout ten o'clock." It was now past noon.

Transitory idlers grouped about him and joked. "I had a truck do that to me once," said someone. "It was a dump truck. Dumped when I was driving it."

"Didn't you ever see a convertible dump truck?" spoofed another. "There it is." He pointed at the wreck and earned a laugh. A short, grizzled, elderly Irishman engaged the driver in conversation. Was he going to junk the truck? No, he could fix it, said the Negro. He could bore holes through the chassis frame, and rivet new plates across the break. The Irishman tried to look grave as he listened, but every once in a while would burst into a gleeful cackle—and a moment later, grave again, assure the Negro that a half-inch plate was all he needed to mend the break.

"I been drivin' since 1918," said the Negro, "but I never had a wreck like this."

"What kind of wrecks you have?" asked the grizzled Irishman.

"Different kinds. I had a piston break through the head. I had an axle break, and the truck drag behind me."

"Like a sled," prompted the Irishman.

"Yeah, throwin' sparks too, they told me. But I never had a break like this."

A small blue pickup truck rolled to a stop before the red light.

The driver leaned out the vehicle's window: "I never seen nothin' like that before," he called out. "Hey, is that your rig?"

"Yeah!" Laughter induced laughter.

"I never seen that before."

"Well, you seen it now."

"What do you call it?"

"Broker. It get broker all the time."

Merriment rolled like a wave between them, and spread among bystanders. With red light changing to green, the pickup went its way.

"I had different kinds of trouble," the Negro resumed, speaking to the Irishman. "I had all kinds o' trouble. But I never had this kind o' trouble."

"No. I'll bet," the Irishman cackled.

Ira told the Negro that he thought the upper part of the load might have rammed the El structure. He assured Ira that it hadn't. There was a crack on top of the chassis frame; that was the trouble.

"Well, when that happens, the top flange goes, and the rest'll break like paper."

The man who spoke had arrived just a minute ago. He was the IRT structure inspector. His voice carried a trace of censure. "You had her loaded bad to begin with: all on the tailboard."

"You don't always have time to load her just right."

"I'm pretty sure your load hit the El. You can see the plaster marks underneath," said the inspector.

"No, I think that happened after she broke."

"I don't know about that."

The inspector appeared disgruntled. For the first time anxiety haunted the Negro's eyes. And now the news photograper appeared, and simultaneously from nowhere a troop of kids. Yelling, "He's from the *Mirror*!" they tried to climb up the tailboard of the already

HENRY ROTH

precariously loaded truck. The Negro moved swiftly through traffic to shoo them off.

"Them newspaper photographers, they're the worst goddamn pests," said the inspector. "There's people in the IRT office does nothin' but search for items like these. They'll wanna know where's the report."

"They don't print everything." Ira deprecated. "That's no big accident. It hasn't done much damage to the El."

"Well, maybe." He frowned, raised his eyes to the smudged El crossties. Standing just beneath them, the Negro had unlashed the rope and was trying to tighten it around the back of the load: a plank slid down to the pavement; a wheelbarrow tumbled.

"Jesus, he's in a helluva mess," Ira said.

The inspector looked from side to side reproachfully, looked up at the El structure, and back at the Negro—and walked away.

A taxicab with a flat tire clumped slowly past, constricting the already constricted traffic. Drivers shouted at each other, demanding, "Hey! You blind? Where the hell d'ye think y'are? A museum?" Passengers craned from cars, laughed. A bumper was dented. The Negro stood on the sidewalk talking to a uniformed chauffeur. "Lucky you weren't going fast," said the chauffeur.

"Yeah, lucky I wasn't goin' down a grade."

"You might have broke clean away and done a somersault."

"Yeah. I could feel myself goin' up," said the Negro. "Just liftin' up."

"Felt like an airplane I bet."

"Sure did."

"I bet you thought you needed a parachute."

"No, I wasn't goin' that fast. Jitterbug," said the Negro, and they both laughed.

"What the truck cost you?" asked the chauffeur.

"Twenty-five dollars."

"Lucky it's your own rig."

A man joined them. "Anybody loads a truck like that on the tailboard is crazy," he said. "The water leaks in behind the cab, and rusts the chassis frame. I had a load of twenty-foot pipe once, and the truck broke just that way."

"Did he say anybody did that is crazy?" said the Negro, after the newcomer walked away. "Man, they been givin' me advice. One come over an' say: why don't you burn that rig up? Another come over an' ask me: Say, how would you like to buy a truck? I'll sell you one. But nobody come over an' say: Here, I'll give you a hundred dollars. Buy yourself a new one."

A police prowl car made its round. "When're you movin' that job?" asked the cop at the wheel.

"My cousin be here any minute now."

"He better. We're gonna have to tow it away. Start movin' the stuff to the sidewalk, will ye?"

"There's a lot o' traffic to get through, officer."

"An' there's a lotta traffic ain't gettin' through. You better start unloadin' right now. You're gonna have to unload it anyway. You can't tow it that way."

"Yes sir. I was waitin' for my cousin to get here to help."

"Nothin' doin'."

The prowl car drove off. Ira waited, while the Negro dragged mortar-caked mixing tray, barrel, and barricade from the tailboard of the truck, and in the lull of red traffic lights, conveyed the gear to the sidewalk.

Mirth, infectious mirth of predicament, announced the cousin's arrival—in a truck as mauled in aspect as the other. The pair set to work loading the equipment on the sidewalk aboard the second truck, which was then maneuvered in position ahead of the first, and the two vehicles chained together, front to rear. By the time the prowl car made its return tour, both trucks were already under way, rounding the corner into the side street, the rear one's tailboard bobbing up and down in burlesque leave-taking.

At the rooming house, Ira had a letter from Dalton, dashed off on a large, lined, yellow sheet of the kind of stationery that seemed de rigueur for lawyers, and to Ira disagreeable, both the canary glaze and the size. He wrote that he had just finished reading a section of Joyce's *Work in Progress*, and thought him insane. He added that Ira's trying to write "for money" was just as insane. What he ought to do was persist in "being the artist." In proof that he was earnest about his injunction, he said that if Ira would apply the money for purposes of creative writing, he would be glad to help him out financially (Dear Edith, speaking through him, like an unseen prompter). He suggested they meet for a drink.

They met the next afternoon at the Woodstock, a fashionable drinking place, and had a couple of glasses of beer. He wore a lustrous Abercrombie and Fitch gray suit, and sported a black walking stick. Ira congratulated him on his marriage, or rather, asked him how he felt now that he was married. He answered: No different. Their excursion to Florida, he said, had wrought quite an improvement in Edith's health and mood. Ira was glad it had. She had sent Bill fifty dollars, and Doris had sent Bill fifty dollars.

He took Ira to a Chinese place for luncheon; and no sooner were they seated than he inquired, in his edged, direct way, how much money Ira needed to live on. His questioning made him seem even more Jewish than he was, and he was unmistakably Jewish enough, with his hawk nose, eyeglasses, his restiveness and trait of chewing his nails, and then immediately scratching his balding head. Ira said he thought he needed sixty dollars a month to get by. Which, above what he received from Home Relief, would mean an additional thirty dollars.

"Well, that can be arranged," Dalton said.

Ira became lost between acquiescence and presumption at such times: of the allure of the luxury of having a reasonable supply of cash, and the recognition of the conditions attached to having it. He became withdrawn and inattentive. Dalton was already on the subject of the futility of Ira's trying to write short stories, and he only became cognizant of his words when he asked what Maxwell Perkins thought of all this. It was Perkins, Ira said, who suggested that Virginia N might make a helpful literary agent. She had been Thomas Wolfe's literary agent, and had been useful in placing Wolfe's shorter pieces in magazines.

What were M's financial resources? Dalton changed the subject abruptly. Not much. And her parents? he asked: What could she expect from them? And what were her prospects? To all of which Ira's answers were anything but encouraging, especially since M was without a paying position at the moment.

"You'd better get an eight-hour job," he said. "You'd be better off with an eight-hour job than writing cheap things."

Eight-hour jobs weren't to be had just for the asking, Ira reminded him, and he was wrong in his view of the short story as cheap. Ira praised the form for the discipline it imposed, the necessity to maintain a pace, interest, the necessity to satisfy the reader's demands with economy and immediacy.

"What would you do?" Again with an attorney's shift of tactics, he asked. "If you were free to write as you pleased. Absolutely free to write as you pleased. What would you do?"

"My main interest would be to continue the childhood of my first book into adolescence."

"Why don't you?"

Was that a trick, or a knack one mastered in law school, the knack of the trial lawyer who fixed you, fastened you down from point to point, like Gulliver by the Lilliputians, so that you were at liberty only to disclose the truth—or lie so flagrantly that your credibility was destroyed. It was a long-drawn silence over the egg foo yong. "I think I need the discipline of the short story," Ira evaded.

"Even if you could write what you pleased?"

"Of course; now it's a question of survival—"

"Let's leave that out of it."

"I'd probably write short stories anyway."

"Why?"

"I said why. The discipline of the form would benefit me."

"You're sure you're not glorifying necessity—struggle versus security?" Dalton rolled a hot morsel of sweet and pungent shrimp between tongue and palate through as many turns as he could, and then reached hastily for a glass of water.

"No, I don't think so."

Tongue quenched, he set down the tumbler. "You've done it before: glorified Bill Loem, his puritanism, his dedication, selling the *Daily Worker* on Fourteenth Street at night."

"But I haven't any alternative," Ira said testily.

"Again, we're not talking about that."

"No, I'd rather write short stories."

"In other words, you're interested in portraying the adolescence of the child character in your novel, but you won't do it, even if you could."

"I'm not ready for it. I thought I'd be, after I wrote of Bill's adolescence and youth, but that went to pot."

"You mean you need time to recover—"

"From the debacle. Yes."

"Well. Why punish yourself in the meantime? Why waste your talent turning out commodities for slick magazines?"

"They're not commodities. I thought I made that clear. Besides, I've got to feel I have my independence in every way, that's all."

He desisted. He harped on his favorite thesis: the progress of the novel from the product of the man of affairs, the businessman like Richardson and Defoe, to the modern day aesthete who rejected today's man of affairs. Ira gobbled and listened, more or less. Dalton was seriously considering running an ad in the *New York Times* to convince businessmen that it was time for a change, to participate again in holding up the mirror of society to society, which was what the novel really was.

Ira snickered, glad he was on that tack. "Revolution by ad," he commented.

It could easily be that, Dalton maintained. He was sure he could demonstrate by a graph how the esteem of the businessman had waned with his declining participation in the writing of literature. "He's on the inside of business, something the aesthete isn't. He's the industrialist, the technologist, the banker; he's the one responsible for the efficient working of society. There's no one who knows it better, more realistically. It's dramatic material, as full of meaning as anything the aesthete ever does. Who's there to give his point of view, give it form? No one but himself."

"All right, run an ad," Ira smirked from the sanctuary of aesthetic superiority—or was it simply because of restored complacency, of averting his probes.

There was more: Yes, he thought he would run an ad. Businessmen and practical people in industry were by very definition sensible people. They would—many would—respond favorably to an appeal for them to resume their former role in literature, and many could. The aesthete was bankrupt. Witness Joyce. Why leave the field open to the so-called proletarian writer preaching violent revolution. "There's no virtue in violent revolution," he accused.

"No."

"I prophesy that ten years from now you'll say to hell with all that. You'll think that making money and living an easy life is a virtue."

"Maybe. But I'll still be in the soup."

"What do you mean?"

"Psychologically."

"You mean you need psychoanalysis. We can help you there."

"No, just get your businessman on the ball."

He chewed his nails, scratched his bald spot, swiftly as always, paid the check, and they left.

With the two glasses of beer and the more than ample repast, Ira fell into a heavy sleep. And when he awoke, he seemed to have a vision of the impasse he was in, perhaps because Dalton's cross-examination had roiled up that particular area of psychic silt. The best he could do was to skirt, to detour around the years of his own growth, avoid it. Virginia N was right: Keep the I out of it, but not the eye. The scene he had witnessed the other day came back to him: The broken-down truck, the Negro driver, the comments, the cops, the low trestle of the El overhead. What was the posted clearance? 11' 6", 12' 6"?

12' 6". He read his notes on the episode. 12' 6" the clearance. Could he pass under it intact? Or more to the point, shape the incident into a *New Yorker* sketch, Dalton be damned. God, you couldn't help being moved by the apparition of Edith behind him, doting ventriloquist, still proffering her love and tenderness and protection, and financial assistance. Pity of it, that boundless maternal cherishing she so eagerly proffered, as if she held out her girlish breast to Ira, so churlishly spurned. But it conjured up the whole lump of his trouble, of what was wrong with him. And compromise with it, he couldn't. So: to the task. Broker. Try that as a title.

He worked on it for a few hours, getting nothing that would stand up when finished, nothing that seemed inevitable. He began to doubt himself, his fitness for the task, and the task itself as a proper goal to aim at, despite his brag to Dalton; it came back to mock him. Stymied, he left the apartment and walked to the Model Cafeteria. Morris was on duty, Ira's oldest uncle, heavyset, fair-skinned and bald, slow-moving and imperturbable, his voice reduced by heavy smoking to a wheezy treble. It was about three in the morning. Ira ordered a chicken salad sandwich and coffee.

Life—the kind of life Morris had led—its relentless treadmill, its compulsion, had transformed Ira's favorite uncle from the jolly, permissive, immigrant youth he had been to the stolid counterman he had become. On his broad shoulders Ira had ridden when he swam out into the surf at Coney Island (and Ira had grabbed his blond hair in fright at the depth beneath them).

Immigrant simpleton, he bought five cents worth of the biggest plums he had ever seen—at a pushcart—and years were to pass before he could bring himself to eat a slice of tomato again. Simpleton, Ira's jocund uncle, trudging home on Ninth Street after a twelve-hour stint as a busboy in a sawdust-spread, swing-door saloon; he would stop at the candy store at the foot of the family's tenement, strip off the wrappers of six or seven newly bought penny Hershey bars, and stuff all of them into his mouth at once, so that they radiated in brown spokes of ineffable bliss from his lips. He had been transformed into this disenchanted, hardheaded drudge behind the counter, and not unaware of what life had done to him— stoic and unforgiving both. Ira had the feeling that for all of his kin their coming to this country had turned into a kind of pedestrian tragedy, although he couldn't say just why. Had they misspent their lives here, their hopes all thwarted? Max's "Oh, I know when I'm licked. Some people don't know when they're licked, but I know when I'm licked." What was it? They seemed a sacrifice to something Ira couldn't name. America? The American way? The American Dream? They seemed a sacrifice to success.

On the other side of the counter, in his white counterman's apron, Morris plodded about, waiting on customers, saying little—regarding Ira in passing with steady, blue eyes, as if he were seeing not him but the someone Ira had been long ago—and between times, picking up his cigarette from the cash register ledge, and smoking. He stopped to ask about Mom. "She's about the same," Ira said.

"You go home?"

"Oh yes, Pop and I have gotten over our squabbles."

"He's not a bad fellow," said Morris. "I like the man. But it doesn't help. You can't do anything for him. His heart's in the right place: I never saw a man so softhearted about colored people. But he's *zerdreidt*." He used the Yiddish word for twisted.

"That's true," Ira nodded—and squinted: Behind Morris, on the floor under its chromium hood, the garbage can's open surface trembled, as if it were full of watery swill. He trudged off to wait on a middle-aged woman customer who had just entered. Once again the surface of the garbage can trembled. And looking closer, Ira saw it: a rat—no mistaking the glint of beady eye, the dragging tail, and loathsome shape. And as Morris went by, Ira signaled to him furtively. "Maybe you ought to cover that garbage can. There's a rat in it."

But instead of keeping Ira's confidence secret, he said in full normal tone of voice, "What's a rat? I had to live with them for two years in the trenches."

"Shaah!" Ira tried to hush him in Yiddish. "Your patrons, your customers."

"What's the matter? Didn't they ever see a rat?"

"They make me sick," objected the woman customer at the other end of the counter.

"I lived with them when I was fighting for democracy," Morris said phlegmatically. "That's how I lost all my hair." He picked up his cigarette from the marble cash register edge.

Later, Ida, Morris's wife, came in. Distraught, haggard, for all her peroxide bleached platinum hair, the lurid plug of the large wen beside her nose glowing like a fanned ember, she had come to take Morris home at the end of his shift—so she said. But in fact, she had gambled most of the night away—her consuming passion, Mom told Ira—and judging from her hectic demeanor, she must have lost. It was Pop who had brought them together, when he owned an ill-fated delicatessen on 116th Street, and been bewitched, as he still was, by her fawning and her stylishness. She had lived in the apartment house above the store. Rapturous marriage broker, Pop had commended her to Morris, praising her virtues to the skies.

"Does she have entrails?" Mom had cynically asked. "Go away. They've been removed. Every ladies garment traveling salesman on Division Street knew her when she was a saleslady." And Morris, poor dazzled yokel, had been taken.

Keep the I out of it. How could you when the implications came shimmering in on you? He finished his coffee and headed back to his room, determined to finish the story that day, without sleep. The coffee, and his ruminations, kept him awake:

Look, any story has to have suspense: there's a big hunk o' junk lying in the path of traffic, in a bus lane of a great city, a great metropolis, impeding the flow of vehicles; and the cops come around, and the cops go away. Finally, finally, the cousin arrives; the mason's gear is removed, transferred; the truck's chained onto the truck and, hind end jouncing, towed out of sight into the colored guy's history.

Do you realize what that would look like from his standpoint?

No, I don't. I can scarcely envisage it. What he would do when he got home, how he would appear to his wife, kids, neighbors in the climate of his neighborhood.

That's what I mean. That's the trouble with you, your immense shortcoming, limitation, that you don't.

I know that only too well. Still, I can plead that the populace has these mutually exclusive spheres, the American populace: the Negro, the Irish, the Italian, the Jew, the Pole, the Oriental, half a dozen others; and we carom off each other all the time. The only one I know anything about, and that's not much, is the Jew, mostly this Jew . . . and not too proud of him either.

He sat apathetically, frowning, first at the blank, lined white page of paper on the table, then at the cage of fingers resting tip to tip on his thigh.

Outside the window, young boys, some in their underwear, and breastless girls in petticoats ran shrilling in and out of the bright foaming water rushing from the hydrant someone had already turned on. Forget it. Give it up. "Every time somebody look at that truck it get broker," the colored man said. Where would that lead? Can you imagine when he was finally towed home, the kids come running out of the dilapidated house. What happened, Pappy? And the wife at the door saying, Law's a mussy, or something else as stock and trite as that. Or laughing, the way they laughed.

Get to work. You gotta get to work.

Broker. If it was really so, if he could make it seem genuinely applicable that his thesis worked: the trick of the truck become broker every time somebody looked at it, *there* was a thread, a guiding principle, that would give cohesiveness to the whole—at least in his mind. He demanded that everlasting sense of unity, sequence of inevitability—he couldn't define it. Anyway, the kids jumped on the truck just as the *Daily Mirror* news photographer appeared. The loaded rear end had teetered. Whee! There was an approach. If only he had other ways of viewing the incident, more sophisticated ways, that would appeal to the cultivated and subtle mind, to the intellectual, the philosophically capable, the abstraction wielders, how different his approach would be—or not at all. The doing might not have seemed worthy to the ideologically competent: a mishap, a traffic obstacle. Or to the sociological: rather dwell on the status of the Negro, economic, social, demographic. Or to the Party, especially to the Party: his oppressed status, his potential for revolutionary change, natural ally of the revolutionary proletariat, maybe voicing approved slogans: "Jim Crow must go." "Down with the cross burners and the lynchers." But he didn't say a word about any of it: of course he wouldn't, in that setting. And he was a petit bourgeois besides: he owned his own truck, owned the masonry implements. Oh, woolgathering. What if a black man saw it? No, now you've got something: a black aspiring writer. The entire picture would be different: a sense of identity would pervade, a sense of plight, different from his, a sense of folk with whom the self was integrated. Say the guy was a Jew, Moe Cohen, his old clunker piled up under the Second Avenue El, and the cops come calling. Let's see your license, Moe; you're in violation, Moe; don't give me no argument, Moe; tell it to the judge. And the pedestrians on the sidewalk: Heh, heh, heh, see that Yid. Oh, Jesus, if he ain't a card. And maybe, for all you know, one of those sub-rosa Nazi stooges you meet everywhere: What'd I tell you? The kikes spoil everything. They got money, but they puts it in de benk. Now what? I'll bet you five bucks you would have been out there to help the poor bastard: Come on, let's unload it; let's do something. Lemme give you a hand. And his answer: *Oy, gewald*. I got such lousy luck. You know what they say in Yiddish: A poor man should never be born. You understand Yiddish? *Oy, khallas auf iss*. (What the hell is a *khallas*? a plague?) But then it would never do for *The New Yorker*.

It was midafternoon; his head throbbed with the heat of the torrid, little cell, but he did have a draft, a rough first draft, a track. It was a light-year away from a finished piece, but at least a direction. He had eaten nothing since the chicken salad sandwich, drunk nothing. He hadn't even urinated. Well, get up, take a leak, get outdoors, blow the stink off you. He had a rough draft.

A uniformed fireman had turned off the gushing hydrant in the street. Somebody with a wrench would sure as hell turn the water on again. A stroll to the East River seemed like a good idea in the heat, the thought of the breeze blowing over the water enticing. He turned east. Swank apartments, and more new ones rising, now stood where the run-down slums had been. Who would have believed it? The crummy tenements gone, once occupied by the corned-beef-and-cabbage Irish, like Veronica with the ravishing beauty spot on her chin, mincing through 119th Street, now with grubby hand on baby carriage handle, saying to frumpy friend, while the great iron nutcracker slammed into toppling brick walls amid slither of debris and cloud of dirt, exposing grimy rat refuge, and greasy wallpaper cockroach haven, speaking. "Remember, Kitty, what dumps was here?"

Muscles bright in running swan dive, sixteen-year-olds plunged off the dock into the water. An excursion boat that circled Manhattan, *The Sylph*, was sailing by, and the swimmers made haste to catch the rollers that came off the vessel's sides. The lads gamboled in the waves, snorted, spewed river water, falsettoed for rescue. There were girls on the dock, too, the same age as the boys, Irish, Italian in appearance, looking on with a kind of self-protective severity that soon gave way to high-pitched giggle, after the boys climbed up the rickety ladder to the dock and began their horseplay. They were dressed in trunks. They pawed each other with hands grimy from the rungs of the ladder.

"Gimme my soap. I gotta go to work soon," said one.

"Is it fairy soap?" asked another.

Said someone stretching out on the dock: "Let me lay here in peace, will ye."

"He wants to lay wit' a piece," said another.

It was all out in the open for them; that was the difference. Natural. Uncorrosive. And they went to confession: Father, I did it to her. Father, I let him do it to me. Tch-Tch! Drop a quarter in the *pishkeh*; recite a hundred Hail Marys; tell your beads, your rosary. All the Jew of today had was psychotherapy.

Ahn, he'd gone astray. Ira puffed at the billow of heat that met him when he opened the door of his sweltering little room. He sat down at the table. Might as well bring the typewriter into play, see if he could get started toward a more definitive draft, see how far he could get before he knocked off to go to M's for supper. He interpolated the carbon paper and inserted the pages in the heavy Underwood.

He and M had gone for a walk, after a light supper the night before, strolled to Central Park, and sat on the lawn near the Tavern on the Green. Enclave in the city, it seemed a little odd with its greensward so near the electric signs and the eighteen-story buildings only a short distance away. They chatted languidly. One thing he remembered: something she said after they listened for a while to the happy din coming from the mall where young people had gathered, and from the others in the roller-skating and cycling enclosures. She said that her motto for some time had been a quotation from Baudelaire. It was to the effect that if one didn't work out of desire, still it was better to work anyway, if only to escape the boredom of pleasure.

Boredom of pleasure—what a bourgeois, stagnating society the guy must have lived in. That black truck driver he had just had the cops hail in the sketch couldn't have felt that way about pleasure: a glass of beer, a game of pool, maybe an excursion to a beach allowing colored people, tar beach.

And back in her room, she made a pitcher of lemonade. And when he said he thought he'd go back to work, she tried to dissuade him. "You've done enough. Please don't overdo."

"Boredom of pleasure," he had spoofed.

"Seriously, darling," she insisted. "I don't want anything to happen to you."

"No?"

"I'm depending on you for a center." She was extremely earnest. "I haven't any of my own. And you do."

"But I'm a cauldron," he had objected. "Just a churning cauldron."

She had lifted her face, features so angelically serene, they'd deceive you. "You're my center. You're my funny Ira."

Promising M he would spend only an hour or so—just to get his mind prepared for the next day—Ira had left and returned to his room. He knew he'd survive. Confidence grew with exhaustion. He'd survive it; he was meant to bear it. A kind of savage pride swelled within him. He was singled out for it. Jesus, he was tired: his ankles, his legs. That bed was gonna feel good; that little lair, stuffy and airless, felt good in prospect.

CHAPTER 17

A note from M, which she left at Ira's rooming house, informed him that her parents were in town, and that Father had said he would take them all out to dinner. Would Ira call for her at six? They would then go to Betty and John's at six-fifteen for a snifter. Her parents were expected to join them there at seven.

Ira bathed, and shaved with a new blade. Then, with necktie in his pocket, and not yet daring to risk putting on a clean shirt, but dressed in his faded, blue polo shirt, blue slacks—Macy's basement bargain—the Wanamaker English jacket of gray-and-black plaid that Edith had given him, his tan shoes, and his gray, weathered felt hat, in want of cleaning and blocking, and with a small vent hole at the front of the crimp, Ira sallied forth.

At the last moment he remembered that M's note instructed him to "bring pipe." So he pocketed pipe, and in typical, absent fashion, deciding not to take the Bull Durham cigarette tobacco along, left his pipe in his room instead, and had to return and fetch it. He bought a small tin of more expensive pipe tobacco than he usually indulged in, Revelation, eighteen cents, out of the dollar forty he had left until his next Home Relief check a week or more hence. Then he knocked at M's window.

She wore a print dress, completely sleeveless. She had cut the half sleeves away when they tore at the seams under the armpits. The material was of some cottony stuff printed with a design of little brown and black circles. She smiled at him on the other side of the open steel door. Ira looked at her questioningly and indicated her room. She said, "It's safe."

They went in, and she clung to him and told him the day's news: John and Betty had been to call on her, also Mr. and Mrs. P, her parents. They had all had a light lunch there, swiss cheese and Jewish rye bread, and liked it. She had been copying music before Ira arrived, and one of the sheets was still wet—he almost touched it, lying on the table under the gooseneck lamp, but she said just in time, "It's still wet, darling." It looked beautiful though (her cantata, which she was preparing to have blueprinted), the black India ink notes contrasting strongly with the thin white paper. She remarked on the three-pointed pen she used, its tendency to clot: the ink coated the pen like paint. Ira suggested that the musical notation would make a fetching design for a cloth. She thought she could make a million dollars on the idea.

They walked over, went into the elevator and up two flights, and rang the Millers' doorbell. Betty looked pretty, tip-tilted nose and blond hair, and comely in a kind of postcard way, pale yellow dress made of rayon and topped by a small jacket that for some reason seemed to go with the word "bolero." John wore a brown suit of gabardine and a chocolate brown shirt with a bold plaid McCrossen tie. Ira was relieved to note that he was not wearing a white shirt (a white shirt was something Mother favored, that and tobacco pipes). His shirt was open, necktie loose. Their phonograph was playing as Ira and M came into the living room—the "Beer Barrel Polka," John's favorite for the week. Their living room was large, nicely furnished, semi-moderne, plate-glass coffee table on wrought iron legs and Scandinavian chairs. John's photographic equipment was discreetly spaced about, and on the white walls his commercial photographs: a hunting arrow with broad-headed tip hanging down, which he had photographed for an insurance company over the caption of their always hitting the mark; a row of test tubes in a rack; a photo done for Consumers Union analyzing the ingredients of a candy bar. He had also taken and enlarged, for his own enjoyment, several pictures of the East Side, teeming as ever with pedestrians halted or in passage before pushcarts. Ira studied them nostalgically, and in one he thought he could make out the word "mohel" in Hebrew lettering on a sign above the doorway of a tenement.

"There are an awful lot of people born in New York. Were you born here?" John asked.

"No, I was born in Austria-Hungary, but some years ago, after the World War, I was born again in Poland."

They laughed.

"What's the name of the town?" John asked.

"Too many *z*'s in it to pronounce," Ira said.

Betty recalled crossing over the border into Canada with a party of social-service workers. The rest of the people were born in New York. But she said proudly: Portland, Oregon.

"That's when Father was a minister in the logging camps," said John. "But you weren't born there." He addressed M.

"Oh, no, I'm a true Brahmin," said M. "Somerville, Boston."

"And you?" Ira asked John.

"In suburbia, New Jersey."

The levity and small talk only seemed to accentuate their nervous anticipation, like tics of uneasiness. What did they want to drink? John asked. No one could decide between vermouth and abstaining, and the question languished there. John gave up. Ira thought M would benefit by having a vermouth cocktail, and she agreed. With John's permission he made her one, and served it, but had none himself. Ira drew out his pipe.

"Oh, yes, that's right," John immediately followed suit.

Everyone wandered about, or sat uneasily, as Ira did, nursing the spruceness of his shirt collar. He had taken his English jacket off when he had come into the apartment, as primary means for keeping cool; but, as time approached for the guests to arrive, Ira fetched it again and put it on.

"Do you really want to wear your jacket?" asked John.

"No," Ira said, "but they'll soon be here."

"Don't be silly," Betty admonished. "Here give it to me. I'll hang it up." Ira surrendered the garment.

"The Ps are human, you know," John assured him.

"Well, I'm trying to accept the rules of the game, and behave accordingly."

And just then the door buzzer strummed.

A woman came in, sharp-featured, spare and quick, moving through the slow haze of Ira's confusion as if her acute brown-eyed countenance were a blade cleaving into the room. Attired in a red hat and a blue-and-white vertically striped shirtwaist, she carried a red handkerchief, and her lips were rouged the same color carmine. She greeted her daughters with a kiss, and her voice was light and sweetly cordial, and completely stylized. Followed a man, heavy-shouldered, bulky and corpulent, clad in a gray suit of thin weave. He had a bulbous Socratic nose, and a sunburned bald head surrounded by a horseshoe fringe of gray hair. Compared with him, in almost all respects, features and figure and grace of bearing, his wife epitomized delicate rearing and aristocracy; he had plain strength, unembellished but well trained for service. He was deliberate in his movements, as befitted his ponderous physique. Ira shook hands with the one and with the other.

Father was big and brawny, had played guard on the football team for Brown while studying for the ministry. That was way back in 1900, and he'd walked off the field once when the coach swore. One of that burly, husky type of American males, descendant of old stock, with a ratchety timbre to his voice: He had put himself through the university by breakfasts of shredded wheat and canned milk. What he ate the rest of the day, Ira never asked. Father, M may have remarked in passing, was chosen all-American guard that year. But that was in 1900, another country, when it was astonishing what people would do for free, do without payment, for the cheers of the crowd and the sheer glory of it.

And he belonged to the time, belonged to the age, not only belonged, but was shaped by it, rigidly so: Everything was either right or wrong, black or white. He had been an avid baseball fan, but when the Chicago White Sox threw the World Series in 1919, he was so outraged that he never attended another big-league game the rest of his life. A brawny, staunch, dauntless American, upright and loyal. And intelligent, too. Intelligent enough to let his wife, née Grace Reid, of similar pure American stock, direct his life and finances. Grace was silkily cunning, politely acquisitive, and sweetly sanctimonious. Father was such an innocent, M once remarked. Thanks to his wife's tutelage, he grew shrewder in time. A little. They both learned to play cards, drink cocktails, smoke, attend musicals.

Father sat down in the easy chair before the window. He settled himself comfortably and drew out a briar pipe, heavy, but seemly and fitting in his large hands. Mother began talking rapidly and brightly about their lovely boat trip from Boston to New York, and the perfectly glorious weather they were blessed with. Betty, who had been in Buffalo recently for the social workers' convention, said that the weather there had been positively cold. Had she looked up so-and-so while she was there? Mother asked. No, she hadn't, hadn't had a chance to. Some talk followed of Niagara Falls and their beauty on the Canadian side.

"A big piece fell off the American side," John remarked.

"Oh, yes," everyone agreed, with Mother saying, "Wasn't it too bad. The Cave of the Winds is gone. The king and queen of England were there when we were," she added.

"We could have come within ten feet of them, if we had wanted to," said Father. The royal pair, he went on, were staying in the Regency, and had he chosen to go to some sort of Kiwanis reception there, he and Mother could have been inducted into the presence of British sovereignty itself.

Mother had declined to go. "I'm too much of a democrat to think it's worth the trouble," she said. "A democrat with a small *d* of course."

There followed talk about the holding and conducting of different kinds of conventions, with Father chaffing Betty about belonging to a social workers' organization, "a kind of union, heaven help us." He had a deep, jolly laugh that, like his voice, vibrated with masculine authority.

While Father was talking, Mother stood up and began circulating about the room. She stopped to inspect a photograph John had taken for *Field and Stream* magazine; it was a photograph of a camping scene, a tent beside a woodland stream with a canoe pitched on its bank. "That's very pretty, John. How much did you get paid for that?" she asked.

"Must you know?" John parried.

"Yes. Now, don't be coy, John. It's all in the family."

"For your benefit, Gracey," John addressed her by her first name, "I was paid fifty dollars."

"That's a tidy sum." And now her quick eye came to rest on the window. "Why, John, what a window!"

"I just didn't have a chance, Gracey," said John. "The day the window cleaner was here, I forgot to tell him, and when I was here, he wasn't."

"Betty," Mother advised. "You could easily train ivy to go up the window. Try it, why don't you?"

Betty didn't seem interested.

Ira felt quite depressed listening to this piling up of allusions to a world in which he shared not the remotest part, and cared nothing for, either, though that was beside the point. He could only sit, feigning alertness and keeping his fingers unlocked in his lap because they stuck together otherwise. In later days publicists and sociologists would speak of a generation gap. There was no such term then. It was taken for granted that, in general, American parents—not Ira's own immigrant ones, of course—middle-class American parents expressed attitudes no longer in vogue. The younger generation for the most part saw nothing absolutely wrong with the older generation's attitudes—nothing absolutely wrong, but decidedly at variance with their own. And they were at variance, because they were taken up with traditional concerns, the positive concerns of American business, American drive, the overcoming of obstacles, forging ahead of competition, getting to the top. Succeeding. Ah, succeeding. Though he was scarcely aware of it, because of the strain of the unfamiliar social setting he was in, the same kind of sacrifice was taking place that Ira felt in the presence of his own partially estranged kin. It was the same sacrifice of personality for aims ignoble. The idealistic clergyman, with a self-imposed mission of salvation to the benighted woodcutters of Oregon's logging camps, had become the executive secretary of Kiwanis International. He no longer preached the Gospel; he dispensed a kind of spiritual gloss, a veneer meant to cover the fundamental crassness, mercenary ugliness, the base complacency, and the self-satisfied callousness and insensitivity of conservative American business.

Only that tall girl in her homespun dress, who sat across the room, was Ira's nexus here. Otherwise he had none; to her parents he was an alien. It was easy to conjecture what they thought of him: Home Relief indigent, dubious scrivener, Jewish neurotic. A Jew and a ne'er-do-well. What could rate lower on their scale of values? No matter. Not they but M was his future. She summed up his hopes and needs, all his aspirations.

There had been some talk—before the choice of restaurant was decided on—about the delicious fish dinners the Ps had enjoyed in Boston: clams, lobsters, and cod. At one point, the convention committee had ordered soft-shell clams—

"Crabs?" M asked.

"No, not crabs, clams." Father meant steamers, not quahogs, and the way some of the people who had never eaten clams before ate them was a scream.

"Of course, they weren't New Englanders," Mother palliated. "Some dug them out of the shell with a spoon instead of stripping off the skin and discarding the neck."

Ira made a mental note of how to eat soft-shell clams.

Father mentioned the name of the coastal town in which the committee had partaken of the seafood banquet.

"Oh, no, it was another town," said Mother, mentioning the name of the other town.

He gazed at her sternly for a moment. And then, as if depicting the unswerving momentum with which his mind moved, he circled his index finger at her, and then jabbed it forward. It was the town he had mentioned.

"Oh, yes," Mother acquiesced.

And now the subject of dinner moved definitely to the fore. John recommended a new Swedish restaurant, where one helped oneself to an interesting assortment of smorgasbord. Betty recommended a well-known steak house. But Father announced that the dining place had already been decided on: It was to be Zum Hofbräu, a German restaurant. It served hearty, wholesome food and was near at hand. Still, he was open to suggestions, or a vote on the matter. Everyone acceded to his choice: Zum Hofbräu it was.

Half-timbered on the lower floors, after the style of a period dining place in Germany, Zum Hofbräu occupied an old three-story converted town house. The effect of exterior quaintness was carried into the interior: dining tables made of stout, wide boards duly defaced by carved initials, stag horns on the walls, a long succession of ornamental steins displayed on high shelves. A small orchestra occupied a platform at the center of the dining hall. During dinner, a vocalist, a smiling fellow who looked French, accompanied himself at the piano in a rendition of French, Russian, and German songs. Later, the small orchestra, comprising a violin, piano, cello, and accordion, played "My Indiana Home," at which Father shouted approval, followed by the "Blue Danube"—for Ira's benefit, said Mother. Singing waiters sang. Mother told him that when Web, her older son, currently head of the Igleheart Flour sales division, and from all accounts a dynamo of conviviality, had brought them there, he persuaded all the waiters to perform in chorus, and before the evening was over, he knew all their names and how many children each had.

There were six at the table, a table for eight. Mother asked John to get rid of the extra two chairs by sliding them over to the next table, which was unoccupied, thus leaving more room. John obliged her, and the chairs were displaced. But the waiter promptly slid them back again. Whenever Ira was waited on, he thought of Pop, his waiter father, and was always constrained thereby—in this case, he felt the chief target of the waiter's dander.

They left the restaurant, and Ira walked with Father toward Beekman Towers, the hotel where they were staying during their visit to New York. Ira asked him whether he was constantly on the move, or did he travel only intermittently. He was on the move whenever occasion demanded; Kiwanis conventions were seasonal for the most part and, of course, during the height of convention time, he traveled more. How long did he plan on staying in New York? Until Wednesday. He had prepared an address scheduled for delivery to the Boy Scouts of America. Ira asked some other appropriate questions about the organization, and the reply took eight city blocks.

Ira thought, as he sat watching them in Betty and John's living room after dinner: These are the people who made America so wonderful, over the centuries. They built America, and these others, Ira's kind and other mongrels, were ruining it.

That out of all this, a hand should have been extended to him, hers, the very grace, the last grace of her tradition. It did no good to ponder the mystery, even if geologic time were vouchsafed in which to ponder it, the impish fidelity of her gaze, so knowing, at Ira's teasing. One became inert before the sheer magnitude of her trust, became overborne by the perception of it. Were they both still children, each in their own way, that she would have him, and he so passionately her?

When the evening was over, and they had exchanged good-nights, John proposed that M and Ira go up to the roof of his and Betty's apartment to view the city's night skyline. From a photographer's point of view, the true massiveness of the city, the way it piled up its huge shapes, was marred by the stagy lighting of the RCA Building. How high were the bold letters on the building, they wondered. Ira counted stories: The letters were three stories high. "Thirty-two feet," said the ever factual John.

Before them—from their eyrie atop the multistoried apartment house at Fifty-fifth Street and First Avenue—loomed the sable outline of the city's towers: the Chrysler Building, which Ira couldn't refrain from remarking reminded him of a squeezed boiled onion; the minaret of the Grand Central Building, with its globe of orange light; the Empire State, opaque and solitary. A single window in a lofty office shone against the gloomy, phallic bulk of the Empire State rearing up against the background darkness.

Alone again, in the street after they bade John and Betty good-night, M and Ira turned toward her rooming house. The sidewalk of the last block before they got there was beneath the covered shed of a new apartment house in construction. It closed in above them like a tunnel under the very night that only minutes ago had spread so immensely. They talked of the evening and of her parents. "Well, how did I do?" he asked.

"Oh, I think you did fine." She took his hand.

"My shirt collar didn't get sopping with sweat for a change."

"No, that was wonderful," she congratulated.

Ira repeated as much as he could remember of the conversation with her father on the walk from Zum Hofbräu to the Beekman Towers.

"I think Father is an unusually fine person," M said as they came out from under the covered way, and she added, "I think he's a pretty swell person."

"I think so, too. I feel sorry for him though—for reasons I'm sure he'd never accept."

"It makes me sick to think of the kind of thing he has to do now: be everybody's friend at the Kiwanis International conventions," said M. "I'd almost rather he remained the poor clergyman, or even the YMCA administrator in Chicago. There was still a little idealism left in him doing that."

Thoughtful and silent, she pressed Ira's hand while they walked. And just before they reached the rooming house, she asked, "Do you love me?"

"Of course I do. If I loved thee not, chaos is come again."

"Oh, that's so beautiful. Promise you'll say that to me every day?"

"Day and night."

They parted, agreeing to meet for breakfast.

CHAPTER 18

Ira took M home a week later for Sabbath supper. It was a deliberate decision to go there Friday evening, when Pop was sure to be home and they could, as it were, keep the reconciliation thriving. It was dusk when they got off the train. Ira slipped M's hand through the crook of his arm. Around the corner, in houses adjoining Mom's, lived the Gypsies. They saw the flounce of gaudy skirt, men in drab clothes sitting on the porch steps. Mom had said that the young Gypsy woman in the neighboring house had lost her husband recently. She screamed her grief incessantly hour after hour, inconsolably—until the day he was buried. And then, said Mom, always observing life with such utter absence of self that her recount was fraught with primitive eloquence, it was as though the young widow had wiped the slate clean. You would never have known that yesterday she was shrieking and lamenting in bereavement. Wiped the slate clean of her grief, and over with.

Mom welcomed Ira and M at the door. As usual, Pop lurked in embarrassment in the front room, apparently until he had mustered up the necessary social self-possession to appear in the kitchen and say hello. Mom thanked them for bringing back the empty jars that had been full of homemade jelly, which she had given Ira when he was last there.

The Sabbath candles in their brass candlesticks were already tipped with flame, the table covered with an embroidered white tablecloth, and on it, shiny new silverware, set with all the professional skill of Pop's calling. As they stood talking, Mom's ancient, decrepit poodle crept in. Newly shorn of its scraggly curls, it looked like a clamshell. Ira quipped to that effect, in English, of course, for M's benefit, and Pop's incidentally.

Nevertheless Mom, though she may not have understood the exact meaning of his words, divined their import. "That's my friend," she said staunchly, in English, and laughed when M did. And perhaps because diverted by that moment of rapport with M, for once Mom refrained from adding her usual gibe at Pop: That's my *only* friend.

There was, as always when Ira's father entertained guests, guests whom he had been expecting, and in the expectation accrued a degree of tension, that nervous, abrupt air about everything he said and did. It was at such times, when he was close to being overwrought—and most apt to fly off the handle at a trifle—that Mom seemed to insist on doing things her own way, with an obstinacy, an intransigence nothing short of deliberate provocation. Supper was a reenactment of an ancient, grievous sequence: First, contrary to Pop's expressed wish, she broke off irregular chunks of the Sabbath loaf, the lustrous, braided challah, instead of cutting neat slices, as he urged. With company present, Pop always concealed his anxiety (anxiety over his own volatility, Ira suspected, his fear of the imminence of his uncontrollable fits of temper) by adopting a super-mild tone of voice. It purred with humility and inoffensiveness. The poor man evidently thought, if he thought about it at all, that his unctuousness would create an image of himself that he would give anything to be: the composed, polite, and entertaining host. Instead, his show of meek cordiality had an air of the unreal about it; anyone could sense another person behind the wheedling, obliging front. Which showed itself when Mom insisted on tearing off hunks of challah. His voice shifted instantly to the harsh, rancorous sound Ira had known for so many years. He glared at her, his benign countenance becoming leathery with hate and exasperation.

He urged her not to place all the "appetizer" dishes on the table at once: the small meatballs in jellied gravy, the gefilte fish in their clotted and spiced aspic, the chopped eggs in rendered chicken fat, the cucumber salad. He pleaded that she bring out only one or two at a time. She refused to heed. They were all brought to the table at once.

"All at once, all at once! She has to pile up everything at once," Pop criticized.

"You serve your customers the way you wish in the restaurant, I'll serve the way I choose at home."

That glare: the volcanic fury pent beyond Ira's father's endurance. Tortured spirit, and Mom's, too, both of their lives wrecked in different ways. M sensed it all, and sat there quietly, her tender brown eyes toward Ira. The pity of it. Pop's lower teeth were almost all gone now, and his cheeks had the toothless sag of old age.

They talked about the World's Fair that had just opened. Ira had been there, and Mom had, too, but Pop and M had not. They discussed the exhibits, and Pop said he had heard that the fair authorities had contemplated lowering the admission prices. "What about those who've bought books of tickets?" M asked.

"That's what they're waiting for—till they use them, so there shouldn't be no squawk," he said.

M said she was looking forward to going, if that were the case.

"The trouble is," said Pop. "I only have Saturdays off."

"Yes, it's crowded weekends," Ira sympathized.

"I think I'll go there, and spend the whole day," said Pop.

"You'll have to, if you're going to see anything." Ira advised. "But I don't know whether your legs will hold out that long."

"As much as I'll see, I'll see. I know I won't see half of it. But I'll spend the day."

"Good," said Mom, in Yiddish. "Even two days. I won't miss you."

Pop's face darkened, but he made no reply.

"I'll be rid of you for a day," Mom pressed on. It seemed gratuitously cruel, so unnecessary—so unnecessary, and yet so ineluctably compulsive. Ira snapped at her in Yiddish. "Why do you have to say that!"

She laughed, and with flagrant mockery: "What did I say?"

"Oh, you're always starting these things. Why do you irritate him?"

"Ah, you're being a fool!"

"You don't have to torment him," Ira growled—and was glad M didn't understand. "Leave him alone."

"You're also a distraught one," Mom retorted. "The way he is, you are. He flares up at a single word. You flare up at a single word."

"Well, anyway, I think I'll spend a day there," Pop resumed. And to M: "Later in the season, we'll all go there together, hanh?"

"That would be nice," M calmly replied.

Talk turned to Ira's cousin Stella's house-warming party. Mom found fault with the spread; not too plentiful a showing, but she liked the rooms. Pop remarked that there were too many guests and it was too hot, so he had left early. Ira commented on Stella's loss of weight, that she had acquired a slimmer figure. Pop's face softened, and he chuckled. "Yes, she's getting a shapeleh," he said in Yinglish. "She took off eighteen pounds already. She's going to lose twenty more. She was too heavy."

"What did she weigh?"

"I think a hundred eighty pounds," he said. "She has big bones, like her father, Zal. He has big bones."

"It wasn't all diet, was it? I think she said something about injections."

"No, she gets a needle," said Pop.

"That's what I mean." And to M: "We're talking about a cousin of mine, Stella, whose house-warming party I went to."

"Yes," Pop waxed tender. "Dr. Weinberg used to give her a needle in the arm; but her arm got so sore, now he gives her a needle in her back—on her *tukhis*," he said to Ira in Yiddish, and smiled.

Said Mom satirically, "She's become his private secretary and bookkeeper."

"*Azoy?*" Ira made light of her remark.

"Ask him," she advised.

He didn't. But at such times awareness became too condensed for separation into components, streaks of implication barely distinguished: Of what Pop was and was up to, plied with glimpses of Mom's vengeful bale, her relentless spite—all crisscrossed by what these had instilled in Ira, of what he was.

Outside, the Gypsies were singing. Evidently sitting on the running boards of parked cars as well as on porch steps, they sang something Ira thought vaguely familiar, some currently popular song, but they sang it with typical throaty Gypsy quaver.

They got up from the table and went into the front room, where they sat and talked awhile. Pop wanted Mom to let the dishes go, but she insisted on doing them. "I must make my exercise," she said to M in English, and again both laughed. Everyone was thirsty, and Mom proposed they quench their thirst with seltzer water. Ira offered to fetch a pitcherful—but with little show of alacrity. No, she would go, said Mom, and Ira acquiesced. M looked at him in surprise. "My mother'll get more," he excused himself sheepishly. Pop said that seltzer left a bitter aftertaste in his mouth; so did ice cream. Ira recalled Saratoga Springs, the summer mornings only a year ago when M and he had driven from Yaddo in the Model A to the free sulfurous "seltzer" burbling in spurts out of the pipes of the public founts.

It came time for Ira and M to take their leave. At ease at last, Pop saw them to the outer gate. It was night. He shook hands with both of them, and told them to take care of themselves, and then watched as they walked to the streetlight on the corner. Ira thought of the tragedy of the immigrant experience in the New World, just as he had felt in the cafeteria talking to Max and Harry. Some kind of immense sacrifice—and for what and to what? Success. The only word that came to mind. Success. An immolation of self to success, to Mammon. One could hardly envisage the hideous, vast ritual of it. Not all the pyramids of skulls of Aztec victims could compare to the victims of success. Millions of immigrants from all over Europe streaming toward the ports where the ocean liners of the 1900s were berthed—Ira among them in Mom's arms—in eagerness, yes, Dante's eager hordes straining toward the boatman Charon. Jesus. Was it the Jews alone, who threw themselves forward with such abandon? No, of course not. It just seemed that way. The Scandinavians traveled out to the Dakotas, to the far West. The Nordics spread out, they took to the soil, they farmed, they homesteaded. Tradition, that was it: that was their tradition, extracting a living from the land. The Jews swarmed on that narrow limb of the East Side like migratory bees about their queen. That was their tradition, seeking success in business, commerce, trade, moneylending.

Back at M's room at about ten-thirty, it was the hour for Ira's departure—according to house rules, but he lingered. And presently, as he embraced her, they heard the landlord leave. He and his wife keep to a set schedule: he left at ten-thirty, and she returned for a final inspection and to spend the night at twelve-thirty or one. "He's gone," Ira said.

"I'm tired," said M.

"Are you? Then I better go." But she didn't want him to. She wished he could stay with her.

"Where?"

"On my couch." Someone else had stayed there one night, a woman friend. Irresolute, he tarried a little longer, and then decided to stay on. She said she was afraid of loving him so much.

Afterward, the landlady returned prematurely, and there was no way for him to slip out. "It seems so silly to have to do this," said M.

And Ira aphoristically: "It's better to do it, and be silly, than not do it."

And as he looked at her in the dark, through the swirling crepuscule of the city, in which light from somewhere was held in suspension like a restless sediment, her features wavered so that, though she slept, she appeared to be smiling. Brown swirling night made her tall, small-breasted figure like something carved out of speckled porphyry. He thought of his parents, of their abysmal unhappiness, which yet did not deter Ira from seeking love. Or was it because of their disastrous lives that he did seek love? He felt as if he had indeed found peace within himself. And hearing the passing of automobiles, of footsteps scraping on the pavement outside her open window, the accompanying crackle of voices, Ira thought as he lay beside her of Ulysses' exclamation in the Divine Comedy, of having reached the west through a hundred thousand perils.

It was a defiance of fate, really, to come away from such grievous unhappiness at his parents' home, and to reflect that it was within the realm of the possible to end that way—and without a shadow of a doubt to end old and doddering merely on account of living long enough—and yet to venture. But it was incomparably worse not to venture. Fortunately for him, Ira only seemed to have a choice; in actuality, if he meant to survive, he had none—or only one: M.

CHAPTER 19

"*I've got a job!*" *she* exclaimed.

"Don't tell me." Ira leaned over the table in mock-daze.

"Yes, it's playing for a dancing class," she said. "It's an hour a day."

"How many days?" Ira asked.

"It's one day a week."

"Oh, for Christ sake. One hour a day, one day a week. What do you get paid?"

"A dollar and a half an hour."

Later, Ira carried her bassoon to the subway station where she would take the train to Columbia for a course in orchestral instruments. About her job, she explained as they walked, the chief thing to commend it was that she had broken the ice: The hardest thing about embarking on any new line of work was to find that first opening, to make a beginning. Ira agreed. She was to play improvisations on the piano for her first dance class Monday.

This came on the heels of the rejection by *The New Yorker* of a story, "The Apostle," based on the street kids Ira had witnessed a few weeks earlier. Ira and M both felt rather downcast, and he was worried seeing her so troubled. He tried not to tell her about the rejection until after lunch, but as always she saw through his feeble attempts at dissembling. She asked whether he was feeling in low spirits, and Ira showed her the letter. Maxwell had written that the story was slight.

Before showing the letter to her, Ira had read it, of course. But not until he had walked over to the East River and watched the crews of men building the new highway that would skirt the eastern shore of Manhattan. The river between its Brooklyn and Manhattan banks stretched blue and languid upstream and down. A motor dory ferried the men to a pile driver, mounted on its huge scow, which floated amid clusters of newly driven piles. With a thud and a belch of steam, a black pile was driven into the water, alongside those previously driven, its protruding top forming another step in the multitude of dark stepping-stones lapped by the river. So the old East River waterfront was scheduled to disappear and, with it, all the picturesque, massively timbered docks that once projected into the river.

Ira remembered the old dock at the foot of Ninth Street. Of the very few occasions in early boyhood when he had felt at ease with Pop, one or two had been spent sitting with him on the dock in the late afternoon of midsummer, enjoying the fresh, briny breeze off the river, and studying the sinister whorls the rising tide made among the slimy green piles. *"Alles ändert sikh,"* said Mom.

Ira hadn't read the letter, but kept debating with himself what he would do—or rather he kept impressing on himself that contained in the letter was bad news and nothing but bad news, and thus prepare himself for the disappointment to follow. And follow it did, the words under the elegant *New Yorker* letterhead driven home with each thud of the nearby pile driver.

From the river, Ira took the long walk back to Fiftieth Street, tapping at M's window, this being his signal. And then ensued their shared disappointment—plus sliced bananas and canned milk for his luncheon, which she served him. She looked very stately in her pale-green figured wash dress of muslin, stately and girlish at the same time.

But then, not two weeks later, in the morning's mail, after returning from breakfast at M's, there was another letter, this time from Virginia N's office. It was signed by N's secretary, and read, "Mr. Maxwell of *The New Yorker* called this morning to say that he would like to buy your story 'Broker,' but that he would like to speak to you about some little changes. I therefore made an appointment for you to be there Monday morning some time after ten o'clock." Ira finished the rest of the note in that state of elation in which he could have cavorted about, whooping for joy.

Ira rushed over to M's room and, of course, perversely put on a forlorn countenance. He could see her stricken look out of the corner of his eye and, at her query, handed her the note. She cried out with joy, then wept, and clung to him.

"It isn't all sold yet," Ira warned.

"Let me read the note again," she pleaded.

He handed it to her.

"We won't say it's sold," she counseled wisely. "If we mention it at all, it will be only to show the letter."

"What about my coming to live in your room. I don't mean here. I mean when you go to board with Betty and John in that Twenty-third Street loft building?"

"I don't think they'd object. You're going to be my honey lamb always."

"I'll have to get off Home Relief, obviously, with a story in *The New Yorker*. What about our getting married?"

They babbled. Ira blew on her oboe in glee; it sounded like a steamboat round the bend, and he writhed in mirth. Then he left, predicting that neither of them would do any work the rest of the day.

Ira returned to his room and at once sat down and wrote a postcard to his sister so that she could tell Mom the good news, and then both might rejoice at his success. And getting up to go mail the card, Ira saw himself grinning exultantly in the mirror. "Well, you did it, you sonofabitch," he said to his image. And then he thought of all his friends and nonfriends, who would read the story in due time, Edith and Dalton, and others, and their response to it. He felt his damaged status salvaged to some degree.

That Monday morning brought nervous anticipation for Ira. Scheduled to be on location at eight-forty-five; M had already gone on her first session of performing terpsichorean improvisations on the piano. Sweating clammily under the armpits, Ira wondered how M was faring in her new capacity. She had had very little opportunity for practicing improvisations over the week, and yet she went off confident and unflustered; whereas Ira, in her place, having to give an account of himself in a novel situation, would be quaking.

The voices of children in the school playground on the corner came through his open window, and he paused, then gazed at the whitewashed rear wall of the apartment house across the yard, the striped orange awnings, the fine blue air above. A butterfly fluttered erratically by. His heart throbbed. The time was now five after ten. He had a Home Relief check to cash, and Maxwell to confer with. Ira's gray plaid jacket was in the dark closet. He thought of Mom, to whom he had yet to tell the good news in person—and to leave some of his laundry with. "Broker"—he'd have to translate the title for her into Yiddish: *Tserbrokhen*. That meant broken. Not quite the same thing. And sans misleading pun.

It was time to go.

He returned from the interview with Maxwell with instructions to devote a full page of exposition describing the scene of the mishap in greater detail: in which direction was the truck headed; the approximate rise in the crest of the hill; the load aboard; its general color and appearance; the features of the second cop; in short every element of the situation clearly presented. He worked at it most of the day, but still no satisfactory result. He thought he had better borrow the method M's father had recommended as the one he followed: Notify his subconscious of the fact that he had a problem for it to solve, and consult that same subconscious the next morning.

In the afternoon, as a break from the strain, and also in the hope of collecting some further data out of which he might fashion a sketch, Ira walked over to the Model Cafeteria, where he listened to, and participated in, a lively discussion on the subject of intermarriage. Said Max, "What's the matter? Aren't there enough Jewish girls for you? What have you felt in that one that's so special?"

"Oh, something," Ira testified.

"Yes?" Max became all eagerness.

But Rose intervened, upbraiding Ira first and concluding with the old standby: "At least you ought to make her Jewish."

"What difference would that make?" Ira asked.

"Your children would be Jewish. You'd be sure of good Jewish children."

"I'd like good, healthy children. I don't give a damn if they're Jewish."

"A goy," said Rose.

"You mean me?" Ira queried.

"You it goes without saying. I mean her. How do you know she won't have a goyish lover in secret?"

"How do I know that a Jewish girl wouldn't?"

"Hitler, may he be destroyed," said Max devoutly, "did the Jews one good service: He decreed that Jew and gentile should no longer mingle."

"A great thing," Ira scoffed. "In that case we ought to have a Hitler here."

"We don't need a Hitler," said Max. "All we ask is for the goyim to leave us alone."

"That's all they ask of us, too. In fact a lot of them wish we'd leave the country."

Rose spared them further increments of acrimony by shifting the conversation, while indulging herself in a corned beef sandwich, with a wedge of huckleberry pie to follow. After ingesting this, she locked her hands in front of her inordinate girth. "Zaida already knows," she said. "'You think I don't know what Ira is up to?' Zaida asked me. 'What?' I said. 'Don't pretend you don't know,' he said. 'What?' I said. 'Do I have to tell you whom Ira's going with?' he said. 'Who?' 'You always wash your hands of everything,' he said. 'I don't know what you're talking about.' 'He's going with a shiksa.' 'How should I know that?' I said. 'May I never live to see them married,' he said. 'Oh, till marriage,' I said. 'That's a small worry, Father.'"

Stella, Rose's daughter, who filled in at the cafeteria sometimes, chimed in from the cash register. "Oh, that old guy. He likes his misery."

"You antisemite," said Rose. "You're an antisemite from way back."

"Of course, he likes his misery," Stella clung to her thesis. "Listen, Ira, if you're sick, and you tell everybody about it, don't that mean you like your misery?"

"My daughter," said Rose. "May no harm overtake you, and may you enjoy a thousand blessings, but you never had any sympathy for anyone."

"Look, Ira," Stella persisted, "your uncle Gabe came here from St. Louis. When did he see Zaida last? In 1927. So the first thing Zaida begins to tell him is how lousy his grandchildren are, how lousy he feels, and how lousy life is. Now if you talk like that right away to someone who's nearly a stranger, it must mean you like it."

"You have no heart," said Rose. "And you're an antisemite

besides. Comes in an old Jew with a beard," Rose buttressed her argument for his benefit, "and what does Stella do? She wants to chase him out."

"No, I didn't. I gave him a penny, and that's enough," said Stella. "I should have all the Jewish panhandlers coming in here? Nothing doing. But she, my darling mother, right away she gives him a dime! Give him a dime? Why? Just because he's got whiskers? Let him work for a dime, like me."

Rose wagged her head as if she found refutation pointless. "Say what you will, at least I married off my two daughters to good Jewish men."

"And the only reason I started going with Lester was because I thought he was a goy," said Stella. "My poor Lester, before he could get married he had to take his pants down and show Papa he was circumcised, and show him his bar mitzvah certificate, and say a *barukha*."

"What does your mother say to this?" asked Rose.

"Haven't you talked to her?" Ira parried.

"No, I haven't. To me it would be anguish. And they say the girl's not even good-looking."

"I think she is. And goodhearted, too."

"They say she's not good-looking," Rose maintained.

"She is." Stella came to Ira's assistance. "She's the English type."

"You didn't see her," said Rose.

"I did," Stella lied. "She's as tall as Ira, and she's blond."

CHAPTER 20

The couple who drove them home after a party were to be married soon. He had a concave bend in his nose, she one of those startling, little gray swathes in her brown hair. At the party, M had engaged another of the guests, Fanny M, a woman lawyer acquaintance, in earnest and private dialogue. And now in the car, slack with food and drink, Ira asked M, "What was the big secret about?"

"You didn't really forget?"

"Yeah, I did forget. What?"

"I asked Fanny about marriage laws in New Jersey," M prompted.

"Oh, that's right. What did you find out?"

"She didn't know. Except that the costs were the same as here, and a blood test is also required there."

They mulled over the information for a few blocks as the car bowled along, and then Ira decided to ask the couple in the front seat, "Say, inasmuch as you contemplate matrimony in the near future, what's the minimum rate you can marry at?"

They laughed. "I really don't know what the minimum is," the woman said.

And her fiancé at the wheel added, "I know the license is two dollars. I think the marriage ceremony is two dollars, too."

"No, I think that's optional, dear," said the woman.

"No, I don't think it is," he disagreed. "Back a few years, the marriage clerk used to pocket the fee for performing the marriage. Now, I think the city makes the charge."

"What the hell, you're paying two bucks for a license to get married, why do you have to pay any more to get married?" Ira asked.

"Well, the license isn't the marriage," explained the woman, much amused.

"That's right, you've got to convert that into a marriage certificate," said her fiancé.

"Oh, I know what the other fee is for," said the woman. "It's for an engraved marriage certificate."

"It's not engraved, sweetheart," said the man. "It's more like citizenship papers."

"Anyway, that's very funny," Ira said. "You pay two dollars for a license to pay more money for a certificate."

"It can't be more than a couple of dollars or so," they both said soothingly.

"Well, I'll tell you," Ira said. "If it's optional, the clerk gets nothing. I need the money more than he does. However, I'd like to be prepared with enough funds to pay for the service."

"We thought we could get married for five dollars," said M.

"I think you can," said the man.

"When do you plan on doing it?" asked the woman.

"When shall we say?" asked M.

"Soon," Ira said.

"As soon as possible," said M.

But after three drinks of Black and White Scotch that night, smooth as honey, and a buffet supper of sliced turkey, smoked tongue, cheese, raw carrots, olives, potato salad, Ira awoke early and slightly crapulous. He felt as though he were slouching more and more, perhaps even putting on weight. He pondered, in his logy state, on the

wisdom of getting married; but when he thought of his obsessions—
and how they continued to haunt him in varying degrees, in season
and out—he realized marriage was the only right course, the only
sensible one. Apart from everything that her love had already done
for him, and there was no sense in trying to assess that kind of benefit, without M he might have wound up in a padded cell.

He walked over to the East River again before breakfast for the
sake of the view and the fresh breeze. To reconcile Ira's welcoming
of change, his welcoming of scientific and social advances, with the
regret felt at the displacement of the quaint and familiar, antiquated
by that selfsame change, created a division within the soul, and set
it at odds with itself. Charming, the bright sparkle of wavelets in
midriver against dingy, sprawling Brooklyn on the other side, domi-
nated by smokestacks. Inescapable, too, the yearning, the untenable
yearning to live on that little island in the stream where warning
bell and beacon were mounted, yearning for protected snugness. Ira's
greatest obstacle to growth probably was resistance to change, with
its concomitant strife, resistance to growth that drives the fetus from
the womb.

When he returned home, doubts dispelled, M surprised him with
the welcome news that the upper floor of John and Betty's penthouse
was free for them to live in. It would be tricky to move in together
in advance of their marriage without M's parents' finding out, but M
had decided it was worth the risk of familial opprobrium.

And so, early in the morning, a week later, Ira left his lodgings
at 351 East Fifty-first Street. A last glance about the tiny room where
he had sweltered so much of the summer, a last glance out the window at the brick stodginess of tenements in purdah of fire escapes
across the backyard, and again the dusty green walls and sparse furnishings of his room, the grayish curtains to which he had pinned so
many bedbugs as incriminating evidence to show his landlady. Then

down the creaking stairs with bags, cartons, and typewriter. He left the stuff in the foyer, and hailed a cab at the corner. The fare was sixty-five cents to Twenty-third Street. Ira felt a little as if he were leaving prison.

The night before, he had covered all his belongings with camphor against the chance of a bedbug tucked in among them; and on the way to the drugstore he encountered Mrs. Compirt, his landlady, and told her he was leaving. She complained about the short notice; she had turned away a woman that afternoon who was looking for a small room. Ira was sorry. He explained that his girlfriend and he had decided to get married. He mentioned that he had sold a story to a magazine called *The New Yorker*, and her daughter said that he should have stayed, because she had some life story to tell him.

To Betty and John's place, and the excitement of entering new surroundings, airy, inviting, unique, a penthouse on the seventeenth floor of a Twenty-third Street loft building. "You're prompt in getting here," John observed.

"I had a good reason." Ira looked about gratefully. There was M—fond and competent M—getting his breakfast.

"Boyoboy. I'll try to fit in," Ira promised.

"Now, don't eat too fast," M set the bowl of cornflakes in front of him.

"No." Ira could feel it was all so experimental, his being here, so tentative. He would try to behave, observe bounds, be inconspicuous, compatible; but knowing himself, his blunders, his surges of ego, his traits and tantrums, behaving satisfactorily, or acceptably, wouldn't be easy. He'd have to try. Keep calm, in check, be cheerful, be reasonable.

After breakfast, M showed him the room, a small one, but adequate, that he could use for his study. It was a spare room on the main floor, where kitchen and John's photographic studio adjoined, and it still lacked a table. They would canvass the secondhand furniture stores on Second Avenue for one the next day. Meantime, if he wanted to write—and Ira did, for a variety of reasons: to compose himself, to be out of the way, and also because he felt inspired to write—M suggested that he could repair to her music room upstairs. She had a card table there, beside the upright piano.

It was more than a music room. Upstairs—at the head of an internal flight of stairs—a wide balcony overhung the music studio where she composed and played. On the balcony was her bed; that would be theirs now. Ira climbed up the stairs for a quick look about: From the window, New York's midtown towers crowded together in a bid for sky. A door opened on the roof. Truly a penthouse, with an accessible sky, with a water tower on lofty piers rising from the roof. All that had seemed just so much pleasant and unlikely speculation a few months ago was now realized. He actually lived here. Ira lived with M in a penthouse.

And tonight he would share the same bed with M. It was no fantasy. Exhilarated, Ira sat down at the card table. He had been dissatisfied with the first draft of a sketch he was writing. But now it seemed to him that he could treat the same narrative in a greatly improved fashion by relieving it of its linear intensity, resorting to a kind of spiral approach. About two hours later, he had finished scribbling a rough draft. As he sat reveling in the aura of innovation, M knocked, and tall and gentle and fair, she stood in the doorway below. She hadn't had a chance to practice today. Would he mind if she warmed up her fingers on the piano for a few minutes?

"No, no, go ahead," Ira urged. "I'm only mulling things over."

It was bliss, just listening to her fingers strike crisp notes from the keyboard. Ira knew he would need that sound, that pianistic reassurance all his life. Maybe it was just fancy, but before the entire notion blurred in his mind and became nonsense, she and the scales she played raised a saving barrier between him and his obsessions, his *mishigoss*, or call it what you would—anxiety, neurosis, dybbuk. What a strange way, what a strange reason to love a woman.

For an hour or two before lunch M and Ira looked through the Bible for a suitable quotation for her cantata, *Chorus for Exiles*, which she intended to submit as her entry to the competition sponsored by a Jewish choral group in Cleveland. And they laughed at the many inappropriate ones they encountered. Finally they settled on a quotation that ran, "Why do you cry unto me? Tell the sons of Israel to go forward." Ira fell into fantasizing about M's cantata; trying to imagine what it would mean to old Zaida, if he photostatted the Hebrew originals, in order that he might read them while the oratorio was being performed. Afterward, Ira felt a sense of release, and spoke of feeling an accession of courage at the words "Tell the sons of Israel to go forward."

"How long do lovers go on loving each other?" M asked in reply.

Ira didn't know, but supposed as long as they both felt unconstrained with each other, felt free and happy and needed each other and could function. She sat across the table looking at him with her steady, soft eyes that he felt sure saw him for what he was, and unbeguiled, nevertheless accepted totally the joining of their lives.

Later came the emptying of satchels and M's trunk. Sorting, folding, tucking clothes in bureau and closet, they discussed marriage. Ira thought, since she had left the decision to him, that the best time to marry would be after her father and mother, who were due for a return visit in a week or two, would have come and gone, leaving them free to marry without parental encumbrance. They had a light snack for supper, and then returned to their room, talked about marriage again until bedtime. Betty was of the opinion, so M reported, that it might be more appropriate if they were married at exactly the time that Mother and Father were in New York. Ira didn't relish the idea much; he didn't think it concerned them. In fact, Betty annoyed him with her firm social-service approach: Both she and John, though younger than M, seemed to arrogate to themselves the role of mature counselors.

"Our marriage," Ira submitted with usual determination, "doesn't concern your parents any more than it concerns mine."

But M, always sensible, moderate, said she wished they could consider the subject free of spite and malice, because marrying after they left would seem like a slap in the face. Ira didn't think so, clung stubbornly to principle, and so the question remained open—until a brilliant solution struck him. Why not get married before they came? Not only would the marriage be a fait accompli, but the normalcy of Ira's relation here could be established that much earlier.

M smiled, tenderly, calmly, when he broached his proposal, and said, so simply that her words blunted the edge of his disappointment: "I don't think so, darling."

CHAPTER 21

The Ps were due Tuesday, and Monday evening Ira decamped for Frank Green's domicile, to spend his time there in conventionally unmarried state while they were here.

There was a great to-do about Ira's going off before the advent of the Ps. A driving autumn rain was falling, beating against the windows. Ira had already packed suit and work clothes in canvas bag and shopping bag, and was prepared to go. The rain beat ever harder against the panes. He was also suffering from a severe crick in the back, as a result perhaps of working at his writing without an extra layer of clothing on. M deplored his leaving: It would be just too mysterious to the elevator man, his going off into the night in the pouring rain. Ira complained about going off in the rain, too, but what other way was there of appearing to be properly separated?

Ira decided to get the rest of his clothing still at Edith's, because he might need more decent clothes to wear when engaged with the Ps. Frank's wife had died a year previously, and he had moved to the top floor of a four-flight tenement on East Second Street, not far from Greenwich Village. On Home Relief, he scratched out a precarious existence with sporadic, unreported carpentry. He had kept some of his wife Flo's belongings, in particular, her two adjustable draftsman's tables, on which she had drawn dress designs. The tilted, unmarred, flesh-colored surfaces seemed to look askance at the rest of Frank's messy, heterogeneous furnishings.

Frank complained of a headache and a sleepless night. Someone had climbed down the fire escape soon after he had gone to bed, which had made him wakeful, and the roof door had kept banging all night. His stomach was bad again, and he was unwilling to get out of bed—even when Ira told him that he was going to Edith's to get his clothes, and if he wanted that gray suit Ira had promised him he'd better come along. However, when Ira told him Edith and Dalton were married, he sat bolt upright and got out of bed. Frank smiled speculatively and wiped errant strands of tobacco from the corners of his lips. He looked so much like James Joyce: gray mustache, eyeglasses, distinguished and sensitive features. Irishmen both. "Well," he said sympathetically as he pulled on his clothes, "you've burned all your bridges behind you."

"Yes. I felt a wall go up forever when Doris told me she was married."

"You've burned all your bridges behind you, and you've burned all your boats, too. You'll have to face life on your own now. It's life for you now," said Frank.

"What they call the struggle," Ira tried to make Bill's oft-repeated shibboleth sound facetious.

"It certainly is," said Frank. "And you know, Ira, I had the idea you two would get together again sometime in a few months."

Ira laughed at his fond hope. "No, I knew I wouldn't. Oh, I came close enough—when I was flat broke in LA. But it seemed something else in me wanted to survive more than I did."

"Well, it's just a kind of business arrangement, that marriage of theirs. There's no telling. It may not last at all."

"I think it will."

248

"No, he's too much of a businessman for her. A lawyer and a businessman."

"He was there all the time I was."

"Oh. He was?"

"Yeah. Ménage à trois is the French name for it."

"I still don't think their marriage will last. Well, anyway, you're facing life on your own now," said Frank. "It'll make a great writer of you."

Ira shook his head. "Unmake, you mean."

"Yes it will. You're having to go through life again." Frank rummaged through a sprawling pile of back numbers of Irish periodicals on the washtubs, and pulled out a large, paper shopping bag, the kind with fiber handles. They took that along, and walked over to Edith's.

"The trouble with you was you let yourself get mixed up with a man who'd lost his balance," Frank chewed reflectively on a bit of cigarette stub as they crossed Washington Square Park. "I've always noticed that those people who've lost an arm or a leg—or a hand, the way Bill did—become unbalanced. They lose their natural balance."

"You think so?" Through foliage on the right Ira could glimpse the off-white wall of the main building of NYU, where Edith taught. "I know this: He domineered the hell out of me, and I let him." Students brushed by carrying briefcases, women pushed prams, kids rollicked, pigeons strutted, a squirrel clung to the bark of a tree. Washington Square Park with its literati—fake or genuine, one couldn't tell—dilettantes, poetasters in seedy attire posing on green park benches. Ira remembered his enchantment when first viewing the scene, in high school. How utterly intriguing once, to behold real bohemians flouting convention. Old stuff now. "I've missed the boat, Frank, that's all."

"You have not."

"I have, too. I'm thirty-three years old."

"What's that!" His face turned pink with restrained mirth, as though he were laughing at a juvenile. "Wait till you're fifty-three and the contractor turns you away because you'll drive up the insurance premiums. And me with a seven-year apprenticeship served on the other side. Thirty-three! You've got all God's time before you."

They came out from under the leaves of the large trees at the northwest corner of the park, the corner of MacDougal Street and Waverly Place. Directly ahead reared the utilitarian, high-rise apartment house, like a block of masonry. Diagonally across MacDougal Street, on Waverly Place, stood the Hotel Earle, typical gray stone, glass doors. Several houses to the west, in midblock, after the outdoor staircases of the brownstones, there jutted out the marquee of the remodeled apartment house where Ira had last lived with Edith—until last year—yes, last September. The rooms weren't very gracious, she said; it was chiefly their proximity to the university that recommended them. Even so, because of her slight frame, it was all she could do to cross the park safely before the brunt of a wintry blast.

Ira was reluctant to go in, but with Frank along—and promised Ira's gray suit—retreat was no longer possible; he had no alternative but to go in. Ira had telephoned Edith before he went to Frank's, and received an invitation to call, her voice on the phone cheerful and brightly forced. He gave Frank his hybrid topcoat-raincoat to hold, the one he had promised to treat with linseed oil, but, characteristically, hadn't got around to doing it. Telling Frank to wait, Ira rang the bell and went in. The entrance was warm and carpeted, the doorway white, the woodwork white, the walls green—and all of it charged with estrangement and farewell. Her door on the third floor was open, and before Ira saw her, he noticed in the mirrored foyer a heap of garments: his shorts, polo shirts, neckties, dress shirts, the gray suit promised to Frank, socks, slacks. Edith appeared, smiling in greeting, her olive skin bright, and looking very trim and slim and dainty in a plaid skirt. The plaid was small, almost like the checks of an old-fashioned apron, and of a pink hue; above it she wore a pink sweater.

"I keep running out of underwear," Ira fumbled. "I thought I might as well clear out everything I owned."

"Yes, of course," she said. "I don't know whether I have it all."

"I took one huarache along with me. And I apparently left one. I wonder if it's still here?"

"I'll look in the closet," she said. And she went and fetched it. "Did you bring a valise?"

"No. I brought this." Ira displayed the paper shopping bag.

"You can't get it all in that, can you?"

"I'll wrap up what's left in the bathrobe. Tie it up in the monk's cord, I guess."

And it was fortunate that there was something to do at a moment like this, something to occupy one, clothes like relics to gather up, to stuff together in a shopping bag. The hem of her skirt hung down into the upper periphery of Ira's vision, as he kneeled to cram things into the shopping bag. Garments that remained he piled up in the middle of the bathrobe, knotted the rope, and by main force was able to knot sleeves and corners together like an immigrant's pack or an old-clothes buyer. Sweating, and with the gray suit over his arm, Ira rose to his feet.

"Can you manage it all?" she asked.

"Yes, Frank Green is down in the street ambling around. He'll help me."

"Oh. Why didn't you ask him up?"

"It didn't seem appropriate."

With solemn, protrusive, brown eyes, she appraised herself in the mirror, as was her wont. "Dalton and I have been married. Or don't you know it?" She said.

"No," Ira lied. He had asked Frank's advice on what to do when she told him she was married, whether to say that he already knew or not. "No," said Frank. "Pretend you know nothing about it—and look shocked." Frank mimed how to look shocked: His lower lip dropped below his carious and scraggly teeth, and his nose all but fell into his mouth. "Look shocked," he repeated, and say, "Oh!" He paused. "And then say, 'From the bottom of my heart, I wish you all the happiness in the world.'"

"Oh, for Christ sake!" Ira had sneered at him. "Here he comes with his flowery prose. No, I'll say, 'I wish you all the happiness that you missed with me.'"

"Oh, no, don't say that!" Frank winced. "That's too bloody prepared."

"Well, to hell with it," Ira had snapped. "I'll say whatever seems, right to say when I'm saying it."

"Didn't you know? Really?" she asked.

"No," Ira said. And it seemed that having been told by someone else didn't matter as much as her telling him. Ira put out his hand, and she held out hers, gave him stiff, tiny fingers to grasp, which when he kissed them, relaxed, and she sniffed. "I hope it goes well," Ira said.

"It may, if we both use some sense. Dalton hasn't told his family yet. We'll be leaving on a quasi-honeymoon, probably for the beach."

"Oh, yes."

"Apparently Doris still hasn't been able to locate you. Or you would have known."

"No, I'm staying at a Mills Hotel."

Ira complimented her on looking so well. She admitted to feeling well. They had gone on a motor trip to Virginia, and there had decided. Ira nodded comprehendingly. And while he stood with his bundles in the doorway, she told him that Bea had written from LA that she was seriously worried about Bill. He was surly, ugly; his rages were almost maniacal. She thought the beating Bill had received at the hands of the police during the anti-Franco demonstration had had a more serious effect on him than anyone realized. She feared for both his ulcer and his mind.

"He may be going through some kind of mental crisis," Ira ventured.

"You think so? Why?"

"It's just a hunch. Because I have, he may. He feels the Party treated him shabbily."

She shook her head, without removing her protrusive brown gaze from his face.

And Ira took his leave.

"Fare you well, for ill fare I." A. E. Housman's words came to mind again when Ira thought of Edith on his way home, of her brief, touching flurry of tears after he had wished her happiness in her new marriage. And he shook his head at himself, at the spectacle of a man thirty-three years of age, without a vestige of economic independence, or even the necessary faith in his aptitude or ability to achieve it, or the self-confidence that comes with having done so for a while, at least once in his life. Nothing. Only a colossal diffidence and uncertainty.

Back home, the evening meal finished and the dishes washed, Ira listened to M play the fourth movement of her *Chorus for Exiles* as transcribed for the piano. It was very exciting, but seemed to him too short. Uncertain, and on unfamiliar grounds, he ventured to express his opinion.

To his surprise, she shared it. "Yes, the piece is too short," she said. "It needs much more development. It's something I'll have to overcome, this tendency to curtail."

Her long frame, her slack, pianist's wrists crossed in the lap of her brown dress, her shadowy blond hair—she looked beautiful seated on the piano stool, her back to the dark upright.

"There are only two things I want," she said. "To marry you, and write music."

CHAPTER 22

Ira spent the night with M and went off to work in the morning. Then after work, back to Frank's, where he changed clothes, put on his best front in preparation for seeing the Ps, and hurried to Betty and John's apartment, only to learn that Father and Mother weren't coming for dinner that evening, but might drop in later instead.

"Oh, I have so much news!" M said excitedly. (He hoped it might be that one of his stories had been accepted, but no.) "I don't know where to begin." Luminous with animation, she separated lettuce leaves into the salad bowl. "Shall I begin at the high point?"

"You'd better finish getting the meal ready," Ira suggested. "Is it bad news?"

"No, not exactly."

"Well, I'm sure it can keep."

After she set the table and waited for John to finish work in his studio, she told him that Mother had asked her, "M, what do you expect to do? What do you expect to live on?"

"Why, Mother," said M, prefacing her answer parenthetically that this was exactly the chance she had been waiting for to bring up the subject, "I expect to get married." Mother continued to talk about other things, almost as if she hadn't understood, and then said, "When?"

"In a week or two."

"Well, why not get married while we're here?" said Mother. It would have been too much like a slap in the face to have refused, so M acquiesced, pending Ira's agreement.

Then Mother took M out to the best women's stores, and bought her a set of apparel: a pair of brown shoes, suede uppers trimmed with cordovan leather; a bluish-green dress of corduroy that looked like velvet and, like velvet, changed the color of its shimmer in lamplight or daylight; silk stockings, underthings. What did Ira think? He confessed that he felt rather chagrined that what he had sought to avoid had come to pass. But, as M said, to refuse would have been a deliberate, uncouth affront. So after a minute or two of silence, while her soft brown eyes pleaded with him, and he strove to regain composure, he agreed. Principle would have to suffer suspension for a higher cause.

Still, he couldn't help twitting her about her feminine duplicity, under guise of innocent coincidence, and especially at Mother's suggestion that they get married by the renowned Reverend Fosdick, popular radio person. Ira seized a lock of her dark blond hair and said, "Nothing doing. You've got to become kosher."

Later, after supper, in came Mr. and Mrs. P, and Mother asked at once what Ira thought of her proposal. "Oh, just grand!" he commended.

"I have another idea. Do you know a Reform rabbi?" Father asked.

"I don't. Sorry, I don't know any rabbis." And then a counter-idea, or rather, a squelcher occurred to him: M would have to become a Jewess, would have to convert, Ira declared. Mother didn't think so. Ira wasn't really sure how relaxed the tenets of Reform Judaism were. He had never given the matter a thought; maybe a Reform rabbi would marry them without M's having to profess Judaism. He suspected not.

The next morning, after a shorter night's sleep than usual, Betty and John, M and Ira all went down the elevator, got into the Ps' automobile at the curb, and were driven by Father downtown to the Marriage Bureau. Everyone remarked on the beauty of the day: how crisp and limpid it was, October's bright blue weather.

They drove through Mott Street on the way, Chinatown, and both Father and Mother reminisced about the missionary work they had engaged in many years ago among the Chinese. The little Oriental kids in the street, Mrs. P thought, were cunning, and proclaimed in her light, high, cheery voice that the Chinese children didn't have birthdays, but became a year older on the Chinese New Year's Day.

M and Ira were dropped off in front of the Municipal Building, and climbed up to the Marriage Bureau, where they found seats. Next to them sat another couple, and they turned and asked, "Is this the right place?"

"If this is the place you want, it's the right place," Ira chortled flightily. "We're getting married."

A few minutes later, Betty and John and the Ps joined them. The Marriage Bureau waiting room was a large, white-painted, boxlike chamber whose high windows let in ample sunlight on the many benches arrayed between entrance and chapel. In the chapel, sansevierias and potted plants could be seen behind the glass set in the oak door, and above the plants a patch of ceiling covered with painted garlands. They were about a half hour or more waiting. Father became restless; he wished he could get out for a few minutes. Then their names were announced, and they were called to a desk in the rear of the room and asked to register. The Ps signed the document as witnesses. The clerk asked them to pay the two-dollar fee— and couldn't change the ten-dollar bill that Father first proffered. The man had a deep, growly, bureaucratic voice, but Father's was a match. The transaction was completed. The couple who had been sitting beside them was called into the chapel, and then, at last, Ira and M were summoned. The clerk there, whatever his official title, blotchy complexioned and puffy, went into his spiel. He began with typical New York Irish-American speech, but after looking over the Ps, shifted to an unctuous, anglicized intonation that gave the rite a phony, pious, and slightly ominous tone. Ira had to smirk, though, at the disconcerted stare with which he viewed the Navajo ring (Edith's gift to Ira), which Ira tendered as token of holy wedlock.

They were pronounced man and wife. Father tendered the clerk a five-dollar note, and they left. Betty departed for the office, while John remained. Driven in the Studebaker to the Gramercy Hotel, they had a wedding breakfast, courtesy of the Ps. It would be memorable always: calves liver and bacon. They discussed Steinbeck's Grapes of Wrath, which Ira hadn't read. Mother thought it was a terrible book, and Father that it was much exaggerated. John countered by pointing out that agricultural commissions had found that the conditions portrayed in the book were true.

"Yes, but not in the sense Steinbeck portrays them," said Father.

"Why can't writers write of beautiful things?" Mother asked. For a writer, one with middle-class background, brought up in the midst of such attitudes, and once loyal to his origins, it must be a harrowing experience to have to reject his former allegiances as false and hollow. The world must seem then desolate and forsaken: sterile. For minds outcast in this way, few options were open, among them the obvious one of silence—or religion.

John said he thought the struggle of Steinbeck's characters to retain their family ties was beautiful in its way.

Mother conceded it was, but there was so much else in the world that was beautiful. She had seen so many beautiful things. Why didn't writers draw upon those? Could Ira explain? She turned to Ira. "You're so quiet."

"Well, in the first place," Ira said, "beautiful things as you regard them are things that have been done. They're the creations of others. We try not to imitate—if we're any good."

"There seems to me plenty of room for originality in depicting the life of the man of sound character," said Father. "I mean the forward-looking, community-building, dedicated type of American citizen."

"Undoubtedly, and I know other people who think so," Ira replied. "But I'm sorry, Father, he's at the opposite pole of the life of many of us who write. We were brought up on the seamy side. We were drug up," Ira palliated by way of the facetious. "And we write about what we know. Unfortunately, I'm not too well acquainted with the community-building type you just cited."

"Doesn't any writer know anything about the millions of service-minded individuals in the country? Aren't writers interested in character building at all?"

"I don't know where they are."

Evidently he didn't either, for he made no comment. Ira felt like a renegade, a backbiter, his mouth stuffed with muffin, delicious calves liver and bacon—of Father's providing.

Mother spoke up, as though she were taking possession of the baton in a relay. "I've made inquiries about your book, but no bookstore carries it."

"No, it's long since out of print. That means they no longer publish it," Ira was glad to elaborate. If the Ps ever read it, with its smut and vile language, he'd be sunk.

"Is that because publishers no longer think it's profitable to print it?"

"I imagine so."

"And is the seamy side of America, as you called it, all that interests you still? Do you think you'll ever find what Father was talking about, the constructive side of America, worth writing about? Doesn't the cloud have any silver lining?"

M sat gazing at him. Too much, too much, Ira thought. What a huge burden, that trust, but he wouldn't have it less. He needed all of it. "A little, uh—" Ira felt a strong desire to scratch under his eyeglasses. "A little silver lining."

"Well, perhaps you ought to turn your attention to that in your writing. Don't you think that would be a good turn to take in the future?"

"It might. There's no telling."

The wedding breakfast over, John took his leave. Father asked the doorman to admit them to the flowery privacy of nearby Gramercy Park, so he could take moving pictures. Nursemaids watched, and little kids drove by on their tricycles.

After the movies were taken, they were to be driven back to the apartment on Twenty-third Street. With M seated in the car, Mother and Ira standing outside, next to the vehicle, they waited for Father, waited amid the greenery of Gramercy Park all about, the children gamboling in the paved lanes where their nannies sat on green park benches, and all ensconced within the fine town houses surrounding the park, under immaculate azure, in the pristine air of October that gave one a sense, not of youth, but of the days just beyond, just past youth—and at the outset of a new venture in life. Striding strongly, Father came up, a bulbous-nosed, imposing, solid man, both bald and gray, his heavy shell-briar pipe clenched between his teeth.

"Here comes the sweetest man in the world," said Mother.

"He's certainly got a man-sized pipe," Ira said.

In remembering this scene, this mix of elation and discomfort that the wedding and the presence of the Ps evoked, Ira flashed forward to the eventual, decisive dissolution of his bonds with these new relatives, a dissolution for which Ira was much to blame.

It happened while Ira and M were visiting the Ps' seaside cottage in Buzzard's Bay, near Cape Cod. How aureate M had looked when they alighted from the train—aureate, shining, her fair hair bleached golden by the sun.

Ira had dug soft-shell clams in the morning, those clams the Ps had taught him about a few years earlier, and with the tide low, he had garnered the better part of a bucketful. Ira had let them sift out the sand from their digestive tract by several changes of sea water. And then, alone for a while, and overcome with a desire to consume them, after steaming them, he did so. O feckless *fresser*.

Came dinnertime, and where was Ira? He wasn't hungry. And in addition, he wouldn't sit at the table. What a wild ass. The elders were insistent. So was Ira. He wasn't hungry. Why should I sit at the table? Then Mother confronted him: If he wasn't willing to abide by their rules, or the rules of their hospitality—and would not come down and sit with them at the table during dinner—then he wasn't welcome to stay in their home. She was severe about it, taut and severe. Said Ira, trapped by himself as usual, consistent as ever to his own detriment, trapped by the logic of self-assertion: Well, in that case he would leave. Humiliated to some extent, impenitent still, but rueful at the unforeseen and disagreeable consequences, Ira went into the bedroom, opened his satchel and began tossing possessions into it. And so he left—that very day, parted from his fondly smiling wife, and grabbed the nearby train back to Boston, from there to New York. How radiant she had been when Ira had arrived, and doting and radiant still when he left. The act was one of the most boorish Ira was ever guilty of. He thought of Joyce, and of his stormy, unbending, agonized refusal to accede to his dying mother's plea that he kneel in bedside prayer for her sake. Tandem idiots—to refuse to comply by a meaningless gesture to a meaningless request, especially when some little kindness could be accorded by doing so, something worthwhile: like comforting a dying mother, like enabling M to preserve her ties with her family.

Father lived only a year longer—felled by a stroke. Mother on the other hand passed through the gates of ninety, and might have reached a century plus, except that in order to get a cigarette, she tried to climb over the rails of the hospital bed, fell, broke her hip, and succumbed to hyperstatic pneumonia. Meanwhile, she had played the stock market so shrewdly she left her heirs, including, it was decided, M, about fifty thousand dollars apiece. She lived out her years in Florida in a co-op called Shipahoy, whither M went to visit her yearly, leaving Ira to develop neurotic symptoms while she was gone.

But all this was in the future, the long filament of years spooling out in front of M and Ira on their wedding day. Time collapsed back on Ira, left him solidly in this happy moment. Ferried back to their apartment, M and Ira waited for the grocery boy to bring the staples for the night's supper, and after he delivered them, they ate quickly and lay down on their bed. Now that they were married, Ira tried, but couldn't get the concrete feeling of what it meant. He was too numb perhaps, auto-lethargic. He related the old joke about their marriage being like the first of the three questions asked on Passover feast. Why was this night different from all other nights? Why had they spoiled their nuptials by being so previous? They had deprived themselves of the joy of Ira's faunlike chasing her through the apartment and out on the penthouse roof. So there was a fallacy, Ira babbled away, citing the Gold Medal Flour ad that declared, Eventually, why not now? Trotsky was guilty of the same mistake also, when he called for world revolution now, instead of revolution in one country. . . . She put her arm around him to quiet his disjointed babbling, and they fell asleep.

PART FOUR

....

Albuquerque

EPILOGUE

As he sat in his study, in his mobile home, this gray day of downpour was so heavy that the Sandias to the east were blotted out by rain and mist, and rivulets streamed down the windowpanes, pools formed in the graveled yards, rain drubbed the metal roof, and flurries pattered against the aluminum walls.

So much went through the mind of this chronically ill old man whom he had become, this creature with rheumatoid arthritis, for whom every night was an ordeal, death staved off only because of one who was so devoted to him, unselfish and constant, so intelligent and cheerful, and in her way dependent on him—who would have believed it? Love and obligation were stronger than the allure of oblivion. But it was over now.

He made and ate breakfast, left the kitchen, and passed his wife's Baldwin piano, its satiny black sheen concealed in part by the ornate paisley shawl draped over it. His wife's photograph rested on a near corner of the shawl. Her lenient gaze followed him as he entered the long passageway to his study. I'll light a candle in her memory tonight, he thought. Crossing the study with its computer and its shelves of books, the words throbbed in his mind with a bleak dolor. He had lost his soul's treasure, or his sole treasure. Either word would do. And whether she was remembered or forgotten could make no difference to her now, could have no meaning for her now. Only the living were amenable to meaning, and she no longer was.

Oh, *difficile est longum subito deponere amorem!* Difficult, indeed, to give up a long love so suddenly.

Pondering, he gazed out of the window. Was that the end of the matter? A quote out of Catullus, like an elegant buffer against the loss of the extraordinary woman whose husband he had been for fifty years? Or was there any deeper meaning to her death that he could discern? He doubted it. He wasn't given to abstractions, to subtle reasoning, to generalizations. Narrative was his only forte, if he had any at all. Interesting though: the word *amorem*—love—could be replaced by the word *odium*—hate—and the statement would lose none of its validity. *Difficile est longum subito deponere odium* was as valid. It was as difficult to get over long hate as it was long love. Then what? *Difficile est*, the poet had written . . . Difficult, yes, but . . . not impossible . . . Not impossible . . . There was hope.

It took out some of the unspeakable sting of recurring existence. That was what those long weeks of her becoming daily more emaciated signified: there was hope. Daily more emaciated, and her lucid, clement mind deteriorating, capable of only a senseless babble, and all because no remedy had yet been found to relieve her of the congestive heart failure from which she had suffered, no remedy that would enable her weakening heart to pump enough blood to body and brain to keep her alive and oriented. Still, there was hope. If *amorem* prevailed over *odium*. His thought seemed to contract into an essence: the scarcely remembered biblical tale of the riddle Samson put to the Philistines. "Out of the strong cometh forth sweetness." Out of the carcass of a lion Samson had slain, he had extracted honey from a hive the bees had built there, honey that he fed to others. So there was hope. *Ahz vey iz mir.* Grief suddenly shook him like a spasm. Oh, woe is me, woe is me, my lost beloved: There was hope.

It was in early January, a few weeks before Ira's birthday, that the ambulance came to take M to the hospital; it was in early February, a day after his birthday, that she died.

A week or two before she was taken to the hospital, she had completed, with immense exertion, immense travail, her last piece of work, a composition for the piano. She would get out of bed at irregular intervals, go to the desk in her little office in a bright corner of the living room, whose window looked to the east, sit down, trailing her plastic oxygen-supplying tubes, and write a few measures, and then painfully make her way back to bed. It must have taken the ultimate in willpower, and—who could say?—her last reserves of vitality. The artist ever, her and Ira's bond, bond of two such divers human beings, holding fast against his fits of raging and ranting, the uncontrollable frenzies in his nature. Ira reflected for a moment on that idea, and then was inclined to deny it; in fact, it became patently untenable to him. The artist in them had the power to tear them apart, as he had seen it do with other married couples. No, it was rather her determination to preserve their marriage that kept it intact, her resolution to subordinate her own art to the needs of spouse and family, to steady her neurotic, frustrated spouse and wholesomely rear their two sons.

"Why, hon," Ira once asked her, "did you always meet my nutty eruptions with such calmness and patience? Did you know I'd come to, finally, come crawling back to apologize?"

"Only in part, darling. I was not going to give my mother the satisfaction of coming back home to her. I wasn't going to appeal to her for help. I wasn't going to prove she was right."

"Is that it?" What good fortune to someone as undeserving as Ira to have been the husband of that superb spirit. He had watched her a moment longer. And all at once, before she dropped her hand, Ira had realized that she had brought into a single focus many of the features of her appearance that made her outwardly what she was: the aging, distinguished face, her gentle brown eyes, the fine, swelling—and now striated—brow, the hair that in younger days he had seen the Cape Cod sun burnish into golden radiance, that was now streaked lackluster with gray. Her once pretty teeth looked irregular and fragile when she laughed, and her bony pianist's hand hung down lankly from her wrist.

The night she went to the hospital, they were expecting visitors, and M had gotten out of bed to spruce up a bit. And so she set out to do. But part way to the living room her strength had failed her, and without calling for Ira at the other end of the trailer where he sat riveted to his word processor, she dropped to her knees, and began crawling toward the living room. Her reason, as she explained shortly afterward, was to get herself there on her knees, and then pull herself up on a chair. But once there, she found herself unable to get up. Ira called an ambulance, and they waited. It was night now. Deep darkness at the window perforated by the simulated trailer court coach lights out front. The minutes went by, leaden and despairing.

The ambulance rolled up so quietly that they didn't hear it. They knew it had arrived only when the doorbell rang. Two men entered, one middle-aged, large, close-cropped, the other still in his twenties, Hispanic, lean, both serious in demeanor. The older man took M's pulse and blood pressure, and then became even more serious, his bearing more important, professionally grave, almost more than his position warranted. The younger man stood by. Very little was said. Was Ira her husband? Did he have their insurance number? It was on the card.

They went out, brought in a stretcher—dropped its landing-gear type of wheels. Speaking quietly, they changed M's oxygen tube to one of theirs. They helped M out of her chair, helped her onto the stretcher, and after covering her with a couple of blankets, buckled her to the stretcher with several straps, then rolled her to the door, maneuvered the conveyance efficiently through it, and out and down the steps.

As if present at some kind of solemn rite, Ira watched mutely. He had an urge to follow them, to see the last stages of her departure, her disappearance. With a mechanical "You don't mind if I just step out," Ira shuffled through the lightweight front door and came out on the small homemade front porch. The air was still, for January, moderate in temperature. Illuminated by one of the coach lights, M lay on her stretcher close to the ground at the rear of the ambulance. The open doors of the ambulance, the senior attendant entering some last data on a page of his clipboard, M lying motionless on her stretcher—especially M lying in seeming tranquillity on her stretcher—all aroused in Ira a powerful urge to take a snapshot, a photo. He was anything but a shutterbug; he rarely thought of taking pictures. Ira had two inexpensive cameras—was there time to hurry back into the house, grab one or the other of the cheapies, and return before M was hoisted into the ambulance? Ira doubted it. Then hang on to the railing, and get down the stairs, he thought. Get to the stretcher as quickly as you can, say, "How're you feeling, darling?" Say, "Good-bye, honey; hope you'll be all right. See you at the hospital first thing tomorrow." No, he would see her tomorrow. What was the point of saying so? Just something momentous about the scene, something fateful: his wife on the ground there, the white-coated attendants, coach lights, night, other lighted trailer windows across the paved road. But more than that—a sense of finality, brooding dread, augury. Would he ever see her back here again? That was it. Would she ever return?

They raised the undercarriage to the level of the ambulance

door, and rolled her in. The younger man lifted her oxygen tank and stowed it in after her. He stepped up and shut the doors behind him. The older man got into the driver's seat, started the engine, and turned the headlights on. He backed the vehicle the short distance to the interior corner of the court, his intent face unwavering in concentration on his rearview mirrors; he backed the ambulance just far enough around so that he could straighten his front wheels in alignment with the gate. Before he drove forward out of sight, Ira caught a glimpse of the word *AMBULANCE* spelled backward on the vehicle's front.

The next weeks were spent at a nursing home. She writhed at times when Ira visited her, when he sat quietly gazing at her. She writhed as if more in impatience than in intense pain, almost completely baring her emaciated body up to her diapers, careless of unwitting immodesty, beyond it, probably unaware of it. He would pull her hospital gown over thighs as fleshless as those of liberated Nazi death camp inmates, a shank bone covered by skin. His wife of fifty years, his M. And yet when he asked her in moments of coherence, whether she was suffering, was in pain, her answer was invariably in the negative—even as she writhed. Then what was it, Ira wondered, that caused her to react as if she were suffering, and suffering so intensely? Dying, he supposed.

A month later, near midnight, after Ira had gone to bed, M's doctor, Dr. Collins, telephoned. He had brought in a specialist to examine M at the nursing home: In his opinion, her condition was very grave. He didn't think she had much longer to live.

"As bad as that?"

"I'm afraid so, Ira. I thought I ought to let you know."

"Thanks. I appreciate it."

"I'm sorry."

"Well, I'm not surprised, Dr. Collins."

"We did all we could. We do that for any patient. But M was special. You understand?"

"Only too well. Thanks again, Doctor."

"Good night."

"Good night."

Ira lay back in bed, aware that he had broken out in perspiration. On other nights Ira had broken out in perspiration the same way as now, assailed by the dread thought that he was going to lose her; this time he really was. His M, unutterably precious M, part of him, intertwined, interwoven, intermingled, inter, inter, inter—torn out of him, ripped out as out of his tissue, his synapses.

His thoughts raced ahead of him, and then doubled back: Hey, pal, get your ass out of bed and hie you to ye Horizon Nursing Home, and watch her expire. As any devoted husband would. You ain't devoted, you prick. Oh, yes, I am. I'm too crippled to drive. Bullshit. You've been driving weekends. And every afternoon when you wanted to. Had to learn again after how many years when she did the driving. Sure it was scary, your taking the wheel. But like swimming, you never forget. After damn near sixty years. Well?

Well? Hell, no. Watch a comatose woman breathe her last? What good would you do? Go to sleep, will you? Sleep, it is a gentle thing, beloved from pole to pole. That's Coleridge, ain't it? Shakespeare says something about the drowsy cabin boy high up in the crow's nest. Macbeth shall sleep no more. Thane of Cawdor, he. The Bible says something about sleep. Purty sure. A little sleep, a little folding of the hands to sleep. Anything in Greek? Yeah, Prometheus riveted to a rock up in the Caucuses, burned by the sun, and frozen. That's right, isn't it? Aw, shut up. My wife of fifty years is dying, my wife is dying. . . . And I thought it would be the other way. She was sensible, so moderate. What did she want for our fiftieth anniversary? A quiet little picnic in the woods. In the Sandias, in October.

But strangely, Ira slept until morning, longer than usual. At about eight-thirty, the phone rang. Ira recognized the voice of the gorgon, Horizon's chief nurse, at the other end.

"Mr. Stigman?"

"Yes, ma'am." Ira braced for the dire message.

"This is Delia, I'm the nurse at Horizon."

"Yes."

"We've been trying to get you since five this morning."

"Is that so?"

"No one answered. I'm sorry to tell you, Mr. Stigman, your wife passed away at about 4:30 A.M. She passed away very peacefully."

"She did?" They all said that, Ira bet.

"Yes. What funeral home do you want us to call, Mr. Stigman?"

"None. Call Dr. Collins. My wife donated her body to medical science."

"Oh, we'll call Dr. Collins, and tell him she's deceased. He'll have her body taken to a mortuary?"

"I expect so. Or a morgue at UNM. That's the arrangement."

"I'll do that."

"Thank you."

Weird. The damned receiving device had blocked out her call at five in the morning, had let Ira sleep: allowed the doctor's call to get through at midnight, but nipped Delia's a few hours later. Ira thought the device was uncanny; it didn't want him to know.

"And leaves the world to darkness and to me." Ira thought of the lines from Thomas Gray. The evening before had been his birthday: the eighty-fourth. She was three years younger than he was, but only during the short period between February and April; then she caught up a year. The same thing was true of Edith. Her birthdays fell on January—and how she hated them. All that was irrelevant.

He had run out of steam; he had begun to feel jaded, depleted of his creative work. Nor could further particulars of the experience be recalled any longer, after this half century and more, especially since the particulars themselves were so obscured and clouded by the continual anxiety that beset him at the time, anxiety, apprehension, vacillation, almost literally like a drifting mist passing between him and events. So the skimpy record would have to do, dissatisfied though he might feel with these mere tokens of the spiritual upheaval he was going through at the time. The few relics that survived, that were extant, would have to do. I am Merlin, and I am dying, said Tennyson in his old age. What else was left for him to do?

Spontaneously, always the symbol of the phoenix stirred in Ira's imagination, recurred, gave substance to his striving: to rise out of one's own ashes. And Shelley's lines: "Shake your chains to earth like dew, which in sleep had fallen on you." Innate and unquenchable hope, expression of life's vitality, or a trust in the future.

Editor's Afterword

The story of Henry Roth has been retold with periodic regularity since *Call It Sleep* was republished, in 1964. The outlines are now familiar: he had the world's most famous case of writer's block, though in fact he never really stopped writing; his literary career enjoyed a marvelous rebirth after Irving Howe praised the paperback reissue of *Call It Sleep* on the cover of the *New York Times Book Review*; and he reemerged, to general astonishment and delight, with the four volumes of *Mercy of a Rude Stream*, the first of which was published in 1994.

An American Type is Roth's last novel, the book he worked on in his dying years. Hobbled by rheumatoid arthritis, grieving the death in 1990 of his wife, Muriel, Roth moved from the mobile home on Albuquerque's New York Avenue, where the two had lived for decades, into a nearby assisted-living facility. He was miserable there, and quickly moved again, into a private home, converted from a funeral parlor, where he spent the rest of his life. Roth was convinced that he had another novel in him, one that would more accurately reflect the aged world he suddenly found himself living in. A new word processor, easier on his gnarled rheumatic fingers, and his precociously wise assistant, Felicia Steele, enabled him to write this novel.

All of Roth's novels are autobiographical, and *An American Type* follows the events of *Mercy*, which ends with Ira Stigman's decision to move in with Edith Welles, which in turn follows those of *Call It Sleep*, which soaringly concludes in 1914. But Roth's range was such that these are three wildly different novels. If *Call It Sleep* is one of the great American Modernist novels—intimate yet sprawling, experiential and experimental in its diction—*Mercy of a Rude Stream* is one of the great modern American novels. Its boundless curiosity mirrors the restlessness of its narrator; it replaces claustrophobia with an intense interest in the world around it, reflected and refracted in the multiple voices of the narrator.

An American Type is a love story, and it's a novel—perhaps the last direct testament—of the Great Depression. But it's primarily a book about Ira's attempt to find an authentically American identity. His childhood and young adulthood behind him, Ira casts about for archetypes, finding a great array of American characters. Bill Loem, his wife M, her parents, his parents, even Ira's adventures on freight trains: all of these are described and evaluated by their essential Americanness.

We follow Ira through his emotional struggles, which are mirrored by his restless travels. He explores America's inherent splendors and its Depression tragedies as he crosses the country and returns home, but even after marriage the question remains: In a country defined by its multiplicity, how does an immigrant—and especially a Jewish one—know what to become?

When the raw manuscript of what became *An American Type*, 1,900 typed pages, came to *The New Yorker* in 2005, I was an assistant in the fiction department, a reader of manuscripts mostly. I was also a Henry Roth fan. *Call It Sleep* was on a college syllabus, but, like many things I read in college, it made only a vague and passing impression. A couple of years later, working a night-shift job in a ski town, I was spending most afternoons at the public library, browsing the fiction shelves for something to relieve my seemingly terminal early-twenties boredom. The first volume of *Mercy* stood face out on a display shelf. That was the beginning of a deeply impressionable week of reading Henry Roth, a week in which I finished the volumes of *Mercy* and then reread *Call It Sleep*. I loved the rhetorical flights that interrupted the gritty description, and Roth's intense belief that a life was worth obsessing over, that self-seriousness wasn't something to be effaced. I was living in Idaho, but I envisioned myself in cold-water flats.

The manuscript that Roth called Batch 2 was sent by *Mercy*'s editor, Robert Weil, who wondered whether the magazine had any interest in publishing excerpts. Batch 2 was the product of Roth's final years and was mostly composed after Batch 1, which became *Mercy*. I made my interest in Roth known, and since I seemed to have some free space on my desk the initial reading of the manuscript fell to me. I read a hundred pages a day with a growing sense of discovery and elation. Much of the manuscript had astonishing vigor, some was repetitive and cursory, and, as was Roth's previous pattern, very little of the material was presented in coherent narrative order. It felt like Roth to me, but a new Roth, one racing against time, needing to get everything down before the page—or his life—ended. Every day I would turn over the hundredth page, put it aside, and go on thinking about its promises and puzzles.

The New Yorker ran two stories from Batch 2 in the summer of 2006, but by that time my attention was consumed by the manuscript as a whole. I had created a page-by-page timeline of the events described, to keep them organized, and would endlessly rearrange scenes in my head. Weil suggested, and Lawrence Fox, Roth's literary executor, agreed, that I should try to make Batch 2 into a novel.

When a posthumous novel appears from a celebrated writer, the critical hunt is on to establish exactly how legitimate the work is, how closely it hews to the divined intentions of the author. To satisfy this reasonable curiosity. I'll try to explain exactly what I've done in editing this novel.

First, I rearranged the manuscript in chronological order. In the last "onerous lap" of his life, Roth wrote scene by scene, as his attentions demanded, and as he struggled, despite crippling infirmities and immense pain, to evoke this fine story. He called this his "aleatory" method. He'd work on an episode from his life, abandon it, go on to something else, and then pick up the scene hundreds of pages later. Out of order, the original manuscript seemed occasionally distracted; but I quickly recognized the arc of a novel buried in unavoidable repetition and digression. I know from my understanding of how his previous works came into being that Roth couldn't leave anything out—he found all personal detail equally engrossing—and so, as with *Mercy*, the work of the editor was to establish what was necessary to the story, and what was extraneous.

There was a very clear beginning to the novel, but it was initially challenging to see where it ended. Roth described his narrator's life through nearly the end, but whole decades were represented by just a few scenes, expressions of remorse for the privations his family had been subjected to by their poverty in the 1940s and 1950s, descriptions of later vacations, and transcripts of phone calls he had made to friends to discuss the Gulf War, in 1990. But it was apparent that the meat of the story rested in the late 1930s, and the natural climax was his marriage and acceptance of the bonds of adulthood.

The epilogue was found toward the end of the manuscript, buried between an account of a literary party in Provincetown and memories of rabbit hunting in Maine. Once I had the shape of the story, I started cutting judiciously, trying to let each part breathe leisurely without overwhelming the reader with minutiae.

In the spring of 2009, I gave Fox and Weil a draft. It was exceedingly important that the two people who most closely knew Roth's intentions and desires, and who were aware of the peripatetic structures of his drafts, approved of the work. They had suggestions that improved the novel and assured me not only that this work could succeed as a novel but that this was the novel that Roth would have approved. It's impossible to know the exact intentions of a dead man, but I can say that during the editing process I felt very strongly the moral implications of what I was doing, and I feel confident that readers deserve this novel, in this form.

An American Type could not have taken shape without the devoted efforts of three of Roth's greatest friends: Robert Weil, his devoted editor; Lawrence Fox, his trusted literary executor; and Roslyn Targ, his loyal literary agent of many years. Mario Materassi, who helped Roth begin to conceive of *Mercy of a Rude Stream*, and Felicia Steele are also owed gratitude by anyone interested in the life and work of Roth. Finally, I would like to thank Hugh Roth for his careful and close reading of his father's last novel.

Henry Roth was a stubborn struggler, never a natural. He needed help to realize his literary gifts: first from his earliest literary mentor, Eda Lou Walton, later from his wife, Muriel Parker. In the end, perseverance was one of his greatest strengths. As his mother said to him, in the epigraph he chose to open this novel, "some fruit ripens at a glance of the sun, and some fruit takes all summer." This is his final fruit.

WILLING DAVIDSON
Stockholm, September 2009

About the Author

Henry Roth, who died in 1995, in Albuquerque, New Mexico, at the age of eighty-nine, had one of the most extraordinary careers of any American novelist who lived in the twentieth century.

He was born in the village of Tysmenitz, in the then Austro-Hungarian province of Galitzia, in 1906. Although his parents never agreed on the exact date of his arrival in the United States, it is most likely that he landed at Ellis Island and began his life in New York in 1909. He briefly lived in Brooklyn, and then on the Lower East Side, in the slums where his classic novel *Call It Sleep* is set. In 1914, the family moved to Harlem, first to the Jewish section on 114th Street east of Park Avenue; but because the three rooms there were "in the back" and the isolation reminded his mother of the sleepy hamlet of Veljish where she grew up, she became depressed, and the family moved to non-Jewish 119th Street. Roth lived there until 1927, when, as a senior at City College of New York, he moved in with Eda Lou Walton, a poet and New York University instructor who lived on Morton Street in Greenwich Village. With Walton's support, he began *Call It Sleep* in about 1930. He completed the novel in the spring of 1934, and it was published in December 1934, to mixed reviews. He contracted for a second novel with the editor Maxwell Perkins, of Scribner's, and the first section of it appeared as a work in progress in *Signatures*, a small literary magazine. But Roth's growing ideological frustration and personal confusion created a profound writer's block, which lasted until 1979, when he began the earliest drafts of *Mercy of a Rude Stream*.

In 1938, during an unproductive sojourn at the artists' colony Yaddo in Saratoga Springs, New York, Roth met Muriel Parker, a pianist and composer, much of which is depicted in *An American Type*. They fell in love; Roth severed his relationship with Walton, moved out of her apartment, and married Parker in 1939, to the disapproval of her family. With the onset of World War Two, Roth became a tool and gauge maker. The couple moved first to Boston with their two young sons, Jeremy and Hugh, and then in 1946 to Maine. There Roth worked as a woodsman, a schoolteacher, a psychiatric attendant in the state mental hospital, a waterfowl farmer, and a Latin and math tutor, while Muriel also taught and eventually became principal of a grammar school.

With the paperback reprint of *Call It Sleep* in 1964, the block slowly began to break. In 1968, after Muriel's retirement from the Maine state school system, the couple moved to Albuquerque, New Mexico. They had become acquainted with the environs during Roth's stay at the D. H. Lawrence ranch outside of Taos, where Roth was writer-in-residence. Muriel began composing music again, mostly for individual instruments, for which she received ample recognition, while Henry Roth collaborated with his friend and Italian translator, Mario Materassi, to put out a collection of essays called *Shifting Landscape*, published by the Jewish Publication Society in 1987. After Muriel's death in 1990, Roth occupied himself with revising the final volumes of the monumental *Mercy of a Rude Stream*. The first volume was published in 1994 by St. Martin's Press under the title *A Star*

Shines over Mt. Morris Park, and the second volume, called *A Diving Rock on the Hudson,* appeared from St. Martin's in 1995.

The third volume, *From Bondage,* which appeared in hardcover in 1996, was the first volume of the four *Mercy* books to appear posthumously. *Requiem for Harlem,* the fourth and final volume of *Mercy of a Rude Stream,* which appeared in 1998, concluded the cycle, which began in 1914 with the Stigman family's arrival in Jewish-Irish Harlem and ended with Ira's decision to leave the ancestral family tenement and move in with Edith Welles on the night before Thanksgiving in 1927. Roth was able to revise both the third and fourth volumes in 1994 and 1995 shortly before his death. The story of Batch 2, which was begun in the late 1980s and completed in 1990 and 1991, is described at length in Willing Davidson's afterword in this volume. Two excerpts appeared in *The New Yorker* in 2006 under the titles "God the Novelist" and "Freight."

While still alive, Roth received two honorary doctorates, one from the University of New Mexico and one from the Hebrew Union College–Jewish Institute of Religion. Posthumously, he was honored in 1995 with the Hadassah Harold Ribalow Lifetime Achievement Award and by the Museum of the City of New York with Manhattan Borough President Ruth Messinger having named February 29, 1996, as "Henry Roth Day" in New York City. *From Bondage* was cited by the National Book Critics Circle as being a finalist for its Fiction Prize in 1997, and it was in that same year that Henry Roth won the first Isaac Bashevis Singer Prize in Literature for *From Bondage,* an award put out by The Forward Foundation. In 2005, ten years after Roth's death, the first full biography of his life, the prize-winning *Redemption: The Life of Henry Roth,* by literary scholar Steven G. Kellman, was published, followed in 2006 by Henry Roth's centenary, which was marked by a literary tribute at the New York Public Library, sponsored by CCNY and organized by Lawrence I. Fox, Roth's literary executor.